"I'm to have my head smitten from my body."

Sarah gave a humorless chuckle.

Anthony's black eyes shifted to her slender, white throat. She could see the muscles of his neck ripple as he swallowed. "That's not going to happen, Sarah. You're leaving here with me...today."

"Oh, certainly. I just walk on out past the guards? A condemned prisoner?"

"Not as a condemned prisoner." His dark eyes gleamed. "As my wife."

Sarah pushed herself up on the bed, her face ghostly white. "Your wife!"

Anthony reached for her hand, but she snatched it away. "I knew you might be opposed to the idea," he said patiently, "but it's the only way. Marry me, Sarah, and you can leave here today, a free woman."

She pulled away from him, against the cold stone of the wall. Her soft gray eyes grew deadly. "I'd sooner rot a thousand years in hell!"

Dear Reader,

Even if you haven't read all of Ana Seymour's books since her debut during our March Madness Promotion in 1992, you are in for a treat with *Moonrise*. With this story, Ms. Seymour turns the considerable talents that brought a sense of excitement and fun to her Westerns in a completely different direction. *Moonrise* is set in England, and is the tale of a beautiful highway bandit who finds herself falling in love with the very man sent by the king to capture her. I hope you enjoy this delightful story.

And speaking of Westerns, with the publication of this month's Women of the West title, *Saint or Sinner*, Cheryl St.John has earned her fourth Gold 5 ★'s from *Heartland Critiques* in as many books. Don't miss this warmhearted story of a man who is determined to right the wrongs of his past and win the trust of a reluctant spinster.

An atmospheric Scottish castle is the setting for *MacLaurin's Lady*, Julie Tetel's romantic tale of a reclusive young woman and a dashing young nobleman who, with the help of his father's ghost, fall in love under the spell of the enchanted castle. And, from Laurel Ames, *Besieged*, a story set in Regency England of a young woman who must convince a world-weary soldier to accept the promise of their life together.

Whatever your taste in historical reading, we hope you'll keep a lookout for all four titles, available wherever Harlequin Historicals are sold.

Sincerely,
Tracy Farrell
Senior Editor

Please address questions and book requests to:
Harlequin Reader Service
U.S.: 3010 Walden Ave., P.O. Box 1325, Buffalo, NY 14269
Canadian: P.O. Box 609, Fort Erie, Ont. L2A 5X3

PRIZE SURPRISE SWEEPSTAKES!

This month's prize:

A FABULOUS SHARP VIEWCAM!

This month, as a special surprise, we're giving away a Sharp ViewCam**, the big-screen camcorder that has revolutionized home videos!

This is the camcorder everyone's talking about! Sharp's new ViewCam has a big 3" full-color viewing screen with 180° swivel action that lets you control everything you record—and watch it at the same time! Features include a remote control (so you can get into the picture yourself), 8 power zoom, full-range auto focus, battery pack, recharger and more!

The next page contains two Entry Coupons (as does every book you received this shipment). Complete and return *all* the entry coupons; **the more times you enter, the better your chances of winning!**

Then keep your fingers crossed, because you'll find out by November 15, 1995 if you're the winner!

Remember: The more times you enter, the better your chances of winning!*

PRIZE SURPRISE
SWEEPSTAKES

OFFICIAL ENTRY COUPON

This entry must be received by: OCTOBER 30, 1995
This month's winner will be notified by: NOVEMBER 15, 1995

YES, I want to win the Sharp ViewCam! Please enter me in the drawing and let me know if I've won!

Name_____

Address _____ Apt. _____

City   State/Prov.   Zip/Postal Code

Account #_____

Return entry with invoice in reply envelope.

© 1995 HARLEQUIN ENTERPRISES LTD.   CVC KAL

ANA SEYMOUR

MOONRISE

Harlequin Books

TORONTO • NEW YORK • LONDON
AMSTERDAM • PARIS • SYDNEY • HAMBURG
STOCKHOLM • ATHENS • TOKYO • MILAN
MADRID • WARSAW • BUDAPEST • AUCKLAND

ISBN 0-373-28890-5

MOONRISE

Copyright © 1995 by Mary Bracho.

Books by Ana Seymour

Harlequin Historicals

The Bandit's Bride #116
Angel of the Lake #173
Brides for Sale #238
Moonrise #290

ANA SEYMOUR

says she first discovered romance through the swash-buckling movies of Errol Flynn and Tyrone Power and the historical epics of Thomas Costain and Anya Seton. She spent a number of years working in the field of journalism, but she never forgot the magic of those tales. Now she is happy to be creating some of that magic herself through Harlequin Historicals. Ana lives in Minnesota with her two teenage daughters.

To my wonderful parents...
and all those swashbucklers we've shared

Prologue

September 3, 1666

From the gardens at Vauxhall to the bustling and smelly streets of Southwark, Londoners agreed that it had been an odd year. The city was tinderbox dry. Instead of fresh autumn winds, a sweltering heat enveloped it like a clinging blanket and showed no signs of dissipating.

Behind three feet of clammy stone wall, Sarah Fairfax felt prickles along her arms where her wool dress clung damply to her skin. She glanced for the hundredth time at the basin of water sitting on the room's single table. It would be heavenly to rid herself of the heavy gown and bathe.

A movement at the small, barred window in the door caught her eye. In the shadowy light she could just make out the features of the warder, the one who had been coming around more and more often. His leering eyes and blackened smile had begun to appear in her dreams...darting in and out amid the other haunting faces.

"Say the word, mum, and I'll fetch ye some fresh water," he said with relish, putting his face right up against the bars. "Won't cost ye nothin'. A lady like yerself needs her baths."

A scar along his left eye made it look squinty and small, while his good right eye had a lecherous gleam that turned Sarah's stomach. "No, thank you," she said calmly. She turned away from him toward the narrow, deep window that had been her only source of light for...how many days now? Weeks? She had lost count.

At the beginning she had demanded candles, blankets, writing materials. Her guards had been only too happy to oblige the beautiful new prisoner, but she had soon discovered that the price of their largesse had been filthy propositions and surreptitious gropings. Finally she had ceased to ask for anything.

She felt the warder's uneven eyes staring at her back. A chill went along her spine in spite of the heat. When she had entered the Tower weeks before, she had been defiant and angry. But day after endless day in the tiny cell had drained the defiance out of her, along with the hope.

Only the hate remained.

Her father would have told her to give that up, too. She could almost hear his sonorous voice echoing around the cell. "My dearest child," he would say, "you must make peace with all mankind before you can find peace with your Maker."

She believed that Jack had done so before he died. He had been possessed of a wonderful serenity during that last sad meeting they had had here in this very cell. But Sarah had reconciled herself to the fact that she simply wasn't as good as her father and brother had been. She intended to take her hate with her all the way to the grave and beyond.

It was early afternoon. By now she knew every angle of the sun's rays through the window slit and could judge the hour more accurately than a timepiece. The warder had at last moved on to torment some other poor victim. Sarah gave a little shudder. Actually, she'd been lucky. She had had to suffer the guards' leers and their hands on her, but some blessed edict from an unknown higher authority had so far kept any of them from bothering her in a more direct way. If she still had an ounce of hope left in her, it was that her death should come before this mysterious protection was lifted.

She stood and walked over to the basin of water, glancing quickly at the opening in the door. Perhaps now, before he returned... She bent and carefully lifted the hem of her skirt to dip it in the water, then brought the wet wool up against her hot cheeks. She closed her eyes, savoring the coolness.

There was a loud thump against the thick wood door. Sarah dropped her skirt and jumped back. A key rattled in the lock. She took an involuntary step backward against the rough edge of the table. Prison routine was more regular than the tide, and it was not the time of day for a scheduled visit. The fear that Sarah had worked so hard to conquer since she had been seized at Leasworth weeks ago came flooding back, leaving an acid sting at the base of her throat.

The door opened with a harsh scrape against the stone floor. The visitor was dressed in solid black, from his hose to his fine silk shirt. His hair was black, too, as were his eyes. Coal, demon black in the dim light of the cell.

"You!" Sarah gasped, bracing herself with her hands on the table behind her.

The black eyes narrowed. "Surprised to see me, my love?"

Sarah forced herself to stand straight and meet the newcomer's gaze. "Not surprised," she said, her voice low and fierce. "Disappointed. I had hoped by now you had been blown to bits by a Dutch frigate."

The man smiled. Without taking his eyes off her, he reached easily back to shut the heavy door. "I've managed to stay out of that particular war so far," he said lightly. "You see, I have some unfinished business yet in the world of the living."

Her chin went up. "Not with me, you don't. Our business was finished long ago."

"Perhaps not."

The softly spoken words made the heat rush to Sarah's face. She put up a hand as he advanced toward her. "Leave me be, Anthony," she said fiercely.

He came like a stalking animal, graceful and deadly of purpose. Sarah's hand shook, then fell to her side. An arm's length away, he stopped. "Now there's a problem, my sweet." His voice was husky. "It appears that I can't let you be. Were old Mephistopheles himself chasing me away, I'd not be able to let you be."

He drew her against him then, and she went without resistance. His lips found hers with the inexorable force of a river seeking the sea. Their bodies molded, clung. For a moment it appeared that they might defy the laws of the natural world to merge themselves into one being.

Sarah's blood ran hot, then icy cold, then scalding. She was held upright only by the steely strength of Anthony's arms around her. Involuntarily her mouth had opened to his onslaught. Her breasts burned against the pressure of his velvet doublet.

The walls of the cell blurred around her, then disappeared altogether. Blood pounded in her ears and lower as her body responded to the hard strength of his arms and the sudden gentleness of his mouth.

It took a long moment for either of them to register the sound of a tin cup scraping across the bars of the door. Anthony was first to pull back. He held Sarah protectively out of view and turned his head toward the sound.

"Glad to see ye enjoying yerself, yer lordship." The warder's black teeth showed in a lascivious grin. "But ye'd best finish it off right quick. I can only let ye have a few more minutes."

With gentle firmness, Anthony set Sarah against the table and took two long strides to the door. He spoke through the opening to the warder in low, even tones.

"My good man, if I see you looking into this room again before I summon you, I will cut out your eyeballs and roll them in my next game of bowls."

The warder winced, and a trickle of sweat started down the squinty side of his face.

"Do you understand?" Anthony asked, almost pleasantly.

The warder nodded once, then disappeared from view.

Anthony turned back to Sarah, his expression troubled. "Have they...bothered you, Sarah? Hurt you?"

Her heart had almost stopped thundering. But she felt weak. Months of confinement and poor food had taken their toll. She'd give anything for some strength at this moment. Desperately she grasped at the table as she felt her legs give way beneath her. In an instant he was beside her and she was lifted in arms that were as familiar to her as her own.

"Sarah!" Anthony cried in alarm. He crossed the tiny cell in a single long stride and settled her on the narrow straw bed. "What is it? Are you sick?"

His head was bent over hers, the window casting its slanting light over the strong, dark features. She took a ragged breath. "What are you doing here, Anthony?"

He smoothed her hair back from her forehead in a gesture that was so loverlike, Sarah bit her lip to keep it from trembling. "I've come to take you out of here."

She gave a humorless chuckle. "In case you've forgotten, *Lord* Rutledge, your king has other ideas for me. If the royal prosecutors have their way, I'm to have my head smitten from my body.''

Anthony's black eyes shifted to her slender white throat. She could see the muscles of his neck ripple as he swallowed with difficulty. "That's not going to happen, Sarah. You're leaving here with me... today."

"Oh, certainly. I just walk on out past the guards? A condemned prisoner?"

"Not as a condemned prisoner." His dark eyes gleamed. "As my wife."

Sarah pushed herself up on the bed, her face ghost white. "Your wife!"

Anthony reached for her hand, but she snatched it away. Patiently he said, "I knew you might be opposed to the idea, but it's the only way, Sarah. Marry me, and you can leave here today, a free woman."

She pulled away from him, against the cold stone of the wall. Her soft gray eyes grew deadly. "I'd sooner rot a thousand years in hell," she said.

Chapter One

December 1665

"Don't be such a stick, Jack Fairfax," Sarah said with a laugh, tumbling her brother off the end of the settle. He landed in a heap in the rushes and groaned a protest. Sarah jumped on top of him, her knees gouging his stomach and holding him pinned beneath her.

"Just look at this," Sarah said triumphantly. One by one she began pulling jewels from inside a knotted kerchief and dropping them on Jack's chest, where they slithered in glittery trails to the ground. "It's a bloody fortune."

"Don't swear, Sarah," Jack said gravely. At eighteen, his arms already had the lean muscles of early manhood. His strength was far greater than that of his sister, and he pushed her off him with rough gentleness. "Father will be resting uneasy in his grave to hear you talk so," he chided as he sat up beside her.

Sarah frowned. "Don't speak to me of Father," she said curtly. Then in a quicksilver change of mood she reached out to give Jack an exuberant hug. "All this from that fat old bishop. Who'd have thought the old toad would have such a hoard stashed away beneath that big belly?"

"We shouldn't have taken it."

Sarah stared at him in amazement. "Shouldn't have taken it? What are you thinking of? This will feed our families for the rest of the winter."

Jack shook his head. "There'll be trouble to pay, robbing a cleric."

"Oh, pooh. A bishop's not a cleric. He's a lackey of the king who cares more for his mistresses and his flagons of ale than for the Bible."

"You don't know that, Sarah. He may have been a godly man."

"Parson Hollander is a godly man, not that old windbag we robbed last night." Sarah's gray eyes and honey brown hair made her look deceptively plain at times, especially against the background of the simple Puritan garb she still favored. But at the moment her hair had pulled loose from its bindings and framed her face in a disheveled golden cloud. Her eyes danced and her flawless cheeks were flushed with her latest success. Even Jack had to admit that he had never seen beauty equal to hers.

He gave a deep sigh. Though Sarah was the older by almost five years, she was nevertheless his sister and it was his duty to be her protector. But how did one protect a maiden who could wield a sword and ride a horse better than any member of the king's guard? And how

did one shelter the sensibilities of a young woman who
had seen her father's head parted from his body?

He picked up a gold necklace set with amethyst.
"These are very fine. Recognizable. Will Parson Hollander be able to sell them?"

Sarah shrugged without concern. "His Dutch contacts will take anything and dispose of it abroad," she
said. "And the good people of Wiggleston will eat well
this winter, in spite of the king's new taxes."

Jack shook his head. "We're at war with the Dutch
these days, Sarah. 'Tis sheer folly to do business with
them."

Sarah picked the last of the jewels out of the rushes,
then jumped to her feet. "The king's too busy playing
with his mistresses to wage a real war."

Jack stood up more slowly. "The war's real enough,
believe me." His handsome young face was sober. "I
might have to go fight in it myself one of these days.
Even Uncle Thomas might be called."

Sarah turned to him, her expression furious. "Never!
Charles Stuart has taken enough from this family.
You'll walk over my grave before you'll ever fight for
him."

Jack smiled in spite of himself. If there was one sight
more beautiful than his sister excited, it was his sister
angry. "Uncle Thomas is one of the finest generals
England has," he reminded her mildly.

Sarah's voice was steady, but her knuckles were white
where she gripped the kerchief full of jewels as though
it were King Charles's neck. "Uncle Thomas and Gen-

eral Monck handed Charles Stuart back his throne on a silver platter, and he repaid them by executing some of the finest men in the land, including our own father, in case I have to remind you, Jack Fairfax.''

Jack knew that his sister's opinions on the subject were somewhat unfair. It was true that the loss of their father had been almost beyond bearing. But John Fairfax had signed his own death warrant long ago when he put his signature on the document condemning the king's father, Charles I. In reality, the executions after the Restoration had been relatively few, the new king proving himself to be more interested in the entertainments of the new court than in revenge and bloodletting.

''And as for Uncle Thomas,'' Sarah continued, ''he will do as he pleases, and shall the rest of his life. The king can't afford to offend him. It's as simple as that.''

She relaxed her death grip on the kerchief and let out a tense breath. ''So no more talk of war, my dearest brother.'' She hefted the kerchief in her hand and gave a grim, satisfied smile. ''Come on, let's go show the good parson this latest evidence of the Lord's bounty.''

''I can't afford to offend Thomas Fairfax, it's as simple as that.'' King Charles stretched out his long legs and looked up at the tall, scowling man standing stiffly in front of him. ''Sit down, Anthony, you're making me tired.''

The newly appointed Baron Rutledge grudgingly sat in a small gilt chair near the king's bed. The royal apartments at Oxford were not as sumptuous as Whitehall, but they were certainly much more luxurious than many of the places Anthony had stayed with Charles Stuart during the long years of exile. And at least they were away from the dreadful plague that had been ravaging London these past weeks. The death toll was up to a thousand poor wretches a day, and the haunting cry of "Bring out your dead!" echoed incessantly throughout the crowded streets of the old City.

By moving first to Salisbury, then Oxford, the court had managed to isolate itself from the devastation. Charles and his courtiers played their games and vied with one another for the most elaborate costumes and hairstyles with only an occasional pang for the sufferings of those left back in London.

"I can't believe you want to send me to the wilds of Yorkshire just when the war is heating up...sire," he added with somewhat belated deference.

Charles smiled. "Anthony, my friend, I have all kinds of courtiers whom I can put to captaining a ship against my foreign enemies, but I have only a few whom I can trust to deal with the enemies from within."

"Are you saying that General Fairfax is your enemy?" Anthony looked perplexed. The famous old soldier had been living in what appeared to be peaceful retirement these past three or four years.

Charles shook his head, his elaborate lovelocks brushing along the tops of his shoulders. "I fervently hope not. But there's been trouble in the area. The people there haven't accepted back the church, and they don't want to pay the new taxes.''

"Very seldom do people welcome new taxes, sire,'' Anthony said dryly. Especially, he refrained from adding, when they know they will likely be spent to buy a new carriage for the king's latest mistress.

"And there's another problem,'' the king continued, ignoring Anthony's comment. "There have been robberies…several. It seems a masked highwayman has been assaulting the gentry. The villagers are making him into some kind of hero. They say he strikes with the full moon. Last month the Bishop of Lackdale was robbed of a small fortune that he had collected to refurbish the church.''

"To refurbish the size of his girth is more likely,'' Anthony grumbled.

Charles laughed. "Impious as usual. Someday your irreverence will catch up to you, my friend.''

Anthony gave one of the slow, lazy smiles that had won him more conquests than any man at court except the king. "I fully intend to repent on my deathbed, your majesty.''

Charles impatiently waved away the formal address. He and Anthony had been in too many escapades across the length of Europe to become sudden observers of proprieties. "Will you do it, Anthony?'' he asked in a cajoling tone that still managed to sound regal. "Will you go to Yorkshire and find out the truth?''

Anthony made one last attempt at refusal. "I've ever been better at fighting than at intrigue, sire. Spying is not to my taste."

"Don't be so dramatic, Anthony. It's not really spying.... Just consider that you're doing me a favor."

"A royal favor." Anthony's tone was of one who knew he had little choice in the matter. His dark eyes looked directly into the king's. There had been times, in earlier days, when they had been mistaken for brothers. Both were tall and dark complected. Both had an innate charm that brought people effortlessly under their spell. But whereas Anthony, five years the younger, had retained his lean form and high energy, the king had mellowed in the four and a half years since the Republican generals had given him back his throne. His face was softer, and he preferred the company of his ladies to sparring with his courtiers.

Charles sighed. "Not a royal favor. A personal favor. If Fairfax is working against me, I need to know immediately. On the other hand, if he's still loyal, I don't want to risk his anger by bearing down too hard on the dissenters there."

"And what about your moonlight marauder?"

"He's just what we don't need at the moment—some kind of romantic hero for the masses, demonstrating once again the age-old disparity between rich and poor. Which was *not*, by the way, invented by my ministers, no matter what the opposition might say."

The king boosted himself off the high bed and started to pace the room, warming to one of his favorite topics. "Oddsfish, *I've* been poor myself, you know. I've passed hunger and thirst and . . ."

"Deprivation," Anthony filled in obligingly. Over the years the script of Charles's adventures in exile had become more elaborated than one of Master Dryden's productions at Drury Lane.

"Yes, deprivation," Charles continued. "No one can say that I don't understand my people."

Gently Anthony tried to shift back to the topic at hand. "You were saying, sire, about the Yorkshire highwayman . . . ?"

Charles stopped in midstride, his mind pulled back to the present. "Yes, blast it. Find the man, Anthony. Shoot him or hang him—I don't care what you do—just get rid of him."

Anthony gave a short laugh. "At least my mission won't be without *some* sport."

The shimmery gray silk of Sarah's dress matched exactly the cold glitter of her eyes. "I don't care what my uncle ordered," she said with controlled fury. "No so-called Surveyor of the Royal Stables is coming anywhere near Brigand. That horse is mine. He doesn't belong to the Fairfax stables."

The old servant shrugged and pulled on his cap. "Begging yer pardon, mistress, but I believe the gentleman is already down there inspecting the lot of them. Brigand along with all the rest."

Sarah jumped to her feet and took off at a run down the path toward the stables. She was breathless by the time she reached the old stone structure, and took a minute to compose herself. She could already picture the scene. One of Charles's foppish cavaliers mincing along through the muck of the stable in high heels, ribbons adorning his artificially curled lovelocks. And putting his hands on *her* beloved horse. It was not to be borne. Her anger building, she stepped over the top of the wooden sty and tugged with all her might on the stable door. It swung open with a crash.

In the darkened interior of the barn, two men straightened up from their perusal of the foreleg of one of her uncle's prized stallions.

"It's my niece," she heard her uncle say to the other man. Then he called to her, "Sarah, come in and join us."

Slowly Sarah walked along the stalls, her eyes adjusting to the gloom. She could now see that the man beside her uncle was, at least, no fop. Taller than her brother, Jack, and handsomely built, he needed no high heels to emphasize his stature. Instead of the lace and furbelows understood to be *de rigueur* at court functions these days, he wore a leather jerkin over a simple, but fine, linen blouse and breeches that molded well-muscled thighs.

Her uncle reached out and took her hand as she drew near. "My dear, this is Baron Anthony Rutledge. The king has honored us by sending Lord Rutledge to review our horses as possible candidates for the royal stable."

Sarah swallowed her angry words as her eyes met the newcomer's. They were magnetic, almost black in color... and, to her dismay, showed a keen intelligence. Her own quick mind did a short reprise of the situation. The only thing worse than a visit from a *foolish* representative of the king would be a visit from a king's man with wits to challenge her own.

"Sarah?" her uncle prompted.

She lowered her eyes from the baron's dark gaze and gave a demure curtsy. "How d'ye do," she murmured.

When she looked up at him again, his expression had become distinctly predatory. A slight smile curved his lips. Inexplicably, Sarah felt herself growing warm.

"I'm at your service, mistress." The words were correct, but they were spoken in a low, caressing tone that made Sarah's toes want to curl up inside her slippers. She glanced quickly at her uncle, but he was smiling congenially as if nothing untoward were occurring.

Perhaps she was imagining things, Sarah told herself. Since her uncle's retirement from public life, they did not receive many visitors at Leasworth. She was sadly out of touch with society these days. For all she knew it might be normal for a court gentleman to devour a lady with a mere gaze, as their visitor was doing at this very moment. Or perhaps it was just that the day was unseasonably hot.

She took a step backward.

"Sarah is the best horsewoman in the shire," Uncle Thomas said fondly.

One of the baron's dark eyebrows lifted in an expression that managed to combine interest with amusement. "Is that so? I would be happy to see an example of such prowess."

Sarah shook her head and tried to clear her mind. Where were her wits? she asked herself angrily. She needed to think what to do with this unwelcome intruder. The last thing she needed was a representative from the king hanging around and discovering the natural riding skills she had inherited from her father. And what about Jack? Since her father's death four years ago, she had fiercely protected her younger brother, trying to keep him from any notice by the king. Though King Charles had said the punishments would end with the executions of those responsible for his father's murder, Sarah had never stopped worrying that the king's vengeance could somehow extend to the families of the convicted men. "I fear my uncle exaggerates," she said finally.

"I hope you'll give me the opportunity to judge for myself."

His gaze had gone from her face to linger briefly on the close-fitting silk of her bodice, then to her narrow waist and the gentle flare of her hips. Sarah felt the heat rise in her cheeks. "I wouldn't want to keep you from your business here, Lord Rutledge. I'll just go up to the house and inform the cook about the midday meal. You will be staying to eat with us?"

"I'll be here well beyond that," Anthony said with another devastating smile. "Your uncle has graciously

invited me to stay at Leasworth while I view some stock
in the area."

Sarah gave a faltering smile in reply. "We're honored to have you, of course. If you'll excuse me..."

She backed up another step, then another, then
stumbled as her foot hit a hay rake. In an instant the
baron was beside her, supporting her with one strong
arm around her back and another at her right elbow.
"Are you all right, mistress?" he asked softly, his face
just inches from hers.

She could see the black stubble along the lean line of
his jaw. A small cleft parted his chin. Through the thin
silk of her dress, she felt the solid hardness of the muscles of his arm. She took an uneven breath. No, this
man was definitely not one of the soft court dandies she
had heard about. It was time to gather her wits about
her.

"Thank you, my lord. How clumsy of me." Deliberately she put a hand on his chest. "I do believe you
saved me from a nasty fall." She looked around her
with distaste and wrinkled her nose. "And in all this
filth. What a dreadful thought."

Anthony felt her soften in his arms and gave a satisfied smile. Perhaps his stay in Yorkshire wouldn't be so
dull after all. This slender beauty would be a conquest
worthy of his expertise. He looked down to where her
soft white hand rested against the leather of his jerkin.
The lass seemed amenable, at least. He wondered how
closely her uncle guarded her virtue. He knew that
many country folk had kept more of the old standards

from the Puritan days of the Republic than had the people in London. As far as Charles's court was concerned, virtue had never been a high priority, even during the days of exile in Europe.

"Dreadful, indeed," he agreed pleasantly. "Would you like me to escort you back to the house...to be sure there are no further mishaps?"

"That won't be necessary, but thank you so much." Sarah's smile was sweet. Anthony's eyes were drawn to her full lips, which were naturally pink and moist without, he was sure, any of the paints used by all the ladies at court these days—and some of the men. He felt his blood quicken.

"I will look forward to seeing you at dinner, then." He lifted her hand from his jacket and brought it slowly to his lips.

Sarah's stomach jumped at the touch of his warm mouth. But at the same time, she immediately thought of the calluses on her palms, which told of endless hours of chafing against leather reins. She smiled at the baron through her long lashes, hoping he wouldn't notice the abrupt way she pulled her hand away from his.

"Yes, until dinner," she said hastily. Then she turned to leave before this unwanted visitor had her in a complete dither.

She berated herself for her foolishness all the way back to the manor house. She had always prided herself on her cool head. When Jack would get into a lather over some slight hitch in one of their midnight forays, she would be the one to stay calm and collected. Now suddenly the presence of a handsome king's man had her feeling like a witless dairy maid.

The best thing would be for both her and Jack to stay out of the way as much as possible while the gentleman was here. That would be no problem at all for her brother, whose comings and goings were little noted by the other members of the household. But in the past couple of years her widowed uncle had come to rely more and more on Sarah as mistress of the house. There was no way she could escape dining with their guest.

She rubbed her telltale palms together and wondered if Baron Rutledge had noted them. She was sure that at court a lady would rather be caught naked than riding without gloves, but Sarah was unaccustomed to such refinements. She had been raised in a thoroughly male household. Her mother had died giving birth to Jack, and John Fairfax had been too involved in his Puritanism and his politics to worry about finding a replacement.

Well, Sarah said to herself resolutely, if Lord Rutledge were to be so ungentlemanly as to comment on her roughened hands, she would merely tell him that life in Yorkshire was not as soft as in the palaces of London. Here in the country ladies worked rather than whiling away their days stitching fine tapestries or planning elaborate masques.

She was so lost in her own arguments that she almost missed seeing Jack skirt around the crumbling ruins of an old enclosing wall and make his way toward the stables. At her call he detoured in her direction.

"Have you just come from the horses, Sarah?" he asked eagerly. "I've heard there's a royal surveyor visiting from the king." His smile died as he took in Sarah's sober face. "What's the matter?"

Sarah motioned with one hand for him to lower his voice. "You heard right. There's a representative from the king. And you're not going anywhere near him."

"Is he very grand, Sarah? Are his clothes as magnificent as they say?" Her brother's eagerness was unabated.

"Do you understand what I'm saying, Jack? I don't want him to know you're here. It's bad enough that he's already got his eye on Brigand."

As the import of her words gradually dawned on him, the smile faded from Jack's face like the dimming of a lantern. "And you think he might have heard reports of the robberies?"

Sarah shrugged. "I don't know. He's supposed to be just a royal surveyor, but it makes me nervous to have a king's man staying here, especially one who knows horses. There's not a horse like Brigand in all the surrounding shires."

"And when the villagers tell their tales of the moonlight bandit, they sing the praises of the magnificent moonlit stallion 'he' rides," Jack added soberly.

"I probably should have ridden one of Uncle's horses," Sarah said ruefully. "Though Brigand has taken me out of more close scrapes than we can count."

"Well, it's too late to do anything about it now. The horse is already known."

Sarah gave a deep sigh. "We'll just have to make sure that master surveyor Rutledge has absolutely no reason to suspect any connection between the highwayman and anyone here at Leasworth."

"And how do you intend to do that?"

Sarah felt her cheeks grow warm again as she remembered her intense reaction to the man back at the stables. "Perhaps I can turn his thoughts in other directions."

Jack eyed her suspiciously. "What do you mean . . . other directions?"

Sarah gave him a determined smile. "Never mind. Let's just hope he won't be here for long. And you, brother dear," she added, putting her arm around his neck, "are to stay well out of his way."

Jack pulled away from his sister's embrace. "It's about time you stopped giving me orders, Sarah. I'm eighteen now—full grown."

"Eighteen you may be, but you're still my little brother."

Jack bristled. "Norah Thatcher didn't think I was so little yestere'en after the Wiggleston fair."

Sarah's eyes grew wide. "Jack! What are you saying?" she asked, her voice rising with shock.

Jack's neck colored just below his ears. "It's just that I'm not a lad anymore, Sarah, and it's time you recognized the fact."

Sarah was still taking in the implications of Jack's earlier statement. Norah Thatcher was one of the more notorious of the village maids. If she had been with

Jack late at night after the fair, there was only one possible interpretation. "Fornication is a sin, Jack," she said sternly.

Jack dropped his defensive expression and gave an easy laugh. "Hadn't you heard, Sarah, love? There's no such thing as sin in the merry reign of King Charles."

Sarah looked at her brother closely. He was no different than he had been when she had broken fast with him this morning, but all at once she realized that he had shoulders as broad as their father's had been. His chin showed traces of a man's whiskers. His clear blue eyes and thick blond hair were no longer those of a boy. "Surely you're not going to pattern your morals on the court's," she said soberly.

Jack, his typical good humor restored, leaned over to give his sister an affectionate kiss. "As I was just saying, Sarah, I'm a man now, and my morals are no longer the concern of my big sister."

Tears stung Sarah's eyes. "Don't ask me to stop worrying about you, Jack. I don't know what I'd do if anything happened to you. You're all I have."

Touched by her unaccustomed show of emotion, Jack took her in his arms. "We'll take care of each other, Sarah. You're all *I* have, too, you know."

Embarrassed by her tears, Sarah pushed at him and gave his chest a glancing blow with her small fist. "I'm all you have? What about Norah Thatcher?" she teased, covering the emotion with a grimace.

Jack grinned. "Norah has become...shall we just say, a good friend."

Sarah shook her head and laughed. "You've ever been bad, Jack Fairfax."

"Now that's funny," he said innocently. "Norah says I was ever so good."

Sarah felt her cheeks grow hot again. This was a side of her brother she was not sure she was ready for. She had been both sister and mother to him for so many years. It was difficult to think of him moving on in life into activities that could not, by their very nature, involve her.

Jack's smile faded as he saw that he had truly embarrassed her. "Don't mind me," he said, pulling her close to him once more. "You're absolutely right. I am bad. But it's just that . . . bad's a lot of *fun,* Sarah."

Unaccountably, Sarah once again had a vision of the almost *carnal* look in Lord Rutledge's dark eyes as he had watched her in the stables. She stepped back from Jack and tried to rein in her spinning thoughts. "Just promise me you'll do as I say, Jack, and stay out of the baron's way."

Jack looked down at her, his eyes full of love. "If it will make you happy, big sister, I'll make myself as scarce as hen's teeth."

She gave his arm a squeeze, taking note of his rock-hard muscle. When had Jack suddenly become so big? "Thank you, little brother. I only wish I could do the same. But, alas, I must be the proper hostess for our guest. And if I don't get up to the kitchens, the grand baron from London will be supping on raw rabbit stew," she added with a giggle.

Jack joined in her laughter. "Run along, then. I'll just take myself off to the village. Perhaps Mistress Thatcher needs some help today in the tannery."

"Jack!" Sarah chastised.

"You said you wanted me out of the way, remember?"

Sarah gave a reluctant smile. "Just mind what you do, little brother."

Jack grinned. "Oh, I intend to mind it very well, Sarah." Then he turned and took off toward Wiggleston in a dead run.

Anthony stretched out his long legs toward the huge fire that blazed in the great room of Leasworth manor. He was tired, though not entirely displeased with the results of his day. Oliver, his colleague on the mission, had reported that his men had made some progress in the village gathering information about the moonlight highwayman. And as for Anthony's own day at Leasworth, it had been more than satisfactory. To his surprise, Thomas Fairfax actually did possess a number of horses that would rival any in London. There was one in particular that was a magnificent animal, a dark gray roan stallion with sleek lines and powerful legs that made it look as if it could run the breadth of the country without stopping.

And then there was the girl. Fairfax's niece. She had the look of a little country dove in her plain gray dress, but she had the features of a classic beauty, and her body... He'd only held her for a moment, but that had been enough. She had all the lush curves of a woman, but with an underlying strength that promised that she would be an exhilarating match in bed.

It was a pity that he was too tired to woo her yet tonight. She should be willing enough, he reasoned. As he'd come out of the stables, he'd seen her with what must have been one of her country swains. She'd been embracing the strapping young lad. She'd even kissed him there in the plain light of day. It shouldn't be too hard to get her to turn her attentions to an experienced courtier like himself. After all, he had wooed and won the most brilliant women at court, at least those that Charles had not marked for himself.

The door to the cavernous room opened. It was she, the niece—Sarah. The name was plain, but it suited her elegant simplicity. So did the gown she was wearing— solid black, with a stark white vee bodice that emphasized her full breasts and narrow waist. Her hair was swept up from her slender neck in a graceful twist. Her finely etched cheekbones glowed in the firelight. She looked serene and dignified, but her gray eyes watched him with the deceptive calm of a wolf ready to strike. He rose to his feet. Perhaps he wasn't too tired, after all.

Chapter Two

"Please don't trouble yourself to rise, sir."

"Why, I've already risen, mistress," Anthony said, masking a rueful grin at the double edge to his words. Without jewelry, without paint, without laces and satin—by the holy rood, the lady was stunning.

"I've merely come to inquire about your sleeping quarters. They are to your satisfaction?"

Her voice was low and pleasant and her eyes now had softened. He could almost believe that he had imagined that fierce expression of moments ago. "I wish you could change your uncle's mind, mistress," he said, walking toward her. "I'd not have him abandon his own bedchamber for me."

"He would have it no other way," Sarah answered, a touch of defiance making its way into her tone. "Uncle Thomas has a very strong sense of propriety. He would never have a visitor of your standing sleep in lesser surroundings."

Anthony shook his head. "Let me talk with him one more time. I don't want to cause disruption in the household."

"My uncle has retired for the evening, Lord Rutledge, and asked me to bid you good-night."

Anthony was silent for a minute. He supposed it was a good sign that General Fairfax still held enough respect for the crown that he wanted to treat its servants with all honor. He would so report to Charles. And in the meantime... the lady appeared to be temporarily without a guardian.

"Your uncle retires early," he said evenly.

"Yes. He works hard and is not so young anymore."

"But he's in good health, surely?"

Sarah could not help the touch of bitterness that crept into her voice. "Years of battle and betrayal wear on a man, my lord."

One of Anthony's dark eyebrows lifted. "I know," he said pointedly. "There are many who say the *king* appears much older than his five and thirty years."

Sarah bit her lip. What *was* the matter with her? she asked herself for the hundredth time that day. She hadn't come here to discuss politics with the baron or open up past wounds. She'd come to try to disarm any suspicions he may have developed during the day about Brigand and the masked highwayman. At least that was the reason she had given to herself when she found her feet directing her inexplicably toward the great room instead of to her own bed. At any rate, she certainly did not want to antagonize their guest.

She made her voice light. "I wouldn't know about that, Lord Rutledge. I've never seen the king."

Anthony cast a quick glance down the length of her black-clad silhouette and his eyes glowed. "That's perhaps a lucky thing, mistress."

Sarah blinked at the unexpected statement. "May I ask why, sir?"

Anthony moved so close that she could see the fine stitching on his black doublet. He spoke softly, bending toward her. "Because the king has a weakness for beautiful women."

It was as if one of the flames from the fireplace had suddenly leapt up and scorched her face. She had never before been called beautiful. Her father had believed that vanity was a sin. While Sarah had always been secretly pleased that her features were comely, she had never remarked upon the fact, nor expected anyone else in the family to do so.

She stammered a reply. "I . . . I can't imagine that his majesty would be interested in a simple country maid such as I."

Anthony reached out a hand and gently ran a finger down her cheek. "You may be from the country, but I'm not at all convinced about the 'simple,'" he said with a curious intensity, then lightened his tone to add, "and I'm afraid that 'maid' would definitely be no longer the case once Charles set his sights on you."

Sarah dropped her gaze from the now teasing dark eyes and took a step backward, away from the touch of his hand. This was beyond her. She had grown up in a society where men and women touched not at all before their marriage, and as seldom as possible thereafter. In her household there would no more have been banter about a maid losing her virtue than there would have been blasphemy against the Lord. "I fear I'm not used to your court humor, Lord Rutledge," she murmured.

Anthony frowned. He hadn't meant to scare the lass. Perhaps she was virtuous, after all, in spite of the scene he had witnessed outside the stables. The fact would not change his intent, merely his tactics. "Please forgive my free speaking, Mistress Fairfax. You are correct. The ribaldry of the court has gotten out of hand these days, and sometimes I forget what it's like to talk with a true lady."

Sarah struggled to regain her composure. "There's nothing to forgive," she said, swallowing over the dryness of her throat. "Now if you will excuse me..."

Anthony grabbed her hand. "Don't go, Mistress Fairfax. I'd have you sit with me awhile by the fire. I promise not to offend you again."

His voice coaxed without pleading. Once again Sarah lifted her eyes to look at him. His hair fell in careless black waves past his shoulders, unlike the cropped Puritan style of the country lads she was used to. But instead of making him look feminine, it merely added to his aura of overwhelming masculinity. Raised with men all her life, she had never been so aware of the difference between the two sexes. Part of her wanted to flee to the shelter of her little room in the west wing of the manor. The other part of her kept her riveted to the floor. "I'll stay awhile," she said finally. "Though I would imagine you, too, are weary after your journey today."

With the expertise of a skilled lover of women, Anthony watched the expressions flit across her face. He saw hesitation, then interest, then curiosity. There was not quite desire as yet, but that would come. He had plenty of time.

"I'm never too weary to enjoy the company of a fair lady." Without relinquishing his hold on her hand, he led her across the room to the leather chairs in front of the fire.

"I'm unused to such compliments, my lord," Sarah demurred, pulling her hand away and sitting in the chair farthest from the one the baron had been occupying.

"Now, I find that hard to believe." He pulled his chair close to hers and leaned so that he was closer still. "I've heard no reports that an epidemic has struck blind all the good men of Yorkshire."

His smile was warm and teasing and Sarah found it impossible not to respond with one of her own. "They are not blind, sir, but neither do they have time to waste on flattery."

"Ah, but 'tis not flattery to merely speak the truth." He paused a moment then added nonchalantly, "Surely the young suitor who called on you today must tell you these things."

"Suitor?"

"A tall blond fellow. I saw you together as I came out of the stables with your uncle."

Sarah's mind worked quickly. As she had expected, Jack's absence at the midday and evening meals had not been noted. Their visitor appeared to be unaware of the existence of her brother, and she intended to keep it that way if at all possible. "Oh, *him,*" she said casually. "Uh...Henry. He's just a friend. His family has an estate in a neighboring village."

Anthony was surprised. Though he would not have suspected Mistress Fairfax of having a devious character, he knew at once that she was lying to him. He considered the fact briefly. Was she just trying to conceal the depth of her feelings for the man? Or was there some darker reason for her duplicity? He could not, after all, forget why he had been sent to Leasworth in the first place. The lady's clear deception put an entirely different tone to the evening.

"Perhaps I should make his acquaintance. His family might have horses of interest to me."

Sarah gave a forced laugh. "I hardly think so. They are not wealthy people. I'm sure they would be quite undone at a visit from a member of court."

She was definitely hiding something, Anthony concluded, surprised to find himself somewhat saddened at the knowledge. He had planned on seducing Mistress Fairfax and then sharing with her his considerable skill—to their mutual satisfaction. He'd even thought he would fall in love with her for a few days. He'd found in the past that being infatuated enhanced the

physical sensations, and it had been some time since
he'd been in the mood. However, it appeared that far
from falling in love with General Fairfax's lovely niece,
he would be investigating her. The seduction was still
not out of the question, but it would have to be done
with his guard up. He would not be able to indulge in
that delicious abandonment of intellect that he had at
times found so rewarding.

"I'll defer to your judgment, then," he said with a
smile. "Though my instructions were to view all the
stock in the surrounding area."

"Oh, take my word for it, sir. The...uh...*Partridges'*
animals are of extremely poor quality."

"Partridge?"

"Yes. Henry Partridge," Sarah said firmly. "That's
the friend you saw visiting me today."

"I see."

Sarah searched his face for any sign of suspicion, but
he just watched her with a pleasant smile. "I should really seek my bed, Lord Rutledge. We are not accustomed to keeping late hours here at Leasworth."

This time Anthony made no move to dissuade her. He
stood and gave a courtly nod of his head. "Then don't
let me keep you, mistress, for I intend to request your
services on the morrow."

"My services?" Sarah asked uncertainly, rising to
stand beside him.

"As a guide," Anthony explained smoothly. "Your
uncle has spoken so glowingly of your riding talents, I
would like to see them for myself, and at the same time

can use your knowledge of the neighborhood to help me in my mission.''

The entire conversation had left Sarah uncomfortable. At first she had been nervous about the baron's disturbing effect on her personally, and now she began again to fear his presence as a representative of the king. She should never had made up that story about Jack, she told herself angrily. This man was too sharp to treat as a fool. She must tread carefully.

''As I said before, Uncle Thomas views my skill with the eyes of a doting relative. However, I would be happy to serve as your guide tomorrow.''

''Fine. Shall we say midmorning?''

Sarah nodded her assent, then turned to leave the room. Anthony watched the graceful line of her back as she walked toward the door. ''Mistress Fairfax,'' he called softly as her hand reached for the latch.

She stopped and looked back over her shoulder.

''If Master Partridge does not tell you how beautiful you are—tell you emphatically and often—then he doesn't deserve you.''

Sarah again felt the heat from the fire all the way across the room. ''Good night, your lordship,'' she said quickly, and slipped out into the dark hall.

''I don't think I fancy 'Partridge.' You could have come up with a grander-sounding name.'' Jack lay sprawled across the foot of Sarah's bed. He grinned at her over the top of the apple he was devouring. It was the fourth he'd consumed in the few minutes she had taken to tell of the previous evening's conversation with the baron. Sarah tried not to think about what nocturnal activities might have caused her brother's inordinate appetite this morning, but she couldn't help a motherly scold.

"What time did you get home last night, anyway, little brother?"

The grin broadened. "You told me to stay away, remember?"

"It's not a joke, Jack. Somehow I sense that this man is dangerous." She pushed herself farther up in bed and hugged a pillow protectively against her middle. If nothing else, Anthony Rutledge was definitely a danger to her peace of mind. It had been hours before she had slept last night, and it hadn't helped that she had heard no sounds of Jack's return to his room next to hers. When she had finally slept, she'd had one of her disturbing dreams. They always started out the same... on that horrible day four years ago, the day of her father's execution. She and Jack had been in the front of the crowd that day—lost, pitiful figures who were about to witness the end of the secure world they had known. But in her dreams she was no longer helpless. She was up on the platform with her father, fighting with his captors, dressed in solid black with a black silk mask covering her face. One by one she fought off the king's men until finally there was only one left... and he stood over her father with a huge sword, more fearsome than any she had ever seen. From there the dreams would change. Sometimes her father changed into an eagle and flew away free into a bright blue sky. Sometimes that horrible sword would descend and then all she would see was red, great bright blotches that filled her vision and her head.

Last night the dreams had changed. Suddenly she'd been watching Jack in the meadow beyond Wiggleston. He'd been entwined hotly with Norah Thatcher, and then the figure changed again and it was not Jack anymore, but the baron. Even this morning she had vague memories . . . The baron's dark hair falling forward as he bent his head toward milk white breasts. And they had not been Norah's breasts . . .

"Sarah!" Jack's voice was insistent. "What's the matter with you? You're pale as a ghost."

She gave herself a little shake and swung her legs over to jump down from the bed. "Nothing's the matter. I just didn't sleep very well last night with a king's man in the house and my brother out prowling the village like an overheated tomcat."

Jack winced at the sharpness of her tone. "Who can understand you, Sarah? You're the one who told me to stay away, and now you're angry because I did as you asked."

She sighed. "You're right. I'm sorry, little brother. It's just that the man makes me uncomfortable. All that nonsense about my supposed beauty . . ."

Jack's smile was tender. "But, Sarah, you can't fault the man for having eyes in his head. You *are* beautiful."

Sarah pulled her voluminous night robes close around her and looked over at her brother. There was definitely a difference about him, a new awareness of her as a woman and himself as a man. He would never have said such a thing even a few weeks ago. It made her uncomfortable, but she found the change intriguing. "Thank you," she said softly.

Jack dropped his eyes. "I guess Father and I were never much good at telling you so."

"It doesn't matter." Sarah shook her head with embarrassment.

"Yes," Jack said firmly. "It does matter. I have the most beautiful sister in all the country and I've never even told her so. I ought to be horsewhipped . . . or at least forced to listen to one of Parson Hollander's sermons."

Sarah giggled. As usual, Jack could defuse the most awkward moment with his good humor. She was tired and more than a little confused by the feelings of the past day and night, but overriding everything else, she felt a tremendous surge of love for her brother. Without him, her life would be barren indeed.

She walked around the end of the bed and leaned over to drop a kiss on his blond head. "Anyway, you do see that it's more important than ever that you keep out of sight. You'll have to stay in the village until the baron is gone. And I want you to talk to Parson Hollander and tell him to spread the word among the villagers. If he asks them to keep your presence secret, I know they'll cooperate."

"What about the servants here?"

"I'm going to speak with Uncle Thomas."

"Get Bess to help you." Bess was the head cook, absolute ruler of the Leasworth kitchens, and the only woman besides Sarah that Jack had ever listened to.

"She'll do anything we ask if it's to help you," Sarah said with a smile. "So, it's settled. Now be off with you."

"And you promise not to be angry with me for spending the night away?"

"You could stay at Parson Hollander's."

Jack's grimace made him look like a little boy again, and forced Sarah to laugh. "Oh, all right," she said. "Stay wherever you please, just don't come back around here until I send word that it's safe."

"But what about you? I don't like the idea of you being with that man unprotected."

"Don't worry about me," she said airily. "I'll be fine. Now get along out of here before the baron shows up for our riding appointment."

"You're sure?"

"Of course. Absolutely sure. I'm not the least bit worried about being able to handle Lord Anthony Rutledge." She turned away biting her lip. As far as she could remember, it was the first time she'd ever told her brother a lie.

"Which of these beauties do you ride, Mistress Fairfax?"

Beneath her smile, Sarah was fuming. She had hoped

to reach the stables before Lord Rutledge this morning to tell the stableboy, Arthur, that she would not be riding Brigand today. But the baron had knocked at her bedchamber door before she had even finished dressing, barely missing Jack's departure.

As she had feared, the words were scarcely out of the baron's mouth before the vigilant young Arthur stepped forward leading her beloved stallion. "This un's Mistress Sarah's horse," he said proudly.

Sarah's smile wavered as Anthony gave a low whistle and said, "He's magnificent. I had marked him yesterday, and hoped to be able to ride him myself today."

"He doesn't take kindly to strangers," Sarah said stiffly.

"Has he learned that from his mistress?" Anthony asked with mild amusement.

Determined not to let the man disconcert her again, Sarah ignored the remark. "I've ridden him since he was a colt. He's used to me."

Anthony reached out to run a practiced hand along the horse's side. "What's his name?"

Sarah gave a swift glance at Arthur, who was listening raptly to their exchange. Reluctantly, she answered the question. "I call him Brigand."

Anthony's hand stopped for a moment, then continued down the horse's smooth flank. "A bloodthirsty name for a horse belonging to so lovely a mistress."

When Sarah made no reply, he asked, "Would you consider selling him?"

"Never!" Sarah responded more vehemently than she had intended.

Anthony straightened from his examination of the stallion and turned to her with a half smile that took Sarah back to her dreams of the night before. "Not even to the king?" he asked softly.

"I'm sorry," she said, regaining her innate dignity, "Brigand is not for sale."

"I suspected as much. Still, it's a pity. Perhaps I will be able to persuade you to change your mind during the course of my stay here."

"You would be wasting your time to try, Lord Rutledge."

"It would be an interesting challenge, then."

His intense gaze was focused on her, not the horse, and suddenly Sarah felt herself unsure as to the topic of the conversation. Once again the baron was standing too close to her. It muddled her thinking. Wedged between the wall and her horse, she was unable to move away.

"Mistress Sarah won't *never* sell Brigand." Arthur's eager young voice startled them both. At many estates, Sarah knew, a servant would be beaten for speaking without being addressed first by the master, but her uncle and father had always encouraged fair treatment and respect for all who worked on their properties. Their idea of Christian brotherhood was not mere abstract theology.

Anthony turned his easy smile on the boy. "I believe you, lad. Though it's been said that I can be very persuasive when I want to be." His dark eyes shifted back to Sarah.

"If we're to get some riding in before the midday meal, we'd best get started. If you like, you may try out my uncle's prize stallion, Chestnut. I think you'll find him a worthy mount," she said hurriedly. She wanted the morning to be over with.

Arthur, now fully under Anthony's spell, rushed to ready Thomas Fairfax's best horse for the baron's use. It was a handsome sable stallion, as high as Brigand, but without quite the breadth of flank that gave Sarah's horse its extraordinary strength.

They left Arthur staring after them in awe, and Sarah had to admit that they must make a striking sight as they made their way along the well-worn road to the village. Brigand and Chestnut were two of the finest horses in the area, and today both had riders worthy of such impressive mounts. They rode several minutes in silence, enjoying the rare December sunshine.

"If I'd known Yorkshire to have such a mild clime, I'd have visited before," Anthony said finally.

"We're fortunate today. Perhaps the sun is shining in your honor, my lord."

Anthony lifted a dark eyebrow. It was the nearest the lady had come to coquetry since that obviously staged moment when they had first met back at the stables. Most of her conversation was disarmingly direct. He found her completely unlike the ladies he was used to back at court. Yet he remembered his impression that she had been lying about something the previous evening. The truth was, Mistress Fairfax had him perplexed and intrigued. It was an uncomfortable feeling for a man who prided himself on his skill in judging women.

It was on the tip of his tongue to answer with one of his courtly comments—to profess that the sun's rays were no brighter than the dazzling brightness of her countenance, or some such nonsense. But he stopped himself and said simply, "If anyone should be honored, mistress, 'tis you."

The unadorned compliment brought color to her cheeks. She answered him with a smile, and Anthony felt his heart skip a beat. "Shall we run a bit, mistress?" he asked brusquely.

"Of course. We can head through the meadow, if you like. The terrain is smooth and flat."

Anthony nodded agreement and followed her as she let her beautiful stallion stretch out into an easy gallop. Her uncle had been right. Even with the constraints of her riding skirts and a sidesaddle, she rode superbly, moving in perfect harmony with the animal. He let his horse fall back a ways just to enjoy the view, then spurred ahead, not willing to let her get too far from him. When he pulled up to her, she urged her horse to more speed, forcing him to catch up once again. All at once it became a contest, one in which Sarah seemed to have total control.

Finally she let him match her speed and stay with her. They raced side by side for several minutes, then Sarah pointed to a low rise in the grass and began to slow her pace. "There's a stream beyond. We'll just let them take a bit of water," she called, laughing and disheveled.

Her hair had pulled loose from its tight coils and fell to her shoulders in honeyed waves. Her gray eyes twinkled, and she looked so fresh and young that Anthony again felt the curious twist inside his chest. "We'll have to arrange a race sometime," she said with a little laugh.

"You'd best me, I fear. You ride like the wind, Mistress Sarah."

"'Tis the horse. No one can beat him."

Anthony nodded. "I'm beginning to believe it."

They had come to the edge of the stream. He jumped from his saddle, intending to help Sarah dismount, but she was on the ground before he could approach her. Anthony shook his head and observed, "The horse is twice your height, mistress, yet you jump from his back as easily as a cat."

He moved toward her, trailing his horse's reins behind him. "You've the eyes of a cat, too, sometimes," he said. "Gray. I've never seen their color before."

With his black eyes intensely focused on her again, Sarah felt the same agitation of the previous evening. In the space of a day, this fancy London courtier had made more observations about her person than she had heard in her entire life. Of course, at Charles's court such talk was probably the fashion. But for a girl raised pure and Puritan in the countryside, it was hard to answer.

Part of the time she thought that her discomfiture served her well. Her uncharacteristic loss for words must make her look a fool in the baron's eyes, and that was probably for the best. However, part of the time, she admitted to herself, she felt an overwhelming desire to impress the man.

Her father had shared his love of learning and books equally with her and Jack. She was educated far beyond what was considered desirable for a woman, and not just in the Puritan teachings of William Prynne and the like. With her father's encouragement, she'd read Shakespeare and Donne, even Hobbes. And she'd come to hold her own in conversations with many of her father's friends, who had been among the most learned of the land. She had a ready tongue and quick wit, and, for the life of her, she could not understand why both seemed to forsake her so utterly when in the presence of Lord Rutledge.

"I've been jumping off and on horses all my life," she answered, for lack of any other response. But Anthony preferred to stay with the topic of her eyes.

"A cat's eyes. But they turn storm-cloud gray when you're angry."

"I don't believe you've seen me angry, my lord."

"Not angry, then, but...incensed. As when you stood up for your uncle last night. I sensed that there was more behind your words. 'Years of battle and betrayal,' I believe you said. And there was anger, deep down." He moved even closer and lifted a finger to point at her face. "And storm clouds there... in those lovely gray eyes."

"The Civil War was hard on everyone," Sarah answered carefully. "It's not something I like to think about."

"But when a king's man arrives at your home, you have no other choice, is that it?"

She shook her head slowly. He was very near again, but this time she had no urge to step back. In fact, she felt almost compelled to draw even nearer. "Perhaps I was ready to dislike you, Lord Rutledge, for being a king's man. But I find that you are not as I would have expected."

Anthony's hand had lowered to settle along her arm. Gently he pulled her an imperceptible space toward him. "And how *do* you find me, mistress?"

Sarah's heart hammered in her throat and ears, making it hard for her to speak. "Not…disagreeable," she rasped.

A glint lit the darkness of Anthony's eyes. "Agreeable, then?"

She nodded.

"I find you *very* agreeable, Mistress Sarah," he said in a voice that had grown husky. He bent toward her, his other hand at her elbow, closing the distance between them. Sarah swayed, her knees suddenly weak.

"Mistress Fairfax!" a shrill female voice called from the road.

Sarah stiffened and Anthony's hands tightened on her arms. They turned in unison toward the sound of the cry. An attractive young woman was approaching them on a lumbering horse with no saddle. She was barefoot and her cotton skirts were hiked up around her thighs.

"It's one of the village women," Sarah said, a lump of disquiet lodging painfully in her throat. She had recognized at once the shapely form of Jack's new friend, Norah Thatcher.

"What does she want with you?" Anthony asked, irritated by the interruption.

Sarah shook her head. Norah slipped from the broad back of the horse and ran toward them, breathing heavily. She stopped in some awe when she got close enough to take a good look at the baron, but recovered quickly and turned to Sarah. "Your...er...Master *Partridge* sent me to fetch ye, mistress."

Sarah felt a stab of fear in her middle. "What's wrong, Norah?" she asked, her voice rising with apprehension.

"Ye's to come to the village right quickly, mistress." She stopped and took a deep gulp of a breath. "It seems that the sheriff has arrested Parson Hollander."

Chapter Three

Sarah rode stiffly alongside Anthony. Their huge mounts had long since left behind the poor farm horse with Norah Thatcher clinging to its back.

"Is it far to the village?" Anthony shouted.

Sarah shook her head. All at once things seemed to be spinning out of control. Gentle Parson Hollander had been arrested. Anthony had insisted on accompanying her to the village, and she didn't know what they would find when they got there. She hoped that Jack would have enough sense to stay out of sight, and that he had had time to enlist the parson's help in making sure the villagers knew about the "Henry Partridge" deception. She was confident that they would cooperate with the ruse. There was little love for the king in the town with the taxes being increased regularly to finance the Dutch war. And Jack and Sarah had been treated kindly since arriving at their uncle's after their father's execution four years ago. Most of the residents of Wiggleston knew how protective Sarah had been of Jack over the years. She could count on their help, as long as Jack and the parson had had time to spread the word.

"Mistress Sarah, are you close to this village parson? You look distressed." Anthony was watching her with a thoughtful look on his face that did not help Sarah's unease.

"He's been the family parson as long as I can remember."

"He's a Puritan, then?"

Sarah hesitated. King Charles had proven remarkably tolerant in allowing Puritans to freely practice the religion that had figured so prominently in the overthrow of his father. But Sarah could not let go of her mistrust. Her father had been killed for his beliefs, and she did not feel comfortable discussing such matters with a representative of the crown. "Parson Hollander is the most godly man I know," she replied at last. "It's absolutely ridiculous to think of him being put under arrest."

Anthony noted the evasiveness as well as the vehemence of her reply and decided to keep his questions to himself. After their near embrace in the meadow, he was more determined than ever to take Mistress Sarah to his bed before he left Yorkshire. He was even prepared to overlook the fact that she obviously knew more about the goings-on in this area than she was willing to let on to him. His mission would be greatly simplified if this Parson Hollander *was* the moonlight bandit. They should know soon—he prided himself on having an instinct about such things. For the time being he would let Mistress Fairfax keep her secrets.

Wiggleston was nestled at the base of a series of limestone crags that led down to the sea. Unlike bustling Kingston-on-Hull to the north, the village's coastline was too rocky to be a commercial port. Except for an occasional poor fishing coble, the Wiggleston coves were occupied only by gannets and razorbills that soared in and out with complete sovereignty. To the west of the village, the cliffs turned into gentle Yorkshire wolds and eventually stretched out as vast moors, which still had a purple cast even in their winter dryness.

Sarah usually loved the moment when the sea came into view as she rounded Bratswick Scar on the road into town. But today she barely glanced out at the water. Her mind was too busy with the complications of the current situation.

"The sheriff's house and gaol is not far. I can make my way by myself from here," she said to Anthony. "Why don't you go on back to Leasworth and spend some more time with the horses?"

Anthony shook his head. "I wouldn't think of it. You're upset. I'll go with you and see what this is all about. Perhaps I can be of some help."

Sarah gritted her teeth and gave a slight pull on Brigand's reins to tell him to head around the big gritstone smithy and proceed along the neat row of brick cottages that made up the most prosperous part of town. At the end was the larger brick structure that housed the town gaol. A number of townsfolk were congregated in the village green just in front of it.

Sarah surveyed the crowd anxiously and let out a long breath when she saw no sign of Jack in the group. She stopped in front of an iron hitching post and jumped from Brigand's back. Anthony was at her side almost at the same instant. He took her arm as they made their way through the crowd.

"Mistress Fairfax, thank goodness you're here." A reedy fellow with thinning hair pushed his way toward them.

Roger Spragg had been the town mayor for as long as anyone could remember, keeping his post by virtue of his untarnished record of absolute inaction. Sarah was surprised to see him so uncharacteristically agitated.

"What's going on, Mr. Spragg?"

The mayor twisted his hands and smacked together the edges of his mouth, which seemed to be devoid of lips. "Perhaps we should send for your uncle, Mistress Fairfax. There's king's men in town and your..." He stopped and looked nervously over at Anthony. "Well, and now they've gone and arrested Parson Hollander."

Sarah put a slender hand on the mayor's sleeve to calm him down. She had the feeling he had been going to say something about Jack, which she couldn't let happen. "I'll go in and talk with Sheriff Jeffries, Mr. Spragg. Why don't you tell these good people to go on about their business? They can't be of any help here."

Spragg gave a little whining sound. "I should go inside with you, Mistress Fairfax. These charges against the parson are outrageous."

"I know." Sarah bit back her impatience with the annoying little man. "I'm sure it's all some kind of misunderstanding. But your duty now is to your townspeople."

Spragg looked around at the gathering and nodded his head several times. "Perhaps you're right, Mistress Fairfax. Duty comes first. I'll try to calm these folks down."

Sarah gave a forced smile and pushed her way past him. Anthony watched her with amusement. She wasn't one to put up with foolishness, that much was obvious. He was looking forward to seeing how she handled the sheriff...and Oliver, if, as he suspected, his friend was behind this arrest.

In deference to the vocation of the prisoner, the questioning was taking place in the parlor of the sheriff's roomy house. By far the fanciest home in the village, the floor had carpets instead of rush mats, and the furniture in the room they were entering was upholstered with tooled leather.

As Sarah and Anthony entered the arched doorway, the occupants of the room turned simultaneously. Anthony's eyes skimmed over the stalwart figure of Oliver, who stood nearest them. He did not let even a flicker of his eye betray recognition. A large man was standing near the stone fireplace, bending over a clergyman who sat stiffly in a straight wooden chair.

Anthony almost laughed aloud when he saw him. This frail, gray-haired cleric was supposed to be the masked robber who rode like the wind and wielded a sword like a pirate?

"Sheriff Jeffries, what's going on here?" Sarah's voice carried none of the mellow tone Anthony had found so pleasing. He looked down at her in surprise.

The man by the fire straightened and then made a slight bow in their direction. He shifted his leather baldric to fit more comfortably over the bulge of his stomach. "We've had an accusation, Mistress Fairfax, against Parson Hollander. And I'm honor-bound to investigate."

Sarah pulled her arm out of Anthony's grasp and briskly crossed the room. "What kind of accusation?"

The sheriff nodded his head at Oliver. "Captain Kempthorne, here, says the parson's been involved in clandestine activities."

Sarah positioned herself behind the parson and looked fiercely at the sheriff. "That's absurd," she said.

"I daresay, Mistress Fairfax. But we have to check on Captain Kempthorne's story."

Sarah glared across the room at Oliver, who was leaning against a trestle table, his arms folded. "And just what is Captain Kempthorne's story?"

Without straightening, Oliver gave a brief nod of introduction. "Oliver Kempthorne of his majesty's guards, at your service, mistress. It appears that your parson has been involved in a series of robberies that have taken place in this district."

"And on what do you base these preposterous charges, Captain Kempthorne?"

"My men have been charged with cleaning up the smuggling in these parts now that we're at war again with the Dutch. Last week up in Hull we had a...er...discussion with a Dutch contrabandist we caught red-handed. The man swore he got the jewels he was carrying from your parson. When we searched the vestry over at the church, we found this." Oliver reached casually into his doublet and pulled out a glittery necklace.

Sarah's mouth went dry. She recognized the piece as one she had taken from the Bishop of Lackdale. She put her hands on the parson's shoulders, as much to support herself as him. "There has to be some mistake," she said, less forcibly than before.

Anthony was watching the proceedings with some dismay. Obviously, this tiny old man was not the robber. But it appeared that he *was* involved in the crimes. And Sarah was disconcerted and upset by his arrest. He hoped that didn't mean that she was involved, too.

"Allow me to introduce myself, gentlemen," he said smoothly. "I'm Lord Anthony Rutledge. I've recently come from court and am, of course, interested in any matter involving the king's business." He addressed the words to Oliver, who nodded impassively, then crossed the room to offer his hand to the sheriff.

"Much obliged, uh, your honor, er, Lord Rutledge." Jeffries gave the impression that two king's men in one day was too much for him to handle.

Sarah turned her direct gaze on Anthony. "If you can do anything about this, I'd be very grateful. Obviously, there has been some kind of terrible mistake."

Anthony looked around at the other occupants of the room. "Perhaps we should let the good father speak for himself." He walked over to stand directly in front of the parson and Sarah. "Tell me, Father," he said pleasantly. "Do you ride the roads at midnight, robbing innocent people of their fortunes at the point of a sword?"

The very absurdity of the statement hit everyone in the room. Parson Hollander looked as if he were having a good deal of difficulty maintaining a seat in the flimsy chair. It was inconceivable to think of him thundering down a lonely highway on a powerful stallion. He gave a gentle smile and shook his head. "No, my son."

Anthony looked at Jeffries. "I think you're going to have a hard time proving your case, Sheriff."

Oliver pulled himself up slowly from his slouch against the table. "He may not be the highwayman, but he's involved up to his holy little neck. Perhaps a few days in the gaol will loosen his tongue."

Sarah's cat eyes glinted like the tips of two drawn swords as she turned to Oliver, her hands on her hips. "How can you take the word of an admitted smuggler against this holy man?"

Anthony gave a half smile as he watched Oliver face Sarah's fury with utter nonchalance. His friend gave a shrug and walked across the room to where a heavy manacle was draped over a bench. He picked up the chains and walked over to the prisoner. "Your hands, Parson," he said calmly.

Sarah's normally fair skin flushed dark red. She moved from behind the parson to plant herself in front of Oliver. "Don't you dare put those things on him!"

Anthony was torn. He was curious to see if she would betray some knowledge of the crimes in her angry state. But at the same time he felt an inexplicable urge to protect her from becoming more involved. The latter won out as he went over to her and put his hand against the small of her back. "Let's go, Sarah," he said softly. "There's nothing you can do here until the evidence has been examined more thoroughly."

Sarah's hands shook as she watched Kempthorne place the heavy manacles around Parson Hollander's white, bony wrists. The cleric twisted to look at her with his serene smile. "Don't worry about me, Sarah. You go on home and take care of yourself. *You're* the one who's important here."

The emphasis in the parson's words was odd, but they seemed to soothe Sarah for a moment. She stood stiffly as the sheriff, who had also winced at seeing the parson locked into chains, helped the old man out of his chair and led him toward the door.

"You won't be there for long, Parson," Sarah said, her voice firm again. "I'll see to it."

Parson Hollander gave one last smile before he turned and meekly followed the sheriff out of the room.

There was a long moment of silence after the two men left. Finally Anthony said, "Mistress Fairfax, perhaps you'd be kind enough to give me a moment with this gentleman. I may be able to get to the bottom of this matter."

"If you're going to talk about Parson Hollander, I'm staying right here." Sarah shifted her feet slightly apart as if to root herself more firmly to the spot.

Anthony could see the amusement behind Oliver's impassive expression. It was not often that a woman refused one of Anthony's requests. He leaned down and spoke low in her ear. "I'll tell you what we talk about later. I might be able to get more information out of him dealing—you know—man-to-man."

Sarah looked from Oliver back to Anthony, then gave a curt nod and left the room with a haughty swish of her skirts.

Oliver resumed his resting place against the table. "I might have known, Anthony," he drawled. "I can't leave you alone for a week without you tangling yourself up with a she-lion."

Anthony was still staring at the door. "Isn't she astonishing? Who'd have thought it... out here in this backwash of civilization?"

Oliver barked a laugh. "You're the astonishing one, my friend. If there's a beauty within twenty shires, you'll land at her doorstep."

Anthony turned his gaze to his friend. "I'd wager there's none in twenty shires to match her, perhaps in all of England."

"Hell, Anthony, you've the look of a lovesick puppy dog. Who is she, anyway?"

"Old Fairfax's niece. My hostess. Charles must not have known about her or he would have come on this mission himself."

"You and the king make a fine pair. England can rot all around you as long as there's a pretty face to watch."

Anthony ignored the barb. "Tell me she's not a beauty, Oliver."

"Her features are fair enough, I guess, though I'd have been better able to judge if she hadn't been eyeing me like a piece of meat she wanted to skewer."

Anthony laughed. "You're just upset because I got to her first. And because you're the villain of the day, while I—" he gave a mock bow "—may yet prove to be her hero."

"Aye. I forgot to thank you for all your bloody support in the interrogation just now."

"Sorry, I figured I'd be better off not to take sides yet."

"Not until you talk the beauteous Mistress Fairfax into your bed, you mean."

"I can't say the idea hadn't crossed my mind."

Oliver picked up a pewter mug from the table alongside him and heaved it at Anthony's head. "It's not your *mind* it crossed, you blackguard."

Catching the mug easily with his left hand, Anthony scowled at his friend. "We're not here to talk about Mistress Fairfax. What have you learned about the highwayman?"

Oliver crossed his burly arms. "The priest's in it somewhere, I'm sure of that."

"But he's not the bandit."

"No."

Anthony began pacing the room. "I don't like this. The town is obviously behind their parson. Why did you have to shackle the old man?"

"For effect. You don't get information out of someone by treating him like a bloody prince."

Anthony nodded. Oliver was right, of course, and it bothered Anthony to think that his own interest in Sarah was already fogging his judgment in this matter. "Well, if he doesn't talk soon, we'll have to move him to London. It will cause too much trouble to have him imprisoned here in his own town."

"And it won't help your relations with Mistress Fairfax any, either."

Anthony disregarded his friend's sarcasm. "Oliver, do you think the highwayman could be Fairfax himself?"

"General Fairfax?"

"We know the bandit is a swordsman. Looking around this village, I'd say there can't be too many here with that particular skill."

Oliver looked doubtful. "The general's not a young man anymore. And somehow it doesn't sound like his style. You don't go from being a leader of thousands of men out on a battlefield to skulking around at night behind a mask."

Anthony sighed. "Perhaps you're right. I'll do a little poking around at their manor house, just in case. In the meanwhile, have your men continue investigating, and keep after the parson. Maybe he'll break down and give us the information we're looking for. Just be sure you don't kill the poor devil."

"Are you sure you'll be all right poking around by yourself at the Fairfax manor?" Oliver asked with a perfectly straight face.

Anthony grimaced. It was the kind of double entendre humor that was rife at court, but somehow it sounded out of place out here in the fresh Yorkshire countryside. Especially when it concerned Sarah Fairfax. "Don't be crude, Kempthorne." Anthony decided it was time to go on the offensive. "Just because you've always preferred your horse to a fine lady."

Oliver's mistrust of women was well-known at court. During the exile years he had fallen so badly for a French countess that he had abandoned his friends for weeks. When he returned to their company, he informed them curtly that, unbeknownst to him, the countess had had a count, and she was not about to lose either the riches or the title he gave her merely for the sake of a fugitive Englishman with uncertain prospects. A few days later somebody had ventured to tease him about his lost countess. The tormentor had ended up with part of his ear sliced off. After that, no one said anything when Oliver refused to join their parties with the ladies.

"Horses are loyal," Oliver said. "They're happy with one master, and they do what they're told."

"Some women are loyal, too, my friend," Anthony said gently. "And I haven't given up on convincing Mistress Fairfax to do as I bid her."

"You just may have met your match in this one, Rutledge. After all, her uncle was one of the men who defeated the most powerful king in the world. And your Mistress Fairfax looked none too docile to me."

Anthony grinned. "It's going to be an interesting challenge."

Oliver straightened up with a snort and started out the door. "Go on back to your courting, Rutledge. I've work to do."

Sarah was outside with several of the villagers who had refused to return to their homes. Her slight form dominated the group, though Anthony could not say if it was her bearing or the regal simplicity of her black velvet riding habit. Her expression was grave as he approached.

"What are they going to do to him?" she asked.

Anthony scanned the anxious faces in front of him. "He's obviously not the masked rider they're looking for. But there does seem to be some link with the stolen goods. If any of you know something more about the thief, you could help your Parson Hollander greatly by speaking to the authorities."

There was utter silence. Anthony could not detect even a particle of guilt in their solemn expressions. He sighed. If the parson really was involved in the crimes, it meant that they were the work of more than a single miscreant. It might even mean that the whole village was involved. And the good people looking at him so earnestly at this moment knew exactly who the robber was.

Anthony looked back at Sarah with something like regret. He had the feeling that she, too, had the answers he sought. Who would hold the village's respect enough to carry out such a conspiracy? Her uncle, surely, but as Oliver had said, he was not a very likely candidate. Perhaps it was the young suitor he had seen with Sarah earlier.

After several moments of silence, Mayor Spragg cleared his throat and said, "We don't know anything about it, Lord Rutledge." Several heads bobbed up and down in agreement.

Anthony turned to Sarah. "You're all willing to let the parson molder away in prison?"

"It doesn't appear that we have any choice," she snapped.

"They ain't going to hang the parson, are they, Mistress Sarah?" The tiny voice came from a boy of about ten years with a dirty cherub face and a thatch of thick brown hair.

Sarah took a step toward the child and knelt down to put an arm around his thin shoulders. "They won't hang him, Benjamin. The parson's no thief, and they'll figure that out soon enough, I reckon."

"He had chains on his hands." The boy's eyes were wide.

"It's what they do to prisoners, Ben. But they'll take the chains off when they set him free. Now, does your mother know you're down here in the green?"

The boy looked down and shook his head.

"Then you'd best run along home so she won't worry. You can't help the parson any by staying here."

She straightened and looked around at the group. "I guess there's not much reason for any of us to stay. I'll talk to my uncle and have him send word to his solicitor."

Mayor Spragg seemed relieved to see the situation come to a temporary resolution. "Yes, indeed. As long as there are king's men in town, we should all be safely back in our homes."

After an encouraging push from Sarah, the boy, Benjamin, took off at a brisk run, and one by one the rest of the group dispersed until just Sarah and Anthony were left. Anthony had a puzzled look on his face.

"What did your mayor mean about being safely back in their homes? Surely the people of Wiggleston have nothing to fear from representatives of the king?"

Sarah gave a humorless laugh. "We never used to be afraid, but now that the king's collectors have tripled the tax, people are wary. Most of them simply don't have the funds to pay such amounts."

"The tax has tripled?"

Sarah gave Anthony a look of exasperation. "You fine folk carry on with your parties and games in the palaces of London and think you are ruling the country, but you have no idea of what is really going on in the rest of England."

Anthony looked around him. He could now see that many of the brick houses that had appeared so neat when he first rode into the village were in a ramshackle state of repair. "When were these new taxes imposed?"

"Months ago. They tell us that the king has run out of money to fight wars with the Dutch over slaving stations thousands of miles off in Africa and the New World. But what is that to us here in Yorkshire? We don't have anything against the Dutch. We've traded with them for years."

Anthony was silent. This mission was proving to be more educational than he had anticipated.

"I'm sorry to vent my feelings on you, Lord Rutledge. I realize that the arrest of Parson Hollander has nothing to do with you."

He felt an uncharacteristic flush of guilt. "Perhaps we should be getting back to Leasworth. You said that you wanted to talk with your uncle."

"Yes. I don't want the parson to spend one hour more than necessary in that awful place."

"Sarah, I can't let you do this." Jack's normally smiling face was grim.

"I don't have any other choice. I can't let the parson stay in prison for something that I did. My only other alternative would be giving myself up to the tender mercies of King Charles's justice. And you'll remember, Jack, just how that ended up for our father." Sarah was curled up like a kitten in the corner of a large sleeping couch. She looked to Jack like a girl of twelve. It was impossible to picture her mounted on a spirited stallion and brandishing a sword.

"I know you're my big sister, but it's time I took on some of my burdens as a man in this family. If it has to be done, I'm the one to do it."

Sarah pushed herself up out of the deep cushions. Jack could almost see her hair stand on end as she glared at him. "Do you think I've kept you out of notice of the king these four years past just to let you give yourself up now? The king can extend Father's death warrant to you with a snap of his fingers. And then what would I be left with?"

"That's assuming I would be caught, sister dear. And though you may not have noticed, I now ride as well as you do, better perhaps."

"I swear, Jack, if I have to get the servants to help me tie you to your bed, I'll not let you do this thing. Uncle Thomas would agree with me. He's always supported me in my attempts to keep you out of the king's way."

"Uncle Thomas doesn't know that his niece is the moonlight bandit," Jack reminded her sharply. "Besides, I thought you were going to get his solicitor to look at the case. Perhaps we won't have to do anything at all.''

"Uncle Thomas has already sent word to Mr. Montague.''

"And...?''

Sarah's head drooped. "He says he doesn't hold out much hope when they caught the parson red-handed with some of the stolen jewels.''

Jack was silent for a moment, then said firmly, "Perhaps you are right that we'll have to do something. But if there's to be fighting involved, I'm the one who will be doing it.''

Sarah sank back into the cushions with a sigh. "My head hurts, Jack. It's been a very long and unsettling day. Why don't you go on back to your Mistress Thatcher and let me alone? We'll talk about this in the morning.''

Jack wasted no time on sympathy. "There's nothing to talk about, Sarah. You're *not* going to ride in single-handedly and break Parson Hollander out of the gaol. The whole idea's crazy.''

Sarah closed her eyes and rubbed the sides of her forehead. "Well, I'm not going to do *anything* tonight, so why don't you just do as I say?''

"Do you promise you won't take any action until we've worked out a plan?''

"Yes, I promise,'' she answered, stopping the massage of her temples to look up at Jack with an expression of pain. "If my head doesn't stop pounding, I'll have all I can do to get to my bed, much less up on the back of a horse."

Jack crossed the room and bent to give her a light kiss on the cheek. "Try to sleep. Perhaps in the morning we'll figure a way out of this coil."

"I will, Jack. Go on and get out of here. Now more than ever I want to keep you out of Lord Rutledge's sight." She looked steadily into her brother's eyes and hoped he didn't notice the flush that had come over her face at the mere mention of their visitor's name.

Chapter Four

Sarah found Anthony in the upper solar. He was making notes on a portable leather writing desk, but looked up with a smile as she entered.

"I fear you have not had the most productive day for your mission of acquiring horses," she said.

Anthony put the desk to one side and stood. "My only complaint about the day is that our ride this morning was interrupted."

Sarah gave a faint smile. "It was a good run, or at least it started out to be. You ride well, my lord."

"War is a fine teacher—for riding, fighting and many other things, as well."

"Yet you did not spend all your youth in battle. You've mastered the skills of the drawing room, too."

"The battles are all far behind us, I hope," he said, reaching to take her arm and draw her to a settle that was placed near the room's tiny fireplace. Sarah had come only to bid their guest good-night. She hadn't intended to stay with him. But she found herself sitting without protest.

"At court these days one must learn the finer ways of life," Anthony continued. "Charles now delights in the more civilized amusements and has left fighting and jousting to his younger courtiers."

He sat next to her, his knee touching her leg and his face just inches from hers. His close presence intensified the pounding in her head and she found it difficult to concentrate on her words. "You admire the king?" she asked.

Anthony nodded. "Charles has many failings, but he is loyal to his friends and generous to a fault. What's more, he desperately wants to be a good king and do what's right for his country."

Sarah had trouble reconciling Anthony's words with the image of the king she had kept in her mind for so long. Her head throbbed, and she lifted a hand to her temple.

"Are you feeling all right, Mistress Sarah? It was a long day for you. You look tired."

"I have the headache, I'm afraid. It was distressing to see such a good man as Parson Hollander treated so poorly."

Anthony made a little circle with his hand. "Turn around," he said.

"I beg your pardon?"

"Turn your head to look at the opposite wall there."

Before Sarah knew what was happening, Anthony's hands were on her shoulders and he had half turned her to face away from him. Slowly he kneaded the base of her neck with his warm hands. Almost instantly, the pain in her head began to subside.

"That feels wonderful!" she exclaimed.

"I know. I can't tell you exactly why, but it does make the pain go away."

His hands moved outward on her shoulders and then back together and up and down her slender neck. They manipulated her body with a wonderfully gentle strength. "Where did you learn to do that?" she asked, sounding sleepy.

"It's a technique I learned in Paris at a...uh..." He hesitated, then said, finishing lamely, "The French are very good with body aches."

Anthony was having trouble holding on to his concentration. Sarah's firm body and silky skin were sending definite messages to his brain and other parts of his anatomy. He could feel her relaxing, melting, almost, at his touch, and he wanted very much to pull her back into his arms.

"You spent a lot of time there?" Sarah asked.

"I'm sorry...?"

"In Paris. Did you spend a lot of time in Paris?"

Yes, he had. But he wasn't about to describe his Paris adventures to the Puritan Mistress Fairfax. In Paris he had discovered the delights of a woman's body and the talents of his own. He hoped to be able to pass on some of this knowledge to Sarah—soon. But he was rather certain that it would not help his case to discuss Paris with her.

"Charles's court in exile was there for a time," he answered briefly.

He turned her around to face him again but did not let go of her arms. "Is that better?" he asked softly.

Sarah nodded. She moved her head in a slow circle. The pain was almost gone. "Thank you," she said. It came out as a whisper.

Anthony pulled her toward him on the bench. His fingers traced the line of her eyebrows, then made gentle circles on her temples. "I'm sorry you were so upset today, Sarah."

Sarah's eyes closed. She didn't want to think about Parson Hollander's arrest or what she might have to do about it tomorrow or the next day. She wanted to continue to experience the sensation of a man's strong hands moving against her. "It's kind of you to be concerned," she managed to murmur.

Anthony's hands moved down from her head to her neck, then to her shoulders and back. It was a natural progression that left Sarah completely at ease as he pulled her against him and bent to claim her mouth. The touch of his warm lips startled her. Her eyes flew open and she started to draw away.

"Don't be afraid, Sarah. Relax. I'm just kissing you good night, nothing more." His voice was low and persuasive.

Her heart was beating heavily inside her chest. She didn't feel relaxed anymore, and she no longer wanted to pull away. But her reactions were scaring her. "I'm not used to your court ways, my lord."

He loosened his hold on her, keeping her just within his arms. As softly as wind on a petal, he kissed each corner of her mouth, then the center. "Ah, Sarah. You are like nothing I have ever known at court, but there's a fire inside you that's going to blaze one of these days."

Sarah scarcely heard the words. Her stomach had begun to feel odd as his mouth continued to touch her. Finally, she moved her own lips in response, and instantly he deepened the kiss into something warm and wet and magical. A wave of heat rode through her middle and her arms clung to him quite without her knowledge.

Abruptly, Anthony pulled away. Sarah's eyes opened, and she looked at him in surprise.

Anthony took a ragged breath. "I find that I want more than a taste of you, Sarah." His thumbs made small circles around the hollows of her cheeks.

His words made her limbs go weak. "I don't...I can't..." Her head was spinning, but not from the megrim this time.

Anthony smiled. One of his questions had been answered. He would wager half the fortune Charles had bestowed upon him that Sarah Fairfax was yet an innocent to the ways of love. He intended to change that. But he would do it with time and care so that he could ensure her full pleasure.

He placed one more light kiss full on her lips, then moved away from her.

"So. Is your head feeling better?"

Sarah had recovered her senses enough to feel some embarrassment. She smiled ruefully. "I'm not sure. It certainly feels different than when I came into the room."

Anthony gave a soft laugh. "I hope I wasn't too forward, Sarah. You've bewitched me, I think."

The churning in her midsection was subsiding, but Sarah still felt dazed. For twenty-three years she had lived among men, taken care of them, debated with them, but she had never had one affect her like this magnetic dark baron. Indeed, she feared she might be the one who was falling under some kind of a spell.

"I've not offended you?" Anthony persisted.

She shook her head and looked over at the fire, avoiding his eyes. In the firelight her hair gleamed like spun gold. Anthony reached a hand to touch it. "I'll bid you good-night then, Sarah."

He rose first and extended his hand to help her from the settle. She took a long breath, then stood without assistance. "Yes, good night."

Anthony watched her leave the room, willing his body to dissipate the rampant desire that had rushed through him the instant his lips had touched her. More than his body was disturbed. He was having feelings for Mistress Fairfax unlike any he had ever experienced. It had given him a fierce joy to realize that she was a virgin, a state on which he had never before put the least value. And yesterday, when he had seen her embrace her tall blond suitor, he had felt a surge of what could only be described as jealousy, a weakness he had always taken careful pains to avoid.

He stared into the dancing flames of the fireplace. One thing was certain. It was fortunate that Master Partridge appeared to be moving slowly in his courtship, because Anthony intended to make sure that it was he, not some Yorkshire bumpkin, who would introduce Sarah to the carnal pleasures her Puritan upbringing had so far ignored.

The dreams had come again, disturbing Sarah's sleep and leaving her feeling tired. She lingered a moment at the top of the steps as if hesitating to descend and meet the day. Memories of her encounter with Anthony in the solar last night did not help her peace of mind.

Nor did it help that his was the first face she saw as she entered the dining room. He rose immediately at her appearance, followed more slowly by the other two men at the table—her uncle Thomas and Oliver Kempthorne.

Sarah stopped in the doorway. What was her uncle doing breaking fast with a king's guard? The last time she had seen such a uniform at Leasworth, it had been on the men who had come to arrest her father for treason. A little scowl furrowed a line between her eyes. Anthony was coming toward her.

"Good morrow, mistress. How are you feeling this morning? Your head is better?" His words were perfectly correct and solicitous, but as he took her hand to lead her into the room, his thumb made gentle circles in her palm.

Sarah pulled her hand away and walked past him to move around to the opposite side of the table. She was far from immune to his touch, but she was determined to come to her senses about this man. She surveyed him dispassionately as he resumed his seat next to Kempthorne. The two men had a similar cast. Though Anthony was lean and dark and Kempthorne was thickset and fair, they both carried the stamp of their cavalier background. Their long hair fell in careless waves and both wore billowing white shirts of the finest lawn. Yesterday one of these men had imprisoned one of her dearest friends. The other had kissed her. She would do well to stay away from them both.

"Lord Rutledge was telling me that you were ill last night, Sarah," her uncle said. "Do you want me to send for the apothecary?"

"I'm fine today, Uncle. I think I was just upset over the arrest of Parson Hollander." She kept her eyes on her uncle and ignored Oliver, whose presence she had yet to acknowledge.

"Yes, well, that's why I've asked Captain Kempthorne to join us. I've been telling him that there simply can't be any truth to these accusations. I've known Parson Hollander since we were boys together."

Oliver reached with his knife for a thick slab of bacon from the serving platter. "I'm willing to listen to all sides, Sir Thomas. The more information we get on this matter, the sooner it will be cleared up."

"I don't think you'll find any information of interest here at Leasworth," Sarah said.

Oliver turned to her and smiled pleasantly. "I don't imagine I will, Mistress Fairfax, but I have to look into all possibilities." Still smiling at her, he brought the entire piece of bacon up to his mouth and tore off a piece with his teeth.

"I believe Captain Kempthorne is making a routine survey of all the houses in the area," Anthony added.

Sarah turned away from both men to serve herself some warm milk. She had no appetite for food this morning. "Captain Kempthorne ought to go on back to London and leave us to handle our own affairs," she said under her breath.

"Sarah!" her uncle protested. "You'll have to excuse my niece, gentlemen. She's upset because she's very fond of the parson, but of course as loyal subjects of the crown we're happy to help in any way with his majesty's justice."

Anthony was watching Sarah's hands as she added cinnamon to her milk then curdled it with a little wine. Her attitude was different this morning. It might just be the presence of Oliver, but her animosity seemed to extend to Anthony, as well. He had been ready to forget about highwaymen and treason and crooked parsons to spend the day riding with her, but now he was not so sure the suggestion would be welcomed.

"I'm sorry if my presence here offends you, Mistress Sarah," Oliver said, chewing. "My men have found a number of witnesses who are willing to talk about the masked bandit. We should have him rounded up within a couple of days, and then we'll be on our way.''

Sarah sipped at her posset, willing herself to be calm. Her gray eyes looked into Kempthorne's without a flicker. "Well now, that's good news. I wish you God-speed.''

For the first time some of Oliver's nonchalance slipped. He glanced uncomfortably at Anthony. "If there's nothing more for me to do here, Lord Rut-ledge, perhaps I should take my leave.''

"Aye, perhaps you should," Anthony agreed dryly.

"Don't forget to be on the alert for that horse.''

Sarah's hands tightened around the mug of milk. "What horse is that, Captain Kempthorne?" she asked with a forced smile.

Anthony answered first. "Some of the victims of the robberies have mentioned a rather extraordinary stal-lion. It's the color of a moonlit sky, they say, though that's probably romantic fantasy.''

"Anyway, while you're reviewing horses, keep the description in mind," Oliver said, standing. "I'll be in touch.''

Thomas Fairfax rose to accompany his visitor to the door, and the two men left the room.

"Some might say that your dark roan is the color of a moonlit night," Anthony said evenly.

Sarah looked at him steadily. "Why didn't you men-tion him to Captain Kempthorne, then?"

"You said that you are the only one who rides him.''

"That's right.''

"What about your uncle? Does he ever take him out? Or your friend Master Partridge?"

"Brigand goes out with no one but me."

Anthony leaned back in his chair. This time he believed that she was telling the truth. He hoped for her sake and for his own that his instincts were correct. "Then there's no point in mentioning him to the authorities."

Sarah let out a little breath. "Thank you. I believe I've had enough of the authorities for the time being."

"How would you like to forget all about them and join me today? We could finish that ride."

Sarah set aside her nearly full mug and stood. "I'm sorry. If you need the services of a guide today you'll have to ask one of the grooms. I'm going to try to take some decent food in to Parson Hollander."

Anthony hid his vexation. "I'll accompany you, then."

Sarah stopped at the door to answer him. "No, thank you. I'm afraid the sentiment in town might be running a bit high against your kind, Lord Rutledge. It's no secret that there's been no great love for the king since his tax collectors started hauling our men off to debtor's prison for the nonpayment of unreasonable taxes. Now they've imprisoned one of the most popular men in town. You'd do well to finish up your business and head back to London where you belong."

Anthony saw no sign of Sarah the rest of the day. The Fairfax solicitor, Francis Montague, a weasel of a man who tapped his fingers incessantly while he talked, had arrived, then left, then come again, informing Sir Thomas that he was looking into the matter of the parson's arrest and would have more news for him in a couple of days.

Anthony had spent a restive afternoon viewing horses at a nearby estate. The owners had been obsequious and annoying, taking pains to assure him every few minutes that they had been faithful supporters of the king throughout the years of the Republic, even in the midst of this hotbed of Puritanism.

At the evening meal Sarah appeared in a severe dark gray dress to preside frostily over the table. She avoided looking at Anthony, whose frustration mounted with each course. Finally, as the servants were clearing away the last of the pigeon pie, he said, "Have I done something to offend you, Mistress Fairfax?"

Thomas Fairfax looked from Anthony to his niece in surprise. He'd spent the entire meal pontificating about the merits of Arabian stock over the more plodding British breeds and had paid scant attention to Sarah's demeanor.

Sarah's neck stiffened inside the high starched collar of her dress. She considered giving a diplomatic answer, but after a day spent first with a disheartened Parson Hollander and then trying to get some action out of Sheriff Jeffries, Oliver Kempthorne and the solicitor, Mr. Montague, she was in no mood to be accommodating to anyone, much less a royalist.

"You, personally, my lord, have done nothing to offend me. It's the system you represent that offends. They say the king's noble cavaliers have revived the art of romantic chivalry. Is it chivalrous to bleed the poor country folk of their hard-earned living so that you can dress yourselves in the finest silks and laces? Is it romantic to let a truly good man go to prison for wanting to help his people survive a long winter?"

There was a long moment of silence at the table. Then Sarah's uncle said, "You are not paying proper respect to our guest, Sarah. The king's taxes have nothing to do with Lord Rutledge. And you certainly can't blame him for the arrest of the parson."

Anthony was silent. For no reason he could understand, he was suddenly picturing the contrast between Sarah and his own mother. His beautiful, vivacious, utterly heartless mother. If she had ever once given a thought to the suffering of the English people during the Civil War it had never been apparent. As long as she could dance the night away at balls and soirees in the most fashionable of Parisian gowns, her world was perfect. He supposed that out of a sense of propriety she must have shed a tear at the news of his father's death on the battlefield at Marston Moor, but he had not seen it.

"Don't chide your niece, Sir Thomas. It's refreshing to hear a lady speak her mind. She would be a rare commodity at court."

"I'm happy to say that King Charles's court is one place where you'll never find me." Sarah rose and gave a rigid nod. "If you'll excuse me, gentlemen, I'll take my leave. Don't get up. I'll send the servants in with more ale."

She was gone before Anthony had a chance to get to his feet. With her departure, the energy seemed to have gone out of the room.

"You'll have to forgive Sarah, Lord Rutledge. She's not had an easy life since her father was executed. She saw the whole thing, you know, up on Tower Hill."

"It must have been horrible for her." Anthony had an uncharacteristic pang of sympathy for that grieving younger Sarah. The knowledge of what she had gone through made it easier to understand the way she felt about the king and his cavaliers. They had taken away the dearest thing in her life, and given her a dreadful, bloody passage into adulthood.

He could do nothing to restore her father or the innocence she must have lost that day on Tower Hill, but he could show her that not all royalists were bad. And he could introduce her to the more pleasing, exciting side of being an adult. Even this night, when she had been upset, he could feel the pull between them. He knew that she felt it, too. He could make her forget her troubles, if only for a few passion-filled hours.

"Please don't think me rude, Sir Thomas, but I'm also going to excuse myself."

Thomas's eyes had grown glazed as his memories had taken him back to the terrible days of his brother's imprisonment. He waved his hand wearily. "Yes, fine. I'm sorry we're not being the most congenial hosts. Perhaps in a few days Mr. Montague will have news for us about the parson and life will resume a more normal course.''

Anthony gave a little bow, then strode out of the room, bent on finding Sarah. He stopped one of the kitchen maids, a pert blonde named Millie who had given him more than one inviting look during his stay. "Do you know where Mistress Fairfax is?"

"Can't rightly say I do, sir, but I heard her say she was tired and would be off to bed early." She smiled up at him, turning her right cheek to show off the dimple. "Sounds like a good idea, if you asks me," she added with a sly wink.

Anthony laughed and gave the girl a pat on the cheek. "You're a naughty one, Millie. Unfortunately I have some business to discuss with Mistress Fairfax."

"More's the pity. It's not often we see a handsome devil like you in these parts."

Under normal circumstances, her bold enthusiasm might have tempted him, but at the moment Anthony only wanted to find Sarah. After assuring the undaunted Millie that he might consider her offer on another occasion, he made his way to Sarah's bedroom, a location he had taken pains to learn.

Sarah was not pleased to hear the soft knock at her door. She had already taken some of her gear out of the old chest where she kept it hidden, and she was trying to get her mind set for the task of rescuing the parson. Her success was dependent on sharp thinking and lightning-quick reflexes. At the moment she felt sluggish and reluctant to act. It would not do. And now there was this interruption.

Hurriedly she stuffed the dark clothes back into the trunk, then crossed the room. It was Anthony, of course. She had known even before she opened the door. He was dressed in the same fine suit he had worn at dinner—black hose and boots up to his thigh, a closely fitted black jacket with underslashes of royal blue silk. He looked powerful, commanding.

"May I speak with you a moment, Sarah?"

She backed away from the door, letting it open after her to allow him to enter. He stepped across the threshold and his presence filled her tiny room. "I was about to retire," she said ungraciously. "What do you want?"

"I want things to be right between us. I want to see a smile in those cat's eyes of yours, as I did that first day in the meadow."

Anthony's low voice flowed through her like a drink of mulled cider. She closed her eyes briefly and remembered how his lips had felt the previous night. Then she took a deep breath. "I'm sorry, my lord, I don't have too many smiles in me today."

Anthony reached to take her hand. "Be fair, Sarah. It wasn't the king who got your parson into trouble. He was in possession of stolen goods. And don't try to tell me he didn't know they were stolen. You don't find jewels of that quality just lying around the village green."

Unwittingly, Anthony had hit exactly on the thing that was most bothering Sarah. He was right. It wasn't the king who had put Parson Hollander in the gaol—it was Sarah herself. *She* was responsible for the good father's plight. And it was she who would have to get him out of it. "I'm not blaming the king, Anthony, or you or even Captain Kempthorne. But it just emphasizes the fact that we are from two different worlds. You don't understand mine, and I don't understand yours."

"Perhaps not, Sarah, but I'm willing to try."

Sarah was surprised at the sincerity of his tone. In fact, it seemed she was constantly being surprised by this man. "To what purpose?" she asked finally. "Shortly you'll be heading back to your glamorous London life and forget all about our simple country ways here in Yorkshire."

"No," he said, shaking his head slowly. "There is at least one thing from Yorkshire that I shall not soon forget."

Sarah was confused. When she had seen him with Captain Kempthorne this morning she had told herself that Lord Rutledge was nothing more than an arrogant representative of a king she hated. All day long, dealing with the parson's dilemma, she had worked to build up a wall of indifference. But now his warm hand was holding hers. His dark eyes were watching her with the same intriguing, predatory expression he had had when he ended their embrace last night. It made it hard for her to think straight.

"How would you ever understand my world?" she asked him.

"By being a part of it. Let's finish our ride tomorrow, and you can show it to me."

"I have some visits to make in the village tomorrow."

"Fine. We'll make them together. And then we can find the sheriff and Captain Kempthorne and I'll see if there's anything I can do to get your parson out of the gaol."

"You would do that?"

Anthony raised her hand to his lips. "Just give me a chance, Sarah. Give *us* a chance."

His lips grazed her knuckles, then nipped softly at the base of her thumb. "All right," Sarah answered, not quite knowing what she was agreeing to.

He straightened and smiled at her. "Until the morrow then, my lady."

"Until tomorrow," she repeated. And he was gone.

She walked slowly over to the bed. She had been resolved not to let the parson spend one more night in the gaol. But perhaps Anthony's suggestion was worthwhile. If he could use his influence to help the parson, it would be less trouble for everyone. It made sense. She did not want to admit even to herself that it was also a relief. Her eyes went to the trunk where the clothes of the masked rider lay hidden. The disguise had seemed so liberating when she had first begun to avenge her father's death by robbing the men who had been responsible. But lately the role was growing more and more difficult. It was true that her efforts had helped a lot of good people through these hard times. But she

92 *Moonrise*

had also complicated her life and those of her brother and the parson. She was tired and ready to lead a normal life, to think about ordinary things such as falling in love and having babies. Perhaps she was even ready to put aside some of the old hatreds.

She took off her dark, straitlaced dress and threw it in a heap in the corner of the room. Tomorrow she would give Anthony the chance he was asking for.

Chapter Five

After leaving Sarah's room, Anthony slowly descended the curved stone stairway to the lower floor. If Sir Thomas was still in the dining room, he would stay to share a cup of ale with him. There was no point in going to his bed for another evening of restless sleep. Last night he had dreamt of gray eyes that at first were Sarah's and then had changed to merge into the face of a beautiful, sleek cat. When he'd tried to pet it, it had lashed out with wicked claws and dug them into his chest until spots of bright red blood dripped to the floor in front of him.

For the life of him he couldn't say how the lovely Puritan had become so important to him in such a short time. Perhaps it was witchcraft after all.

The dining room was empty and dark. Anthony sighed. He had a momentary vision of the maid Millie's smiling blue eyes, but pushed the thought away. He would wait for the real thing.

* * *

The day was not going as Anthony had planned. He had imagined accompanying Sarah on a few minor errands in the village and then enjoying a brisk ride through the rolling Yorkshire wolds. He had made sure to carry along a blanket roll, and his saddlebags were filled with a flask of ale and some honey cakes. He had been looking forward to testing his own mount, Deception, against Sarah's magnificent stallion.

But it was midafternoon and they were still in Wiggleston. They had spent the day visiting the families in the poorest part of the village. Sarah's own horse had been loaded with the items she was delivering—a length of cloth for a tired-looking young woman who appeared to be expecting a baby at any minute, a crock of cream for a family of eight who had lost their only cow to the tax collectors, a strong-smelling liniment for an elderly man who couldn't rise to greet them in spite of several attempts.

"It's just the winter's cold," he'd said, refusing Anthony's offer of help.

Now they were inside a two-room cottage, and everywhere Anthony looked in the dim light there appeared to be a child, each one of a different size. He recognized the boy who had been among the crowd in front of the sheriff's after the arrest of the parson.

"Where's your mother, Benjamin?" Sarah asked the child.

"She's over to the Wyeth place working in the kitchen. They're going to pay her a shilling a week."

"Who's looking after you children?"

"Me and my sister Nancy. We're re-responsible, Ma says."

Sarah frowned. "Which one is Nancy?"

A girl of about Benjamin's height with the same thatch of brown hair stepped forward, her face turning dark red. Sarah's voice was gentle. "How old are you, Nancy?"

The answer was so soft Anthony could hardly hear it. "Ten, ma'am."

"And Benjamin?"

The boy spoke for himself. "I'm nine."

Sarah sighed. "You children take good care of your brothers and sisters, won't you?"

"Yes, ma'am," Benjamin said sharply. His sister was silent.

Sarah pulled a piece of metal from the leather bag that hung at her side. "I've brought you a hoe blade, Benjamin, to tie on the stick you were using last week in your garden. Your mother will be very proud of you if you can grow some vegetables this spring."

"I'm going to grow *lots* of them, Mistress Sarah. I'm the man of the house now."

"I know you are, Ben. Your mother is lucky to have you."

The boy's chest puffed out and he grinned, making him look even younger than his nine years.

Sarah turned to leave. "Tell your mother I'll try to come by again this week." She looked over at Anthony, standing with his head bent to fit under the low wattle ceiling of the cottage. He'd grown increasingly quiet as the day wore on, but he hadn't complained, nor had he suggested that it was time to move on to more amusing activities. Well, fine. It wouldn't hurt him to see the kinds of hardships many of his beloved king's subjects were experiencing. She wished that every one of the king's ministers who lavished money so readily on their ships and guns and armies could spend a day in Wiggleston.

"Is their father dead?" he asked her in an undertone.

Sarah didn't bother to lower her voice. These children knew what had happened to their family. "Their father was impressed into the navy four months ago for failure to pay his taxes. They've not heard a word from him since."

Anthony hesitated a minute, then ducked under the low lintel of the cottage door and went outside. Almost immediately he was back with his hands full of honey cakes. "Look what I found," he said to Benjamin. "I surely can't eat all these. Do you think anyone around here's hungry?"

The child's eyes grew round, but he made no move toward the cakes. "I reckon my brothers and sisters might be," he said.

Anthony pulled over a small stool with his foot and sat, putting himself at a level with the children. One by one they ventured near him, tempted by the sweet smell. He broke each cake in half to be sure there would be enough left over for Benjamin, who waited until the very end to claim his piece.

"Thank you, sir," he said through a mouth full of crumbs.

Anthony unfolded his long frame from the tiny seat and joined Sarah at the door. "If you children are good and mind Benjamin and Nancy, I'll bring you some more cakes."

From around the room pairs of little eyes regarded him solemnly. "That's a promise," he said.

They walked away from the row of cottages in silence, leading their horses. Anthony spoke first. "I've given away my victuals, but this morning I also managed to bribe a bottle of canary wine out of your steward at Leasworth. Would you care to stop for a drink?"

Sarah was impatient to get to the sheriff's office, but Anthony had been uncomplaining and attentive all day, and she decided it would be ungracious to refuse his invitation. "All right. We can sit a spell over by the mill." She pointed to a grassy hillock that overlooked a stream and a rough wooden gristmill.

Anthony led the way and chose a spot where the ground was even and soft. Before Sarah had a chance to sit, he took off his long leather jacket and laid it on the grass in front of her.

"My lady," he said gallantly, offering her his hand to help her sit.

Sarah laughed. "I have no objection to sitting on the ground. As I've told you, Lord Rutledge, we are not used to these fancy court customs here in Yorkshire."

Anthony dropped to the grass beside her. "I'm beginning to learn about your ways, Sarah, but you'll have to give me some time."

She was surprised at the seriousness of his voice. "You were very helpful today," she said.

He stretched his long legs out in front of him. "You were absolutely right when you said that in London we become insulated from the real world of the people of England. I would that the king could spend a day such as I have spent with you."

"I can't think that it would make a great deal of difference to the grand King Charles."

Anthony shook his head in exasperation. "You're determined that there must be differences between us, aren't you?"

Sarah looked down at her hands. "The differences were not of my making. They started before I was born—before *you* were born, I daresay."

Anthony's eyes glinted with humor. "As long ago as that?" he asked in a mocking tone, which then grew serious. "The saddest of the differences between the crown and the Puritans like your family sprang from diverging views of religion."

"Why do you say 'saddest'?"

"Because faith should unite people, not divide them."

Sarah sat up straight, observing Anthony as he reached to fill a leather cup from his flask of wine. This was yet another side of this king's cavalier.

"Most theologians say there is no way to reconcile the beliefs of the Puritans with those of the Church of England," she said slowly.

"Most theologians should spend less time in dusty libraries and more time in the fresh air. Then perhaps their learned brains would function better," he replied.

"You don't agree that Puritanism is bordering on heretical, as your church leaders say?"

Anthony offered her the cup of wine. "If I were a religious man, I'd go along with many of the ideas of your Puritan thinkers."

"Such as?" Sarah could still not believe that Anthony was accustomed to spending time thinking about subjects as weighty as church doctrine.

"Well, for one thing, I believe as Prynne does that a man should look to his own soul for salvation."

"You have read the works of Prynne?"

Anthony took the cup from Sarah's hand with a smile. "Even in London we *do* occasionally occupy ourselves with activities other than games, Mistress Fairfax," he chided gently.

She felt his smile all the way to her stomach. Anthony Rutledge was definitely not as she had imagined a cavalier to be. In fact, she had never met anyone quite like him. For the first time in her life she was having trouble concentrating on her responsibilities. She ought to be seeing to them now, instead of sitting here growing soft in the middle over a king's man with a face like a Roman statue and a tongue like a Greek scholar.

Abruptly she jumped to her feet. "I'm sorry to cut short our discussion, my lord, but it's time we got over to the sheriff's office."

"Kempthorne has ridden out with his men. I don't know where you'd find them. I'm sorry, Mistress Fairfax." Sheriff Jeffries shifted his bulky form in the narrow desk chair.

"I'm going to see Parson Hollander, Mr. Jeffries, with or without Captain Kempthorne's permission." Sarah's face was set in the stubborn expression Anthony had come to know. She folded her arms and waited.

"The captain said that no one was to see the prisoner. They're taking him down to London tomorrow."

"London!"

Jeffries nodded. "Newgate Prison."

Sarah's stomach turned over. She looked at Anthony, who tried to sound reassuring. "They probably want to get him out of Wiggleston. His imprisonment is causing hard feelings in the town. It will be better for everyone if he's gone."

"Better for Parson Hollander?" Sarah asked indignantly.

Anthony was silent. Where the hell was Oliver anyway? He hadn't seen anything of him since yesterday's breakfast at Leasworth. Now Oliver had evidently made the decision to move the parson without even consulting Anthony. And Anthony couldn't countermand his orders without revealing that he was actually the one the king had put in charge of this mission. A fact he was hoping that Sarah would not have to find out...ever.

"Please, Sheriff," Sarah coaxed.

She may not have had the experience of the court ladies at coquetry, but to Anthony's mind the look Sarah turned on Jeffries would have had dozens of courtiers at her feet. The sheriff, however, shifted once more in his chair and shook his head.

"Don't ask it of me, Mistress Fairfax. Captain Kempthorne could well decide to throw *me* into Newgate in the bargain."

Sarah clenched her fists at her side. "If the captain comes back, will you please send word to me?"

"Yes, ma'am. I'll surely do that."

She turned on her heel and left the office, angry at the sheriff, Kempthorne, the king...even Anthony. For all his fine talk earlier, he had proven to be of no help at all. She had felt herself softening toward him as she watched him surrounded by the children at the Whites' cottage and discussing Puritan theology back by the mill, but now her resentment was coming back. Anthony wasn't going to help Parson Hollander. No one was, and by tomorrow the cleric would be out of reach. She smiled grimly. The moon would rise early tonight.

Anthony stared into the goblet of wine he'd been holding for the past several minutes. He'd asked Millie to bring it to him, but had cut her off curtly when she seemed inclined to linger for some conversation. He didn't want to talk to anyone. Except Sarah. And she had retired early to her bed.

He moved his hand in a circle and watched as the deep red liquid whirled around the edge of the cup. He had a feeling the wine was not going to help tonight. There were too many feelings running rampant through him to be quenched with liquor. Images from the cottages they had visited that day kept coming back to him. Little Benjamin White's proud face as he announced that he was the man of the family.

Damnation. The king would never approve of his tax collectors taking a father away from his family. Of that, Anthony was sure. Charles was one of the most soft-hearted men he knew, especially when it came to children and helpless creatures like his beloved spaniels.

He would speak to Charles when he returned to London. The thought was disturbing. Returning to London meant leaving Sarah. Anthony shook his head and laughed to himself. What irony that Baron Rutledge, the notorious rake who had broken hearts across Europe, should fall so quickly and so hard for a simple country lass without fortune or prospects.

No, not simple. He pictured her as she had been today, gently and efficiently ministering to the villagers, providing comfort without pity, charity without humiliation. He banged the goblet down, spilling wine on his hand and the table. He had had enough of these strange feelings about Mistress Fairfax. It was time he started dealing with her on more familiar territory—his territory, one in which no woman had yet been able to gainsay him.

He stood and walked purposefully down the hall to her room. Tonight Sarah would be his, and perhaps the odd demons she had created within him would be exorcised for good.

He knocked on her door. There was no response. He tried again, more firmly, but was met only with silence. Perhaps she was already sleeping. Quietly he pulled on the handle. The door swung open to a darkened room, but one thing was clear enough. Sarah was nowhere in sight.

Clarence Tinker had just begun a great dream. He was back in London at his favorite tavern and the serving wench who had ignored him for months had finally flung herself in his lap and was gently nuzzling his neck. Suddenly the nuzzling became wetter and less gentle. Clarence sat bolt upright, banging his head on the brick wall behind him. In his face was the nose of a gigantic horse. He reached for the pistol that hung at his side.

"Don't move," said a muffled voice.

He looked up to see a figure all in black, a cape billowing around him in the wind. Moonlight glinted off the edge of a drawn saber. It was dark underneath the eaves of the gaol, but Clarence thought the figure's face was covered with a mask.

"Are there other guards inside?" the voice demanded.

Clarence shook his head.

"Hand me your pistol—carefully, from the barrel."
Clarence felt a prick of steel at his throat. Slowly he
pulled the gun from his belt and passed it over.

"Now start running across the green. If you reach the
other side in thirty seconds, I might not shoot."

Clarence jumped to his feet, taking care to avoid the
huge horse, and began to run. When he reached the
other side of the green, breathless and frightened, he
paused and cautiously turned around to look back at
the gaol. The moonlight gave him a clear view. The
door to the gaol was open, and the mysterious dark
figure had disappeared inside. If the man hadn't taken
his gun, Tinker told himself, he would sneak back over
and get the drop on him. But what could he do un-
armed against such a formidable foe? The best course
was to get out to the guards' camp at the edge of the
village and raise the alarm.

He started to run. Captain Kempthorne would have
his head on a platter for this night's work.

Sarah looked around frantically for the keys to the
gaol's one cell. "Parson!" she called in a loud whisper. She couldn't see him in the dark.

She heard a rustling from inside the black cell and
then an astonished, "Sarah?"

"Yes, it's Sarah. I've come to get you out of here."

"My child…" The parson's voice sounded raspy and
weak.

"Do you know where they keep the keys?" she asked
urgently. She had opened every cupboard in the sheriff's desk and had not come across them. An acid taste

stung the back of her throat. This was a problem she had not anticipated.

When she had made her plans for tonight's raid, she had come to terms with the fact that she might be forced—for the first time in her life—to do physical harm to another human being. She had loaded her flintlock with trembling hands, hoping that she would not have to pull the trigger. As long as she could remember, there had never been a guard at the Wiggleston gaol. But then, it had never housed any more dangerous malefactor than Cyrus Green, the town drunk. Now that the sheriff had a royal prisoner in custody, she could expect guards, but she hadn't known how many. She had been immensely relieved to see the solitary figure dozing away on the front porch and had become even more confident when she realized that he was a lad not any older than Jack.

But she hadn't thought about the keys. What if the sheriff had taken them home with him?

The parson took hold of one end of the cot and pulled himself into a standing position. "They're on a ring. He hangs them on the wall, I think."

It was nearly black in the small room and Sarah didn't know where to find a light. She was beginning to regret that she had let the guard go. By now he could be raising the alarm. She fumbled toward the wall and began to grope along it. Her hands had turned cold.

"Which wall, Parson?"

"Sarah, you shouldn't be . . ."

"Which wall?" she demanded, her voice shrill.

"Over there . . . by the door."

She crossed the room, stumbling over a chair, and put her hands out to find the wall. Her hand touched wood, then metal, and she let out a long breath in relief.

As quickly as she could she retrieved the keys and crossed the room to insert them in the big iron lock. "Are you all right, Father? Will you be able to ride with me?"

The parson reached around the iron bars as she opened the cell door and clasped her in his arms. "You foolish child," he chided. "Always putting yourself in danger for another's benefit."

Sarah returned his embrace, but said, "There's not time for that, Father. We've got to get out of here before the guard I let go is back with a squad of dragoons."

Parson Hollander nodded. "Lead the way, child. I'm right behind you."

"It's my fault, Anthony, for not posting more guards." Oliver slapped the sheriff's desk with his leather gloves. "I can't believe my own stupidity."

Anthony's voice gave away none of the frustration he was feeling. "Hindsight, my dear Oliver, will get us nowhere. What about this man who was on duty?"

"I've sent for him, so he should . . . ah, there he is now."

The door opened and a nervous-looking guard of no more than twenty years entered the office. He shuffled his feet and looked at the floor. "You wanted to speak to me, Captain Kempthorne?" he mumbled.

"You were supposed to be guarding the prisoner last night. What happened?" Oliver did not bother to hide his anger, and the guard's nearly beardless face grew bright red.

"I was right there, Captain," he stammered, not looking up. "I never left my post, not till the man threatened to shoot me."

"I've a mind to shoot you myself," Oliver barked.

Anthony stood and walked over to put a hand on the young man's shoulder. "What's your name, lad?"

"Tinker, sir. Clarence Tinker."

"Well now, Clarence." Anthony's voice was calm and pleasant. "We need to know as much as possible about this masked rider. Do you think you could give us a description?"

Tinker nodded vigorously. "I couldn't see his face, of course. But he was powerful, dressed all in black like the bloody devil himself."

"Would you say he was a big man? Did you see anything else of him—his hands, his hair?"

"Big! He was near a giant. His hair was dark, too, I guess." The soldier paused. "It must've been tied up under that big felt hat. And as to his hands... I don't think I could see them beyond the tip of the sword he held at my throat."

"A saber?"

"Aye, but wicked. Looked more like a bloody cutlass, to tell the truth."

Anthony exchanged glances with Oliver. The lad's recounting of the event was obviously colored by the fright he'd suffered, but it did appear certain that the description of the bandit would eliminate the elderly General Fairfax as a suspect.

"What about the bandit's horse?" Oliver joined in the questioning.

Tinker finally looked over at his commanding officer. "A magnificent beast, and giant, as well. Its head was the size of half my body. I ain't never seen such an animal." Emboldened by the attentiveness of his two listeners, Clarence lowered his voice and continued in a more confidential tone. "Some of the men are saying that it's not a real horse at all, but a demon come to earth in animal form."

Anthony turned to move back to his chair, giving Oliver an exasperated look.

"What about the color?" Oliver asked.

Clarence looked puzzled. "Dark . . . I don't know exactly. It was a strange color. Some sort of gray, I guess."

Oliver gave a big sigh. "Do you have any more questions, uh, Lord Rutledge?"

Anthony shook his head.

"You can go, Tinker." Oliver dismissed the man with a wave. After the young guard left he dropped his head into his hands. "Damnation! Now we have no suspects and no parson."

"Do you think you can get some more information out of your informant with the Dutch smugglers?" Anthony asked.

Oliver straightened. "He says they always dealt through the cleric. But we can keep after him."

Anthony stood. "Do so, and this time keep me informed of what's going on."

"What are you going to do, Anthony?"

"I have a few questions of my own I want to ask." Since he had been in the area, he had only seen one man who was big and powerful and would be likely to be skilled with a sword. It was time he met Sarah's suitor, Henry Partridge.

The winter view from Flamborough Head north across the bay to the limestone crags was desolate. In the spring wild daffodils would paint yellow trails almost down to the water's edge. The hawthorne hedges would blossom, forming festive green and white corrals for black-faced sheep, who would peer now and then over the edge of the cliff, never losing their footing. Skylarks would resume their sweet melodies in the surrounding meadows. But today the only sound was the eerie cry of a peewit and, below, the roar of the winter sea. Sarah clutched a heavy leather sack with one hand and used the other to steady herself as she scrambled down the side of the cliff. Her footing was even more sure than the sheep's. She and Jack had been climbing down to Coxswain's Cove since they were children and used the small caves below for their pirate games.

She jumped the final length to the soft sand of the beach and looked around. As usual, the cove was deserted. Though the Dutch smugglers had occasionally landed at this place back when Parson Hollander used their services to help fugitive royalists escape to the Continent, they much preferred the less rocky beaches farther south.

Skirting around a massive boulder, Sarah bent to look into the dark recesses of a small cave. "Jack," she called softly.

Her brother's blond head appeared almost instantly. "It's about time," he said. "We're nigh on to starving."

Sarah held up the bag with a smile. "I brought as much as I could carry."

Jack stepped out of the cave and took the bag from her, giving her a kiss on the cheek. "You're a lifesaver."

Together they ducked under the low-hanging entrance to the cave and went inside. Parson Hollander sat leaning against the cave wall in front of a small fire. "How are you, Father?" Sarah asked.

"Thanks to you, I'm fine, child. But I wish both you and your brother would stay away from me. I can make my way on my own now."

Sarah knelt at his side and reached out her hands to warm them at the fire. "I got you into this trouble, Father, and I'm going to see that you get out of it."

The parson pushed the hood of Sarah's cloak back and put a gentle hand on her head. "My brave, impetuous Sarah. You have such a good heart. But I've warned you for some time that we all just may have used up the good Lord's patience with these crimes."

"I've never taken a farthing from anyone who could not afford to lose it."

"'Thou shalt not steal,'" the parson said gently.

Sarah's lips went together in something close to a pout. "What about 'Thou shalt not kill'? During the Civil War the cavaliers I've stolen from killed my father and thousands of other good Christians."

Jack had joined them, sitting on his haunches. "The war's been over for many years, Sarah. The Puritans and the royalists are at peace with each other. Perhaps it's time you made your peace, too."

Sarah was silent. Parson Hollander moved back to lean tiredly against the wall. "Your brother's right," he said.

"Your parishioners will suffer without the extra money, Parson," Sarah argued.

"They'll have to make do as they have in the past. The Lord visits trials on us all at times."

"Listen to us, Sarah," Jack urged.

"I'll think about it. But that doesn't help the current situation. We have to get the parson away from here so he won't be put in prison."

"That's not your problem, Sarah," the parson said firmly. "After I've rested a bit, I'll make my way along the coast and see if I can find a way to leave this part of the country. The Lord will provide."

"You may want to wait for the Lord to provide, Parson, but while you're waiting, Oliver Kempthorne and his men will be combing the countryside for you." She looked at Jack. "We've got to get him out of the country now."

"The contrabandists?" Jack asked.

She nodded and turned back to the parson. "You'll have to tell us how you contact them."

"It's too dangerous," he protested.

"If you don't tell us, we'll go find them ourselves, which will be more dangerous still."

Parson Hollander's face looked even older than his threescore years. He suddenly seemed too frail to be set out in a tiny boat on the cold North Sea, but Sarah didn't see that they had any other choice.

The parson took a deep breath that rattled in his throat. "All right, but it'll be up to you to talk to them, Jack. I'd not trust Sarah alone with them."

"Of course, I'll go at once. Anyway, Sarah has to get back to Leasworth to entertain the king's surveyor."

The parson gave Sarah a questioning look, but she didn't elaborate on Jack's comment.

"So it's settled," he said. "Listen carefully, Jack, and I'll tell you how our signaling system works. Mind you, it might take a couple of days. The third village to the south of here is Cottleswoode. Just at the edge of the village you'll find a cove much like this one, but twice the size. On the north end there's a big boulder they call the Druid's Skull..."

Anthony had just left his mount with the stableboy, Arthur, when he saw Sarah walking toward the house, coming from the path to the sea. He called to her and she veered in his direction to meet up with him.

"You've heard the news?" he asked her.

"About the parson?"

"Aye. That he was taken from the gaol last night by the notorious masked highwayman."

"News travels fast in Wiggleston," Sarah said with a nod.

"Especially good news?" he asked dryly.

"It wouldn't make sense for me to pretend that I'm not happy the parson is free, now would it?"

Anthony took her arm as they reached the cobblestone walk that led to the side door of the main house. "You might pretend at least a little respect for his majesty's justice."

Sarah did not pull her arm away, but she answered him stiffly. "I believe my uncle has informed you just exactly what that justice meant to my father, Lord Rutledge. How can you expect me to respect it?"

Anthony looked down at her. A gray wool cloak trimmed with black fur hid the curves of her body, but he could see the sweep of her long pale lashes over her cheeks, reddened from the sea breeze, and the ripe fullness of her pink lips. His body stirred, and his mind rebelled against the task he had to do. He wanted to forget all about parsons and masked bandits and spend a pleasant evening in front of a huge fire with a bottle of wine and Sarah by his side.

"I'm sorry about your father. I was only nine when I lost mine, but I remember the pain to this day."

Sarah looked at him in surprise. The baron did not seem the kind of man to have ever suffered pain over anything. "What happened to him?"

"He was killed, fighting with the king at Marston Moor—the old king, Charles I, the one that *your* father and his colleagues had executed."

Sarah bit her lip. "So many good men lost on both sides—and for what? The old king's son is back in power and nothing has changed. What is it that makes men so fond of war?"

"It's not war they're fond of—it's power, and along with it money and lands, I suppose."

They reached the door and Anthony opened it for Sarah to enter. "Your cloak is wet," he said. "You must be cold."

Sarah nodded. "I went for a walk by the sea. It's wet and windy down there this time of year."

"You need to warm up by a good fire."

"But perhaps you haven't supped. I should go to the kitchens and see if Bess can put together some food."

Anthony turned her to face him and began to untie the laces to her cloak. "All I want is some mulled wine and your company by the fire."

His fingers brushed against her chin as he reached the top lace. "I'll go find my uncle, then, to join us." Her voice had grown husky and she gave a slight shiver, though she wasn't sure if it was from the cold.

"I'd prefer to have you to myself."

The look in his eye made her shiver again. She *was* cold, she told herself. And she was *not* going to get herself in a dither over the slight touch of a man, no matter how attractive. Especially not a king's man. Especially not with her brother and the parson hiding out in a cave not more than a few hundred yards below the house.

Briskly she took off her cloak and flung it over a chair in the entry hall. "If you will make yourself comfortable in the great room, my lord, I'll just go and see about the wine."

With a snap of her head, she disappeared down the long passageway to the kitchens.

Anthony paced along the Persian rug that ran the length of the room. He would have preferred a more intimate setting, but perhaps this was for the best. He was, after all, supposed to be using his time to find out more about Sarah's suitor, or any other local who could possibly be the masked highwayman. He was not supposed to be paying attention to the baser demands of his body. He was not supposed to be thinking about how firm Sarah's breasts had felt under the gentle pressure of his knuckles as he had unlaced her cloak....

"I've brought honey cakes, as well, since you were generous enough to give yours away to the children yesterday."

Anthony had not even heard her come in the door. She stood with a heavy tray, and he quickly went to take it from her, noting with pleasure that there were only two goblets for the wine.

"It was hardly my generosity, since the cakes came from Leasworth." He placed the tray on a low table by the fire and drew two chairs up close to it.

Sarah seated herself in one. "But they were to be your lunch, and you gave it away," she persisted. "The gesture gave me hope that not all the king's courtiers think only of their own pleasure."

Anthony smiled. "Have you always been such a candid speaker, Sarah?"

Sarah reached for a cake and grinned. "In my household it was a sin to prevaricate. Even white lies were considered against the Lord's will."

Anthony grew serious. "In that case, my lovely Puritan, I have a question to ask you."

"What question?"

"Will you tell me truthfully if you know anything that would help Captain Kempthorne in his search for the highwayman?" he asked gravely.

Sarah's hand paused with the cake halfway to her mouth. Then she sat back in the chair and finished taking a bite, giving herself time to chew before she answered. "Why is this any concern of yours, my lord?"

"It should be of concern to all law-abiding citizens."

The cake felt dry in Sarah's mouth, and she reached for her glass of wine. "Could we not talk of more pleasant things?"

Anthony watched Sarah's hand tighten on the glass. It was as he had suspected from that first night. She knew more than she wanted to let on. If appealing to her sense of law and order did not move her, perhaps he should resort to a more tried-and-true method of eliciting information. It was another skill he had honed in the boudoirs of Paris, when it was vital for Charles to know how much support he could count on from the French throne. He sipped some warm wine and felt it spread pleasantly out along his limbs. It appeared that his duty and his desire for this evening could follow the same path after all.

Chapter Six

"Aye, let's talk of more pleasant things, by all means." Anthony got up and went to throw a huge log on the fire.

"I can call the servants to build that up, if you like," Sarah offered.

He added another, smaller piece, then brushed off his hands and turned to her. "No. Didn't I say that I wanted you to myself tonight?"

His smile flashed and his eyes had a possessive look that made Sarah want to take a deep breath. She took a sip of wine instead, and it steadied her. "I told you the day we met, Lord Rutledge, that I am not used to the coquettish ways of your court."

He looked down at her, leaning one elbow carelessly on the mantel. "You would be a sensation at court, Sarah. I can just picture you walking in among all those ladies with their ribbons and laces."

"A sparrow among the peacocks?"

"No, a pure gleaming pearl among gaudy strings of cut glass."

Sarah smiled. "You are too practiced at this, my lord. I can't compete."

"Yet you persist in addressing me as 'my lord,' which makes me feel like a silly old man paying court to a young girl."

"Are you paying court to me, Lord Rutledge?"

He laughed. "There! You see what I mean? At court the ladies plot endless intrigues involving all kinds of tangles and machinations to discover if they have caught a particular man's fancy. You simply look up at me with those wonderfully direct cat's eyes of yours and ask."

"It would seem the simpler course," Sarah observed.

"Ah, yes. But simplicity is a rare virtue."

Sarah grew serious. "Here in Wiggleston it's not so rare. We're simple people. Most of us just want to live in peace and provide a good life for our families. But, as you saw yesterday, that's not always easy."

Anthony did not want the conversation to drift back into difficult subjects. It did not suit this evening's purpose. "You were very good with those children yesterday, Sarah. Why is it you haven't settled down to raise a family of your own?"

Sarah hesitated. She could not tell Anthony that she had devoted herself to raising her little brother, since he did not know of his existence. "The Tower of London is not the best place for courting."

"The Tower of London?"

"When I was at the age for romance I was living with my father at the Tower. After his execution, I had no humor to join in wooing games. I came here to Leasworth instead."

"To hide yourself away from the rest of the world."

Sarah thought for a moment. "Yes, to hide away, I guess. I did not think the world a very pretty place back then."

"But now? Four years is a long time, Sarah."

She smiled. "Too long. I would imagine that I'm well past the age of eligibility now. I'll probably live out my life here at Leasworth as a doddering old maid."

When she smiled, there was a radiance to her classic features that took Anthony's breath away. He stepped away from the fire to take a deep drink from his goblet of wine, then, ignoring his own seat, he dropped to the rug near Sarah's chair. He reached across her knee to place his hand over hers. "You'll not be an old maid, Sarah, of that I'm quite sure."

The fire crackled and sent up a shower of sparks. Sarah took another long sip of her wine. The warm liquor was making her heady and utterly conscious of Anthony's arm on her leg. She moved in her chair, but did not pull her hand out from under his. "How can you know that?" she asked, her throat dry.

"I'll show you how."

Deliberately he took the wine goblet from her and stretched to set it on the table. Then he took both her wrists and pulled her from her chair. She slid without resisting into his lap. "I'm going to kiss you, Sarah," he said, his face close. "And when I'm done kissing you,

you can tell me if you still picture yourself as an old maid.''

The fire roared in front of them and the mulled wine had warmed her limbs, but the heat racing through her now came from an entirely different source. His lips were soft as a feather at first, giving her time to protest or pull away. She did neither. Anthony moved to enfold her more completely in his arms, then began to kiss her in earnest—long, deep kisses that had Sarah's head spinning entirely out of control.

She opened her mouth to his and found herself responding, drawing into herself his warmth and passion and letting his desire stoke her senses. His lips moved to the tender underside of her chin, then down her neck. Chills raced up and down her entire right side. She went limp in his arms.

Holding her firmly with one strong arm, Anthony moved his other hand along the side of her closely fitting dress. His fingers massaged her soft stomach, then moved upward to the firm thrust of her breast. She drew in a breath and he stopped the movement of his hand, but brought his mouth back to hers for a demanding kiss. "Your body was made for a man's touch, Sarah," he said huskily as he drew away to look into her eyes. "Let me show you."

Sarah moved in his lap. His hand rested just below her breast, waiting for her signal. She turned her face into his neck.

He pulled her back against one arm and looked down at her tenderly. "I don't want you to be afraid, sweetheart. You're the most beautiful woman I've ever seen, and I want you desperately, as I suspect you are aware. But we're just beginning. We're just playing now—learning each other—having fun.'' He gave a playful nip to the tip of her nose and the end of her chin.

Sarah's voice was shaky. "I've never thought of... what goes on between a man and a woman... as having fun.''

"As I told you before, you Puritans have some very good ideas on a great many subjects, but in this area you have a few things to learn.''

Sarah looked into his bold, dark eyes, which were slightly hooded now, and intense. "I think I'm willing to learn," Sarah said, her face flushing.

Anthony gave a low, provocative chuckle. "I do so like a willing pupil," he said.

Once again his lips were on hers, and Sarah scarcely realized that at the same time his hands were slowly unfastening the small jet buttons down the front of her dress. In the recesses of her mind she had the wickedly vain thought that she was glad she had on the fine lawn overchemise, the one undergarment she possessed that was not of serviceable, unbleached linen.

The upper part of her chest lay bare to the firelight and Anthony bent his head to plant kisses there. Her head fell back against his arm. With his free hand he traced the pattern of her chemise, lingering at the taut swell of her nipples. Through the cloth he kissed first one, then the other. The touch of his lips reverberated down through her breasts to reach some secret part of her that she had never before known. Gently Anthony pushed away the fabric to let his lips follow where his fingers had been. Of their own accord her hands wound their way into Anthony's silky long hair and pressed him to her as he teased her with gentle tugs.

She made a whimpering sound in the back of her throat. "I've not hurt you?" Anthony asked at once, stopping the gentle suckling.

She opened her eyes. She could see the stubble along the strong line of his chin hovering above her bare white breasts. It was shockingly erotic, and Sarah felt a kind of delicious guilt in the pit of her stomach. She hadn't ever pictured herself in quite such a moment, yet in some ways it seemed as natural as anything she had ever done in her life.

She reached out a hand to stroke the slight roughness of his cheek. "You haven't hurt me, Anthony. It's...enjoyable, as you said."

Anthony's smile was pure seduction. "We've barely begun, dearling."

He'd have preferred a bed to the raspy ornamental rug, but he knew Sarah's sense of propriety was too great to join him in his bedchamber—at least at the beginning. He fully intended to finish this evening there with her in his arms, preferably naked and awake. Perhaps a long night of passion would cure him of the curious obsession he seemed to have developed for her. Although so far their lovemaking was merely heightening it. His body was thundering its impatience. If it weren't for the innocence of her eyes and the vulnerable quaver to her voice, he'd have taken her by now.

There were pillows and a blanket on a nearby settle, but he didn't dare let her go long enough to fetch them. She could yet flee. So he merely leaned back against the leather base of the chair and settled her more comfortably in his arms. Her shoulders and breasts were milky white in tantalizing contrast to the healthy color of her face. He bent again to one of the rosy tips of her breasts and worked it expertly with his lips. A flush started up her chest toward her neck and he heard her breathe, "Ah…" He pulled back and grinned at her. "I told you it was fun."

Her eyes were closed and her only answer was a slight smile. He turned his attention to the other breast and then back to her mouth. His own breathing had grown erratic, and he knew that he would not last much longer with her soft little bottom rubbing unconsciously against him through their clothes. Forcing himself to retain some hold on his reason, he decided to slow things down by trying to get some of the information he needed. It was, he knew from past experience, the best time—when both parties were too needy to be cautious.

"Tell me, Sarah, has no other man done this to you?" He caressed her breasts with the warm palm of his hand. "Not even your attractive neighbor, Henry Partridge?" As soon as the words were out of his mouth, he regretted them. He felt as if he had somehow dirtied something fresh and beautiful. But it was too late. Already she was looking up at him, her eyes bewildered.

She struggled to sit up, pulling the edges of her dress together. "How can you ask such a question?" she asked in a hurt tone.

He tried to repair the damage. "It's just that I'm a jealous lover," he replied lightly. "I'm sorry. 'Twas ill-done. Forget that I spoke."

He made an attempt to settle her back against him, but she pulled away. "Is this part of the fun you promised, Anthony? Questions that humiliate? An interrogation between kisses?" With easy grace she disentangled herself from his lap and stood up. He jumped to his feet after her, furious with himself, but keeping his voice even.

"Sarah, I'm sorry. I've apologized. I know that you are innocent."

"And, furthermore, it would be none of your business if I weren't," she pointed out indignantly, buttoning her dress.

Anthony looked at her helplessly. He could scarcely believe that in one ill-timed query he had ruined both his evening of lovemaking and his effort to get more information out of her. Charles would be laughing himself sick if he knew. Their friendly rivalry over who had the greater finesse with the ladies had been going on for years.

He gave Sarah a little bow of apology and respect. "You are absolutely right. It's none of my concern.

Now will you please sit with me and have another glass of wine?"

Sarah looked from the glowing fire to the table with the two goblets of wine. "I think not," she said slowly. "I said I was willing to learn, but I'm starting to think that the lessons may not prove to my liking."

"Just sit with me—no lessons. I won't touch you again, I promise."

Sarah smiled coldly. She didn't know for sure why Anthony's question about "Henry Partridge" had sent a chill down to her heart, but she trusted her instincts more than she trusted these new feelings Anthony had awakened inside her. "I'm tired, my lord. I think it best if I bid you good-night."

She turned to leave, ignoring the irritation in his expression. She would do well to follow the resolutions she had made when she first set eyes on this man—to keep her wits close by and to keep Lord Rutledge at a distance.

The stableboy, Arthur, was waiting in the front hall when Sarah came down the stairs the next morning. It was perhaps the first time he had been in the big house, because he looked around him with eyes wide and shuffled his feet back and forth. Sarah greeted him with a smile. "Good morning, Arthur. Can I do something for you?"

The boy took a hard swallow that Sarah could see all the way down his throat. "I came to find ye, Mistress Sarah. To tell ye."

"What is it?"

"They be lookin' at Brigand again."

Alarm sent a rush through her stomach, but she kept calm. "Who's looking at Brigand, Arthur?"

"The fine gents. The one who's staying here and another one like him with the fancy long hair."

Sarah thanked the lad with an absent pat on the head, then, not bothering to go for a wrap, made her way quickly to the stables. Sure enough, there were Anthony and Captain Kempthorne in serious conversation, standing in front of Brigand's stall. The captain was the first to see her. He stopped talking in midsentence. Then Anthony turned toward her. His expression was hard, almost that of a stranger. She could hardly believe that she had lain half-naked in this man's arms the previous evening. The memory brought heat to her cheeks.

"Good day, Mistress Fairfax. I'm glad you've come," Kempthorne called. "I have a few questions to ask you."

Warily Sarah approached the two men. She kept her eyes off her horse. "What questions?"

Kempthorne motioned toward Brigand. "My men have been getting more eyewitness reports of the moonlight robberies. The description of the bandit's horse fits this one precisely."

"That's absurd." She looked to Anthony for support, but he said nothing.

"You must admit, Mistress Fairfax, that this is an unusual animal."

"He's a roan—there must be many in the area."

"Not of this size and this color. My men have searched. Ask Lord Rutledge. He's been looking over the horseflesh in these parts." He turned to Anthony. "Have you seen anything like this stallion on any of the other estates you've visited?"

Anthony looked at Sarah for a moment, then slowly shook his head.

Captain Kempthorne made an intimidating figure. He was wearing a thick leather jacket that tapered to the waist, then belled out to below his knees and was made even bulkier by a heavy sword belt and yet another for his pistol. He looked larger than life, quite dwarfing Sarah's slender form. "Who might be likely to be riding this horse?" he asked her.

"No one. I'm the only one who rides Brigand."

"Could someone be taking him at night without your knowledge?"

"No," Sarah said firmly. "I'm afraid you're entirely mistaken in this matter, Captain. There's no way anyone else could be riding Brigand."

Oliver reached out and ran his hand along Brigand's long neck. "Well now, that's mysterious. I guess I'm just going to have to confiscate this animal for the time being while we continue to check into the matter."

Sarah looked at Anthony in dismay. They couldn't take away her horse! Since the day he was foaled, Brigand had never been away from her care.

Anthony pursed his lips, watching her carefully, then turned to Oliver. "I'm sorry, Captain Kempthorne. You won't be able to take this horse."

Oliver looked at his friend in surprise. "Why the bloody hell not? Begging your pardon, mistress," he added in a lower voice.

"Because this horse no longer belongs to Mistress Fairfax. I've purchased it for the king's stables. If you want it, you'll have to take the matter up with his majesty."

Oliver's jaw dropped, and Sarah blinked in astonishment. "You purchased it for the king?" Oliver asked. "I mean, you *really* did?"

Anthony nodded. "So now, if you have no more questions for Mistress Fairfax, she and I have an appointment to view some horses at a distant estate and have yet to break our fast."

Oliver eyed his friend skeptically, refusing to believe what he had just heard. "You're telling me that you are taking this stallion with you back to London?"

Anthony's eyes were steady. "Aye."

Oliver paused another moment, then shrugged. "Very well. I'll keep on investigating this thing from other angles." He hesitated, looked uncertainly at Sarah, then asked Anthony, "Are you sure there's nothing more you...uh...need to tell me?"

"No." Anthony turned to take Sarah's arm. "Go on about your business, Captain Kempthorne. As I was saying, Miss Fairfax and I have a prior engagement."

He started walking with her toward the stable door, leaving Oliver looking after them with an expression that was at once angry and baffled.

As soon as they were out of sight of the stables, Sarah pulled her arm out of Anthony's hand and asked, "Why did you lie?"

Anthony continued walking toward the house. "So he wouldn't take your horse."

"But... he's a representative of the king, just as you are."

"I never said that every action done in the name of the king is just."

"But you say the king is your friend."

Anthony finally stopped and turned abruptly toward Sarah, his heel grinding in the dirt. "I'm the king's friend, but that doesn't mean that I have to agree with royal tax collectors who take fathers away from their children or guards who confiscate horses for no reason."

Sarah shifted uncomfortably.

Anthony lifted her chin, forcing her to look up at him. "It would be for no reason, isn't that right, Sarah? You've told me that you're the only one who rides Brigand, and I'm taking you at your word."

Sarah found it hard to meet his potent eyes. They were looking at her again as they had in the firelight last night, and the same odd, fluttery feelings were developing inside her. "I told you the truth, Anthony. I'm the only one who rides Brigand."

He held her chin with his strong fingers a moment more, then released her. "Good. Then there's no reason that Captain Kempthorne should deprive you of your daily rides. Especially when I'm going to request that you join me again today."

She felt a surge of happiness. The suspicions of the previous evening when he had questioned her about her suitor were beginning to disappear. After all, hadn't he just championed her against one of the king's own guards? Last night's query was probably due to jealousy as he had said, nothing more, and she didn't find the thought entirely displeasing.

"I would be honored to accompany you, Lord Rutledge," she said cheerfully.

Anthony looked around to see that no one was in the garden, then bent and gave her a light kiss. "Anthony," he corrected gently.

When Sarah entered the smoky kitchen, Bess was punching a huge mass of bread dough as if it were a mortal enemy. Her huge white forearms were covered with flour and quivered with each punch like molds of white jelly. Sarah hoped she was in a better mood than yesterday. When she had asked Bess to help her put together some food for the parson and Jack she had been subjected to one of Bess's famous tirades. She and Jack ought to know better than to get the good parson into all this trouble, Bess had raged, and now the poor man had to hide away in a cave like some kind of criminal and probably catch his death in the bargain.

Sarah had listened good-naturedly. She and Jack were used to Bess's lectures, and they knew that they were invariably caused by her concern for their welfare. Having grown up without a mother, they usually found the stout little cook's scolding endearing.

Bess was the only member of the household who knew of Sarah and Jack's nocturnal activities. She highly disapproved, but Sarah knew she would go to her death, if necessary, before revealing their secret.

"I need some more food for the parson, Bess," Sarah said to her, surprised that the cook had not greeted her with her customary smile of welcome.

"Well, look around in the pantry, missy. I can't help you now when I'm up to my elbows in dough. A body has work to do in this house, you know."

Sarah looked concerned. Bess did look tired this morning. She was getting on in years, and perhaps all the cooking for such a large household was becoming too much for her. "Where's Millie?" she asked.

"Probably off making eyes at the dairy lads as usual," Bess grumbled.

"Maybe you need to get more help down here."

Bess stopped her blows long enough to fix Sarah with a piercing glare. "I don't need any such thing. What I need is for you to stop traipsing off in the middle of the night so's I can't get any sleep and for you to get poor Parson Hollander out of trouble and—" she stopped and gave a two-fisted pummel to the dough "—most particularly for you to not go *kissing* any king's man in broad daylight as if you were the village trollop."

Sarah felt a flush of guilt. "If you mean just now in the yard," she said defensively, "it was *he* who kissed *me*. And 'twas just a friendly gesture. I'd wager it's the way they do things in London."

"I don't give a cock's crow how they do things in London. You ain't got no business getting anywhere near that gentleman. He's nothing but trouble for you ... in more ways than one."

Sarah hid a smile. "If I promise to watch myself around Lord Rutledge, will you give me some of those raisin tarts to take to the parson?"

Bess's expression did not soften. "You mind what I'm telling you, Mistress Sarah. That man is bad tidings for all of us."

Sarah finished filling her bag with an assortment of provisions, then walked over to extend her arms as far as they could reach around Bess's ample middle. "I'll be careful, Bess," she said fondly. "Though you may be wrong about the baron. I'm beginning to think that for a king's man, he's really a rather decent sort."

Sarah used the technique she and Jack had perfected as children to slide down the cliff above Coxswain's Cove almost without stopping. She didn't have much time before she was to meet Anthony for their ride, but she wanted to take another bag of food to the parson and check on what arrangements Jack had been able to make for his escape.

The cave was darker than normal, and Sarah was surprised that Jack had let the fire die. It wasn't good for the parson's old bones to be in the cold and damp.

"Hallo!" she called. From within she heard a weak reply. It was the parson. She could barely see through the gloom. "Where's Jack? What's happened to your fire?"

Parson Hollander was in the same position as the day before, leaning against the cave wall, but the fire pit in front of him was cold and black. "He hasn't come back yet."

Sarah's good mood vanished instantly. "What could have happened to him?" She crouched next to him and reached for the parson's bony hand, which was ice-cold.

"You mustn't worry about him, my child. Remember I told you it sometimes takes a few days to contact the contrabandists."

His serene voice calmed her as it had so often in the past. "I thought he would have come back, at least to check on you," she said.

The parson gave a rueful chuckle. "I would imagine Jack figured that as a grown man I ought to be able to take care of myself."

Sarah's eyes were becoming adjusted to the dark and she could see that the parson's features were etched with pain. "What's wrong, Father? Are you hurt?"

He smiled and shook his head. "It's nothing. These old bones just don't work as well as they used to." He pushed himself up against the wall, and as he did so gave an involuntary grunt and clutched his side.

"You *are* hurt!" Sarah moved over beside him and took his arm. "Tell me the truth."

"I have, child. It's just an ache in my side. One of Captain Kempthorne's men had boots that were rather heavy when applied to an elderly set of ribs."

"They kicked you!" Sarah felt the fury rise in her throat. How dare they treat an old man so, and a holy man at that.

"Just one of them. It seems he was convinced that I hadn't told them everything I knew about the highwayman they're seeking."

"Oh, Father." Sarah sank to her knees. "I never meant to involve you this way."

The parson smoothed a hand along her hair. "This poor, earthly body is of no importance, Sarah. Your father knew that lesson, and gave up his for what he believed in."

A tear made its way down her cheek. "I'll have to get Dr. Andrews to come down here."

The parson shook his head. "No." His tone was surprisingly strong. "We'll bring in no other conspirators on which the king's guards can practice their gentle ways. All I need is some of the food you brought, and perhaps a rebuilding of the fire, if you would be so kind."

Jack had left firewood piled on the opposite end of the cavern, which meant, Sarah realized, that the parson had been unable to so much as cross the room. He was undoubtedly suffering more than he cared to admit. But she didn't know what she could do to help. The best thing would be to get him to the Continent as quickly as possible. Once on safe ground he could seek medical attention.

She started a new fire and soon warmth was filtering out into the cave's chill. Then she turned back to the parson, who sat with eyes closed. "Your side should be bandaged, Father. Let me help you get more comfortable."

He shook his head without lifting it from the wall. "No, I'm fine. The fire feels wonderful."

She watched him with a worried expression as she transferred the pile of wood to his side so that it would be in easy reach. "This should keep you through the day if Jack doesn't come back. This afternoon, I'll come again, with some hot food and bandages. You're going to get some nursing, whether you want it or not," she said tenderly, her smile faltering.

"What I want is for you to take care of yourself, Sarah. It's very dangerous for you with all these king's men around. Jack says one is staying at your house."

"Yes, but..." Sarah blushed. "But he's not one of Kempthorne's men. In fact he took my side today when the captain wanted to take away my horse."

"Brigand?"

"Yes. The captain said he fit the description of the horse used in the robberies."

The parson's expression became worried. "My child, you see how close they're getting to you? You have to be careful, and you mustn't do anything to arouse suspicion."

"I intend to be careful. In fact, after one last job, I intend to retire the moonlight highwayman for good."

"What do you mean, one last job?"

Sarah hesitated. She didn't want to add to the parson's worries, but she had always been truthful with him. "The masked rider must make one more raid to get the money to pay your passage with the smugglers."

"Absolutely not. I've dealt with these men for years, and I think they'll take me for free. If they won't, I just won't go. It's too risky for you to try anything now. I forbid it."

Sarah smiled. She could see that the parson was in some pain and she wasn't going to argue with him. She knew what she had to do. It was true that he had dealt with the same band of smugglers since the Civil War. Even though he was a Puritan, he hadn't held with the slaughter of fellow Englishmen. If a fugitive royalist came his way, he helped him to freedom. He truly did follow the doctrine of "love thine enemy." It was one of the things Sarah had always admired about him. *She* was certainly not that willing to give love and charity to all sides.

"We'll see what Jack says when he gets back," she said. "Are you sure there's nothing I can do for your side?" She was reluctant to leave him, but Anthony would be waiting for her.

"You go on before someone misses you."

"I'll be back later on this afternoon, Parson, to see if Jack has returned and to bring you some more food."

"God be with you, my child."

* * *

Anthony studied the tapestries that hung along the stone walls of the front hall of Leasworth Manor. He had had time to make a detailed examination of Gabriel and each one of his angels. This was, at least, one trait Mistress Fairfax shared with the ladies at court—an irritating tendency to tardiness. He'd been waiting nigh on a quarter of an hour.

He was normally a patient man, but today his humor did not lend itself to tolerance. After the encounter with Sarah in the great room, he had not slept well. If truth be told, he had scarcely slept at all. Finally near dawn he'd fallen into a troubled sleep filled with visions of her white breasts arching to meet his mouth, then fading as she pushed him away, her gray eyes looking at him accusingly. He'd been interrupted by a servant banging on his door to tell him that a Captain Kempthorne urgently requested his company down at the stables.

Then there was Sarah. The irrational fury with which she had received his questions about her suitors. The flicker of fear in her eyes when Oliver had asked about her horse. It was disturbing and frustrating, but he had come to the conclusion that he didn't care anymore. He didn't care about Oliver or the highwayman or even the king, blast his hide. He just wanted Sarah. He wanted her totally and with a desperation that he had simply never before experienced. And he could think of nothing else until it was done.

The massive front door swung open and Sarah walked in. "I'm sorry to keep you waiting," she said with a distant smile.

Her hair was windblown and her cheeks red. While Anthony had thought she was upstairs primping for their riding appointment, she'd been outside somewhere. Where?

He waited a moment, hoping she would offer an explanation. When she didn't, he drew on his gloves and walked over to her, telling himself that the only thing to think about was the day's purpose.

"Are you ready now?" he asked her.

"Yes. I just stopped off at the stables and Arthur is saddling your horse and Brigand. Thanks to you I can still ride him today. Where did you want me to take you?"

Anthony took a deep breath. "I've had ample chance to explore the neighborhood in the last few days. Perhaps today I'll lead the way."

Chapter Seven

During the first part of their ride, Sarah's mind was so preoccupied with thoughts of the parson's injury and Jack's safety that she paid scant attention to where they were going. It was a rare winter day. The sun was shining so warmly that she had thrown off her cloak and let the wind blow the skirts of her wool riding habit.

"Your eyes take on a violet cast against the blue of your outfit," Anthony said to her as they rode easily along.

The habit was bright blue, not a color Sarah was wont to use. And beyond that, the dress was not at all her usual simple style. It had fashionably puffy sleeves and black silk braiding all down the front. Her uncle had bought it for her from a traveling vendor, saying that it was time she had a garment that might appeal to a young girl's vanity. Both Jack and Sarah had been surprised at his extravagance and his defiance of the Puritan doctrine, but it had been just one of many evidences that Uncle Thomas had mellowed considerably since his days as a firebrand Roundhead general.

"I've never had anyone comment so on my eyes," she said, trying to pull her mind away from the little cave by the sea.

"As I've told you before, Sarah, these Yorkshire men are fools for having left you neglected for so many years. But perhaps we can make up for the lost time."

Sarah looked at him questioningly. He nodded ahead of them, and she suddenly realized that they were coming up on the small hunting cottage that was at the far end of the Fairfax estate. Uncle Thomas hunted rarely these days, and the sport had never been to Jack's taste, so the little lodge mostly lay idle.

"What do you mean?" she asked warily.

"Last night you asked me if I were paying court to you. Your question took me off guard, and I believe I handled the occasion badly, for which I apologize."

Sarah started to say something, but he held up his hand and continued. "But, aye, Sarah Fairfax, I am paying court to you. And today I've prepared a little surprise to show you that a cavalier can be a romantic when he chooses."

Mystified, Sarah followed his horse up to the door of the cottage and slid down into his arms when he dismounted and came to her. "My lady," he said gallantly. "Would you do me the honor of dining with me today?"

He threw open the cottage door and Sarah gave a little gasp. The entire room had been cleaned spotless. Herbs had been sprinkled around the room, giving it the sweet, wild aroma of sage, rosemary and lavender. "I would have wished to bring flowers," Anthony said, "but they're hard to come by this time of year."

In the middle of the scrubbed wood floor sat an elegantly appointed table set with Leasworth's finest French china and filled with dishes of food.

"How did you do this?" Sarah asked with amazement.

Anthony grinned. "I've made a friend or two in your uncle's kitchens."

Sarah wondered briefly if the "friends" Anthony had made included the comely blond maid, Millie. After Sarah's conversation with Bess earlier, she knew that Anthony would have received no help from her. Perhaps she should pay more heed to the cook's warnings about Anthony. Perhaps he *was* bad for her. But she had never experienced the kind of giddy elation she had seen in the other young people in the village as they made their discovery of the opposite sex, and all at once she felt that she deserved the chance to see what it was all about.

Slowly she walked into the room and looked around. The last time she had seen this place, it had been dusty and abandoned. Now it had the warm feel of a little house dearly loved by its occupants. She gave a twirl of delight. On the table was a platter of apple tarts—her favorites. "I can hardly believe it," she exclaimed.

Anthony came up to her and offered his hand. "Are you hungry yet, my lady, or would you prefer a stroll in the gardens first?"

Sarah felt like a little girl playing house. With a delighted laugh, she answered, "A stroll, by all means, my lord. Let us survey our estates."

Hand in hand, they left the little cottage and walked down a gentle knoll to the stream that bubbled just below. They watched as a sparrow landed tentatively in the clear water, then shook its wings as if to protest against the cold.

"My uncle's estate is beautiful," Sarah said dreamily.

Anthony seemed to have caught her fanciful mood. "Today this land is not your uncle's. It belongs to you and me. We're all alone in our own little world."

"And did you arrange for our own little world to be warm and brilliantly sunny in the middle of winter, Lord Rutledge?" She smiled up at him. "Because if you did, I think I'm going to have to accuse you of witchcraft."

He put his arm around her waist as they began walking downstream. "I'm not a witch, but I do think that I'm under a spell."

Sarah sighed. "It may be blasphemous to say, but I feel the same way. It's as if I'd drunk an entire flagon of wine in one big gulp."

Anthony stopped their progress and bent to kiss her lightly on the lips. "It's called infatuation, sweetheart. And there's nothing blasphemous about it. Indeed, I believe it's one of God's great gifts to delight our poor mortal existence."

"Infatuation—not love?" Sarah asked.

Anthony pulled her gently forward to resume their walk. "Ah... love. Now there's a concept that playwrights and poets have tried to dissect for centuries. It's too complicated for me. Simple, delicious infatuation is more to my taste."

"Have you never been in love, then, Lord Rutledge?"

"I've been in love dozens of times, which is to say... never."

Sarah frowned. "But surely love is a far nobler ideal than your so-called infatuation."

"Those are the words, precisely. Noble and ideal. Not of the real world."

"Your view strikes me as overly cynical, my lord."

Anthony was trying to take a bite out of his unruly tongue. He had spent the better part of the morning preparing the perfect seduction of Mistress Fairfax, then when it came time for the honeyed words and false promises, his mouth had taken entirely its own course. Truly Sarah did something to him that no other woman had ever done. He found himself wanting to present his views to her honestly, as an equal. To reveal something of his true self, even if it did not favor his purpose.

"I learned love at the skirts of my mother, Sarah. Literally, at times, when she forgot about my presence as she embarked on one of her numerous affairs."

"Surely not!"

"Oh, yes. A young son was nothing more than a nuisance to the beautiful and unfortunate Lady Rutledge. Left too young a widow, exiled and penniless in a foreign land, she wrenched the hearts of more French nobles than I can count. And when they had succumbed to her charms, she wrenched their pocketbooks, as well, before she moved on to the next victim.''

Sarah listened soberly. ''But she must have loved you—her only son. Perhaps she was forced into the life you describe in order to get enough money for the two of you to live on. Sometimes women aren't given many options in this life, you know.''

Anthony smiled. ''Do you always look for the good in people, Sarah?''

She nodded. ''It's a rewarding activity. I believe if you look hard enough, you can usually find it.''

''Even in the king?''

She hesitated. ''For four years I've tried very hard to forgive the men who killed my father. It's *my* imperfection that prevents me from doing so. But yes, I imagine there's some good even in the king.'' She stopped and put a hand lightly against his cheek. ''Indeed, I know there is good in him if he is your friend.''

Anthony's heart twisted in his chest. Sarah's light touch felt like a burning brand. Now was the time to tell her of his true reason for being in Yorkshire, to open up his heart and be completely honest with her. But he couldn't bear the thought of seeing her face harden with the disdain that had been there when he first arrived. He *would* tell her the truth, he promised himself. But first he would let them both experience the joys of the afternoon country idyll he had planned.

He took her hand from his cheek and kissed the back of it in a courtly gesture. "Shall we dine, my lady? Our meal awaits in the dining hall of our mansion."

Sarah leaned back in the stuffed leather chair and held her hands over her stomach. "Who told you that I liked apple tarts?" she asked laughingly.

"Ah, my lady, a gentleman never reveals his sources." Anthony had watched in amusement for the past several minutes as she finished off the last of the sweet pastries.

"Now I'm far too full to ride. We shall never get back to Leasworth."

"Do you care?" he asked in a low voice. He stood, looking too tall for the tiny room. He had removed his leather jacket and was dressed in a white silk shirt that cinched at the waist and covered the tops of his hose. It made a snowy contrast with his dark skin and hair.

"No, I don't care a whit. I've always wanted to be carried off and locked away by a pirate."

Anthony scooped her up from the chair. "A pirate, am I?"

"You look like one, though you lack an earring. And a cutlass." She made no protest at being held in his arms.

Carrying her easily, he walked across the room to deposit her on a wide cot that ran underneath one of the cottage's cut-glass windows. "I have them stashed away in a trunk. But to no avail. You've discovered my secret."

"So you're not really a baron?"

"No, you guessed it—I'm Black Anthony, scourge of the seven seas." He pulled a kerchief from inside his shirt and tied it around his head at a rakish angle. His long black hair flowed from beneath it and he looked for all the world like a buccaneer.

Sarah lay back against the big feather pillows and laughed. She had never experienced this kind of play with a man before, had not known it was possible. For the moment her worries over Parson Hollander and Jack were forgotten.

"Then I should be afraid of you, Black Anthony."

He knelt over her on one knee and took her hand. "Oh no, not you. For you are my lady, and I'm sworn on the pirate's code of honor to protect you with my life."

Neither said anything for a long moment. Anthony moved from his kneeling position to sit beside her, but their eyes didn't lose contact. "I'm glad to hear that," Sarah said in a near whisper. "For I could swear that the one I most needed protection from was you."

Anthony swallowed hard. In spite of his candor during their walk earlier, the day had gone much as he had planned. Sarah was relaxed, perhaps even slightly tipsy. And she looked more beautiful than he had ever seen her with the sun streaming in on her unbound hair. But her words hit a chord in his heart. She was absolutely right. The one she most needed protection from was him.

He struggled to bring back their playful mood. "Well, you see, you were wrong. You have nothing to fear at all. As my lady, I merely keep you locked up here all day while I feed you apple tarts."

"Until I become too fat to waddle."

"Exactly. Then I know you'll never escape me."

They laughed together, then grew serious again as Anthony cupped his hand behind her neck and pulled her toward him. "You don't ever have to be afraid of me, Sarah. I only want to make you happy."

He kissed her full on the lips once, then again. She opened her eyes. "You do make me happy, Anthony. I've never had these kinds of feelings before."

The fitted blue habit clung to the curves of her body, outlining her long legs, which were stretched out along the cot. Her breasts rose and fell in an erratic rhythm. Anthony gave himself one last chance to allow the newly protective feelings he had experienced since his arrival at Leasworth to take charge, but the demands of his body were gaining the upper hand.

He moved to position himself next to her on the cot, then put an arm around her waist and pulled her closer. "I may not be an expert on love," he said huskily, "but I *am* infatuated with you, Sarah Fairfax."

"Delicious infatuation," she said, repeating the phrase he had used.

"Aye." He kissed her. "Delicious." Slowly his tongue tasted her lips, then moved within her mouth to meet with hers in a warm, liquid mating. Sarah felt herself sink into the pillows as his body covered her. His hard thigh rubbed between her legs, precisely where an indefinable ache had begun to build.

She spread her hands over his broad back, the silk shirt moving under her fingers. His chest pressed against her breasts.

Anthony reached up to tear the bandanna from his head and flung it to the floor. He was done with games. Like a hunter stalking a wild doe, he narrowed his focus to the rough bed they shared. He opened the brackets of her dress to allow him access to her breasts. Slowly, patiently, with his hands and his tongue, he stoked her desire, then withdrew, allowing her to become familiar with the building heat. When she arched toward him, he moved to one side, then stroked one hand down her stomach and lower. There he stopped with his hand resting on her, warm and strong, as if to protect her most feminine secrets.

"I want to make love to you, dearling," he said into her ear.

In that moment every sermon Sarah had ever heard, every notion she had ever had about lovemaking, fled. She knew nothing but Anthony's hand on her body, his lips on her mouth and his voice in her brain. For her answer, she moved beneath him in an age-old plea.

Giving her a bruising, impatient kiss, Anthony pulled his shirt over his head with one swift motion, then began the more tedious process of freeing her from her clothes.

Sarah had turned her attention to Anthony's bare chest. She ran her hand along the taut muscles and was surprised at the silky feel of the dark hair that covered them, tapering to a vee, then widening as it disappeared beneath his soft leather belt.

She moved willingly as he lifted her from the bed to pull her dress out from beneath them. Surprisingly, she felt no shame at her nakedness. Reflected in the hungry look in Anthony's eyes, her body felt ripe and sensuous. Now Anthony's hands were everywhere, showing her sensitive places that she had not known existed. Suddenly he sat up and tugged at his boots and hose. Once he was as naked as she, he fiercely pulled her underneath him and met her mouth in a demanding kiss.

Their bodies molded in a natural harmony, hard against soft, rough against smooth. Anthony fought for control. With expert fingers he made sure she was ready for him. Just as he thought he could not bear another instant, he felt the warmth of her surrender and carefully entered her body.

Sarah had known, of course, what was to happen. She had observed the whole process quite dispassionately between her horses. But she hadn't known about this frightening whirlwind of sensation that had robbed her of all reason. She clung to Anthony with a near sob and clenched her fists at his back as he quickened his thrusts, spiraling the sensation upward through her stomach and breasts until it seemed to explode in every part of her body at once.

She went limp. Anthony lay quiet and heavy, his head on her chest. For a moment the only sound was their labored breathing.

Sarah ran her hands lazily through his hair. "So this is what you call infatuation?" she asked weakly.

For a moment Anthony could not answer. He hesitated to tell Sarah that nothing in his experience with infatuations could have prepared him for an experience such as this one. He slid upward and gathered her into his arms. He had none of his normal desire to leave now that the lovemaking was over and go on about his business. In fact, he found himself suddenly wishing that he could hold her this way forever, sending the king and Oliver and the rest of the world to hell.

Gently he kissed her forehead, then her eyelids, her nose, finally her swollen lips. "I don't know exactly what to call it, Sarah," he admitted.

"But you're sure it's not love."

"It damn well feels like it, doesn't it?" he said in a bemused tone.

Sarah smiled and snuggled into his arms. It wasn't exactly a declaration, but it would do for now. Her instincts were telling her that Anthony Rutledge's usual dealings with ladies were nothing like this. He sensed the difference, too. She could tell. He had grown quiet and was holding her tightly in an embrace that seemed to have little to do with passion.

"Anthony?" she asked softly.

He looked down and smiled, his expression preoccupied. "Yes, sweetheart? Are you cold?" The cot had no coverings, so he reached to the floor for the jacket of her riding habit.

"No, I'm not cold. It's just that you seemed far away all at once."

He squeezed her more tightly. "On the contrary, Sarah. I'm feeling very close. Perhaps closer than I have ever felt before . . . to anyone. It's a little frightening."

Sarah nodded. "I know. I've felt that way, too—so close that it makes you afraid."

"With a suitor?"

Sarah had been thinking about Jack. When her father died it had seemed that Jack was all she had to cling to in a terrible world. And sometimes, she feared, she had held to him too tightly. But Anthony didn't even know of Jack's existence. Perhaps now was the time to tell him the truth—now that they had shared so much.

"No, not a suitor—"

Anthony interrupted her with another hug. "You're talking about your father, of course. And how he was taken away from you so young. But the Civil War and its reprisals are long past. There's no more reason for you to lose anyone you love, Sarah."

His mention of her father and the war made Sarah's confession stick in her throat. To her complete astonishment, it appeared that she was falling in love with a king's man. But while she had entrusted him with her body, she was not yet certain that she wanted to entrust him with Jack's life.

"Let's not talk about it," she said.

Anthony pulled himself up to look at her. The stream of afternoon sun had turned golden and bathed her bare skin with bronze. Her hair spread around them in silky tangles. Passion's flush was slowly fading from her cheeks. He pulled her back into his arms and bent toward her mouth. "We don't have to talk about it, sweetheart," he murmured. "We don't have to talk at all."

The pungent odor of the tannery hit Sarah's nostrils while she was still several steps away from the door. She hesitated before knocking. She had known the tanner, Silas Thatcher, and his family all her life, but she was curiously reluctant to face his daughter Norah, who had so recently become involved with Jack. Especially now that she knew *exactly* what Norah and Jack had been doing during those nights out in the meadow. She had learned the secret yesterday in a long, glorious afternoon that she would never forget. But the feelings and thoughts were still tumbling about wildly in her head. It was at times like this that she missed having a mother or sister, or even a good girlfriend, to confide in.

Perhaps she should confide in Norah. The girl was certainly experienced enough in these matters. Sarah gave a little laugh. What irony to think of the daughter of the great Puritan John Fairfax seeking advice from the "bad girl" of the village. She lifted her hand to the door.

Norah's mother, Merry, answered the knock. She was a drawn, tired woman whose premature aging belied her name. Her lot had not been easy. She'd borne nine children and seen four of them put in the ground.

"Good day, Mistress Thatcher. I'm looking for Norah."

"She be not at home." Not even the ghost of a smile relieved her weary expression.

"Well, actually..." Sarah paused. "I'm here to inquire after my brother. Has he been here? Or do you think Norah might know something of his whereabouts?"

Merry Thatcher shrugged. "A strapping lad, your brother," she said. "But not for the likes of my Norah. He'll break her heart one of these days."

Sarah could not think of an answer. To her shame, it had not even occurred to her that Jack's liaison with Norah would be anything more than entertainment—on both sides. It was well-known in the village that Norah gave of her body freely and often. Furthermore, she was a poor tanner's daughter, whereas Jack, in spite of their tainted lineage, came from much higher stock.

"When Norah comes back I'd appreciate it if you would ask if she has any news about Jack."

The woman nodded and started to close the door, but stopped and looked down the road instead. "There she be now. My Norah."

Sarah turned and saw the dark-haired beauty sauntering along the road. She always walked around town with a kind of sway to her hips and a half smile on her face. It was no wonder that the men sought her out and the women whispered about her behind her back.

"I'll just ask her myself, then, Mistress Thatcher," Sarah said hastily, relieved to turn away from the woman's sad eyes.

Norah was carrying a basket of buns, which swung back and forth to the rhythm of her hips. "Mistress Fairfax," she called to Sarah. "What brings you here?"

Sarah felt an unaccustomed shyness as she approached the girl, observing her now not as just one of the village maids but as her brother's lover. "You can call me Sarah," she said hesitantly.

"Sarah it is," Norah said. "What can I do for you?"

"I . . . I'm looking for Jack. Have you had word of him?"

"He told me he was to stay out of sight as long as you have that fancy gent from London staying up at Leasworth."

"Yes, that's right. Only . . . he was going on an errand some ways south of here and he hasn't returned. I'm just feeling a bit worried."

Worried and guilty. When she had finally made it back down to the cave last night after forgetting herself entirely during her incredible day with Anthony, she had discovered that there was still no word from Jack. The parson's fire had gone out again as he slept, and he looked bad. His face was ashen and his eyes ringed with great dark circles. Sarah had built up the fire and spent several futile minutes arguing with the parson about going for medical help. She had berated herself all the way home. She should have been looking after the situation, finding out where Jack had gotten himself off to, rather than indulging in purely personal carnal pleasures with Anthony.

It had been too late to do anything more by the time she got home, but first thing in the morning she had made a trip down to the cave and then set out to the village to try to find out about Jack.

"Jack's a smart lad, Sarah," Norah said kindly. "Brawny, too," she added with a wink. "I'd wager he can take care of himself."

Norah's assurances and good humor made Sarah feel calmer. "I guess it's just that I've taken care of him for so many years now, it's kind of hard to give up the job," she said with a smile.

Norah nodded sympathetically. "Well, there's lots who would be willing to take over that particular job, if you get my meaning. I'd be first in line. As I said, Jack's a brawny lad."

The words were said teasingly, but Sarah detected an underlying seriousness. "You and my brother have become very good friends . . ." she ventured.

Norah's warm smile dimmed and Sarah could detect a slight trembling of her bottom lip. "Jack's the best thing that ever happened to me, Sarah. He's not like the others—he treats me like a lady."

Sarah put a comforting hand on Norah's shoulder. "He's fond of you, Norah. I can see it when he speaks of you."

"When we're together it seems like the rest of the world just doesn't exist. . . ."

Her big brown eyes filled with tears and Sarah felt the sting behind her own eyelids. After yesterday, she knew exactly what Norah was talking about. But the real world did exist. Was she just fooling herself that she and Anthony had any more hope for a future than Norah and Jack?

In spite of both Norah's and Parson Hollander's assurance that Jack could take care of himself, Sarah grew more and more worried as she rode back toward Leasworth. She considered riding south to Cottleswoode herself, but she couldn't give herself a good reason to go. Jack was undoubtedly still waiting to contact the smugglers, and her appearance there would just complicate matters. Her brother was now a man full grown, and she had to struggle to remember that.

She was lost in thought as she entered the Leasworth stables. Brigand took his own lead to head toward his stall. When he stopped she slid off his back and gave him a distracted pat.

"I thought you had run away."

Anthony's deep voice made her jump. She clutched Brigand's bridle and turned around. He was walking toward her, dark, lean, powerful—looking somehow more dangerous today. Or perhaps it was just the recognition of how much of herself she had surrendered to him, body *and* heart, that made him seem so. "You startled me," she said.

He stopped a couple of paces from her. "You've had a hard ride already this morning?" he asked, pointing to Brigand's muddy legs.

Sarah had an excuse on the tip of her tongue, but it wouldn't come out. She didn't want to lie to Anthony any more than she had to. So she merely nodded her head.

Anthony frowned. "When I awoke to find you'd gone, I had a horrible feeling in the pit of my stomach, as if you had fled and I would never see you again."

"Well here I am, so you see, you were wrong," she answered lightly.

He closed the distance between them and spoke in a low voice. "If we weren't in your uncle's home, I would have had you in my bed last night and there would have been no early morning ride for either of us."

"No?" Sarah felt her throat go dry just as it had the day before.

"No. We'd be there still, making slow, sweet love in the morning light."

She swallowed and backed up a step, but he followed her until their bodies met and his arms went around her waist. "I'm going to want to make love to you at every hour of the day, Sarah." He kissed her softly. "Can we manage it, do you think?"

To her chagrin, Sarah felt her body once again turning to jelly. In another minute she'd be inviting him to lie down with her here in the middle of the stables, with anyone likely to come along at any moment. She had, indeed, lost her wits entirely.

She pulled away. "Someone will be coming," she protested.

Anthony looked around the stable. "Let's go somewhere else, then. I'm not particular."

Sarah laughed. Her body, too, was entreating her to find somewhere that they could continue to explore the delights they had just begun to sample yesterday. But it was absurd. She had too many other things to think about. She tried to keep the mood light. "I've heard that some men are insatiable, Lord Rutledge," she said.

He put one long arm entirely around her waist and held her against him. "Only when the menu is so delectable, my lady," he said huskily.

Chapter Eight

"Ah... beggin' yer pardon, Mistress Sarah."

Neither Anthony nor Sarah had noticed the arrival of Arthur. He stood just inside the big stable doors, looking as if he wished he were anywhere else.

Sarah pulled herself out of Anthony's grasp. "Come on in, Arthur. You're just in time to brush down Brigand."

Anthony appeared unaffected by the boy's arrival. He bent to speak low in her ear. "I was about to invite you on a picnic. With that menu we were just talking about."

Sarah blushed as she handed Brigand's reins to Arthur. "You are remiss in your duties, Lord Rutledge. Aren't you supposed to be out scouting horses?"

Anthony grinned. "I plan on sending word to the king that I've been stricken with the worst malady known to man and need more time for my task."

"I didn't notice that you were experiencing ill health," Sarah said dryly.

"It's not a malady of the body, but rather of the mind. And I believe that it's one with which the king himself is quite familiar."

The banter was making Sarah uncomfortable. Though she couldn't deny that her feelings this morning were every bit as strong as they had been in the cottage yesterday with Anthony, somehow today it all seemed different. She had made the most serious commitment a woman could make to a man, yet Anthony could joke about being stricken with a malady and compare it to the king's liaisons, which frequently lasted less time than an eight-course banquet at Whitehall.

"Perhaps tending to your duty would help you recover from your illness, my lord," she said, her voice grown chill.

"Sweetheart, I was teasing you." He glanced over at Arthur who had begun to curry Sarah's big horse and lowered his voice. "Yesterday was wonderful—one of the best days of my life."

Sarah's mood did not brighten. Anthony had implied that he had proven a good match for the king in romantic conquests. It made Sarah wonder how many times the same flowery words had passed his lips.

"Well, you may not have business to tend to, but I do. If you'll excuse me, I'll see you this afternoon."

Anthony grabbed for her arm as she turned to leave. "Don't go, Sarah. Let's find a place where we can talk. You're upset, and I want to know why."

"I'm not upset. I just have a lot to get done today."

He let her go. It was not the encounter he had imagined when he had awakened this morning wanting her as badly as he had before they had ever made love. There *was* something wrong. But the middle of the stables with the boy listening to every word was not the place to get to the bottom of it. "I'll see you this afternoon, then," he said evenly.

She turned and was gone with a swish of her skirts.

By the time Sarah visited the parson that afternoon, she was nearly frantic with worry. It had been three days with no word of Jack. The parson himself had finally begun to sound concerned. "I should have given him something of mine to identify himself with," he said with a frown.

He still moved as though he were in great pain, although he assured Sarah that his side was much better.

"You don't think the contrabandists would harm him, do you?" she asked in alarm.

"I've dealt with the band for many years, but they can be unpredictable."

Sarah busied herself piling more wood by the fire and arranging the food and cider she had brought so that it would be within easy reach. "I should have gone myself," she said half under her breath.

"Come here and sit by me for a minute, Sarah."

The parson's voice was stern, and Sarah did as he asked.

He took her hand and addressed her admonishingly. "It's time you realize, Sarah Fairfax, that you are a woman. It would have been the height of folly for you to go by yourself and meet with the contrabandists. They're rough men. I don't believe they'll harm Jack, but I wouldn't care to think about what they might do to a lone woman."

"I believe I've proven that I can take care of myself, Parson. With Brigand's help."

"Brigand wouldn't be of much use to you against a whole band of smugglers. Listen to what I'm telling you, Sarah. It's all right for you to depend on others for help now and then. In spite of what you have felt since your father died, it doesn't have to be Sarah Fairfax against the world. Or even against the king."

"You yourself have said often enough, Father, that if it hadn't been for the generous 'contributions' of the cavaliers I've robbed, some of our people might have starved."

"I know your intentions were good, Sarah. And goodness knows, the king's taxes are still an unholy burden on the town, but, curiously enough, the war is causing more prosperity along the coast. Perhaps this winter will be better. By any measure, you've done your part. It's time for you to concentrate on yourself for a while and your own future."

She wondered what the good parson would think if he knew just exactly how much she'd been concentrating on herself with Anthony yesterday afternoon. The thought made her blush.

"I know. Jack's told me the same thing. And I intend to do some serious thinking about our future,

Jack's and mine, just as soon as we get you out of this coil and get the king's men out of our hair.''

The parson leaned forward and kissed her forehead. "Give Jack another day, child. I feel certain that by tomorrow there will be word of him."

She was too agitated to go back to the house. Giving Brigand his head, she raced along the top of the sea cliffs. She had no fear as the path veered close to the edge. She and Brigand had traveled this route together since he was little more than a colt.

Her thoughts were in disarray. The parson's words about her future were mixing themselves with Anthony's protestations about making love to her, and in the midst of it all was the nagging worry over her brother. Jack was the most important, she told herself. No matter what the parson advised, she was through waiting for word. Somehow she would make her excuses to Anthony and go to Cottleswoode to look for him herself. The sudden resolution made her feel better, and she was able to put all the other unwelcome deliberations out of her head. She wheeled Brigand around and headed back toward Leasworth.

When she reached the Bratswick Scar she stopped. A rider was coming toward her, and it took her only one quick moment to see that it was Jack. Joyously she spurred Brigand ahead. "Jack, you're all right," she called with a wave.

Jack brought his horse up to hers. "Of course I'm all right."

Sarah spoke more calmly. "I was . . . uh . . . the parson and I were worried about you."

Jack jumped from his saddle. "Come walk with me and I'll tell you about it."

Sarah dismounted more slowly, and, to her surprise, Jack reached to give her a hand. She couldn't remember Jack ever helping her off her horse in her entire life. But then, she was learning that this was a new Jack.

They started along the cliff path, letting their well-trained horses follow behind with no lead. "Did you contact the contrabandists?" Sarah asked.

Jack looked irritated. "That was why I went, wasn't it?"

Sarah was surprised at his ill humor, but she asked calmly, "Well, what did they say?"

"The younger lads wanted no part of an escaped fugitive, but the leader is an older fellow who has worked with the parson since the war. He thinks they should do it. Finally they decided that they wanted to talk to the parson himself—and to you."

"To me!"

"Well, to the moonlight highwayman. They want to negotiate, I reckon, to try to get a good price for the job."

"Why didn't you just tell them that we would pay whatever they asked?"

"They wouldn't deal. One of the scurvy lot said that they didn't make bargains with nurslings."

"Oh, Jack." Sarah felt his embarrassment. But it was a measure of just how close he was to becoming a man that it hurt so much to be treated like a boy.

"Well, we'll just have to arrange a meeting, then."

"You don't have to arrange anything. They're waiting down by the cove now. I came to fetch you."

Sarah glanced over at the cliffs leading down to the water. "Good. What are we wasting time for?"

"I don't like to have them see that you're a woman," Jack said, sounding reluctant to move.

Sarah waved off his objection. "It can't be helped. The parson is hurt, and we need to get him out of here."

Jack interrupted. "The figure they're mentioning is fifty guineas."

Sarah grew silent.

"I told them it was too much," Jack said apologetically. "But the old man said that with the war on and all, everything is more dangerous."

"That's all right, Jack. Whatever it is, we'll get it."

"I thought perhaps we could get it from Uncle."

Sarah shook her head. "We've resolved never to involve Uncle Thomas in any of this. Do you want him to end up the way our father did?"

"I suppose the sheriff took the pieces of jewelry the parson had left to sell."

"I think so. But it's not a problem. There's more where those pieces came from. The masked highwayman will just have to make one more raid."

Jack stopped and turned to her, taking her upper arms in a bruising grip. "Are you out of your mind?" he shouted.

Sarah's chin went up. "It's the only way."

"There's no way in hell I'm going to let you go out on the roads again with king's men behind every tree. You're finished with that—for good."

"We've got to get the parson out of that cave. I told you—he's been hurt."

"What's the matter with him?"

"They kicked him, the dirty swine. I think he might have some broken ribs."

Jack closed his eyes briefly, then looked at her with a stubborn expression. "If there has to be one more robbery, *I'm* the one who'll be doing it."

"No, you're not."

"Yes, I am."

They glared at each other for a long moment. Finally, Jack gave a rueful laugh. "You are by far the most bullheaded woman in God's creation."

"And you are learning from my bad example, little brother," she said petulantly, pulling his hands away from her arms.

"What about Lord Rutledge?" Jack asked.

Sarah knew that Jack was asking about their guest in relation to the proposed robbery, but she couldn't help the instant blush that heated her face. "What about him?" she asked, trying to sound casual.

Jack grabbed her arms again and looked down at her averted eyes. He was quiet for a long moment, then asked, "Yes, what about him? *You* tell *me,* big sister."

"He's not like we thought he would be, Jack."

"What does that mean?" Jack's tone was skeptical.

"He stood up for me when that Captain Kempthorne wanted to take Brigand, and he says he feels sorry about the parson, and he wants to learn more about Puritanism, and he gave away his cakes to the White children, and..."

Sarah stopped. She had the feeling that she was babbling, and Jack's steady gaze was growing more and more wary.

"And...what, Sarah?" he asked softly.

"And...I think I'm falling in love with him." Until that moment she hadn't wanted to voice the words even to herself, but it was true. She was falling in love with Anthony Rutledge, cavalier, courtier and classic example of everything she had held in disdain.

Jack dropped his hold on her and looked out at the sea. "As bad as that?" he asked finally, his back to her.

Sarah gave a rueful smile. "As bad as that."

"He's only been here a few days...."

"Tell me, Jack. Once you really discovered Norah Thatcher's existence...as more than just one of the maids about the village...how long did it take *you?*"

Jack had no answer. He had "discovered" Norah, as Sarah put it, at a village harvest fair and had made love to her that very night, a night he would never forget as long as he lived. But Norah was a different kind of girl from Sarah. Girls from good families didn't have the same kinds of feelings...or at least he didn't think they did.

"Well, at least this settles one question," he said briskly.

Sarah looked confused.

"As long as Lord Rutledge has his eye on you, there's no way you can go off and become the moonlight bandit."

Sarah bristled. "Jack, I've already told you, *I'm* the one who's going to do it, and that's that."

Jack grimaced with exasperation. "We'll go together," he said, giving up.

"No, we won't," Sarah said, smiling sweetly.

Jack's expression grew stern again. "It's no use, Sarah. I'm just getting too big for you to boss around. Either we do this together, or I do it by myself. Those are the options."

Sarah stood back a step and looked him up and down. He was a full head taller than she, and his broad shoulders blotted out the waning rays of the afternoon sun. He was right about one thing, he was getting too big to boss around.

"All right, you can go with me. But when it's time for the score, you stay back. Brigand and I know what we're doing, and you would just be in the way."

Jack nodded. There would be time enough to work out the details once the deed was under way. "Partners, then," he said, holding out his hand.

Sarah laughed and reached to shake hands, but instead he took hold of her wrist and pulled her into his arms for a hearty embrace. "I do love you, Sarah," he said tenderly.

She turned her face into his wool coat to hide the tears that threatened to well up and answered, "And I you, Jack."

At the same moment they pulled away from each other. Jack took her hand and turned back toward the horses. "Come on, then," he said briskly. "Let's go play pirate one more time."

Deception tossed his head, impatient to be on his way. Anthony pulled back on the reins. He couldn't believe the tender scene he was witnessing. The lovely enchantress who had spent the better part of yesterday afternoon in bed with him, professing at every step to be an innocent, was in front of him now in the arms of another man—her neighborly suitor, Master Henry Partridge, to be precise. The same Henry Partridge he had been planning to find and interrogate about the highway robberies, a quest he had abandoned when Sarah had offered herself to him so completely.

He watched as the two people on the edge of the cliff embraced. They held each other with the ease of long familiarity, not with the stiff self-consciousness of a new courtship.

He should ride and confront the pair right now. Perhaps being caught together like this would take them off guard and he could get the answers he sought. His mind ordered his feet to spur Deception ahead, but his feet didn't move. It was as if he had frozen to the spot. Sarah's skirts were blowing in the breeze, outlining her graceful form. Perhaps the problem was that he didn't want the answers after all.

The wind shifted suddenly and he distinctly heard the man's words. "I do love you, Sarah." It was as if a saber blade had sliced into his chest. He had known since he first set eyes on her that she was different. And yesterday had confirmed it. With her bright mind and kind heart she had somehow reached a place inside of him that he hadn't known existed. Yesterday he had tried to call it infatuation. But now as he watched the two figures mount up and ride off with a tender touch of their hands, he knew that he had been lying to himself. He was in love with Sarah Fairfax. And he had just sat by like a moonstruck schoolboy and let her be wooed by a man who most likely was a wanted criminal.

Sheriff Jeffries and Oliver were playing a game of chess when Anthony burst in the door. "Excuse me, gentlemen," he said caustically. "I don't want to interrupt your important activities, but I was under the impression that we had a bandit and a fugitive priest to catch."

Oliver looked up with a puzzled expression. "What burr has gotten under your saddle, my friend?"

Anthony kicked a chair to bring it nearer the other two men and sat. "I just want to know what's being done."

Oliver turned to the chessboard and took the sheriff's queen with his rook. "See if you can get yourself out of that one, Sheriff," he said with a short, gloating laugh. Then he turned his attention to Anthony. "I told you I'd be up to the house to report in the morning. What's the sudden hurry?"

"I've seen Partridge."

"Where?" Oliver asked.

"Who's Partridge?" the sheriff asked at the same time.

Oliver and Anthony looked at the sheriff in confusion.

"Henry Partridge," Anthony answered. "You must know him—he's from these parts."

"Can't say as I've heard the name."

"Come, man. He's been courting the Mistress Fairfax." Anthony's voice had a raw edge, which brought another quizzical glance from Oliver.

Sheriff Jeffries looked mystified. "*Courting* her, you say?"

"Aye. I've seen them together myself."

"Courting Sarah Fairfax. Well, that's a new one. Yes, sir."

Anthony brushed aside the man's comments and turned back to Oliver. "I want your men to bring him in."

"You say you saw him. Why didn't *you* bring him in?" Oliver asked with a speculative look.

Anthony hesitated. "He was too far away and on a fast horse. But someone around here must know where he lives. Get your men out asking questions."

"Tonight?" Oliver asked mildly.

"All right—not tonight. But first thing in the morning."

"We'll start out at first light. I'll serve him up to you for midday meal, if you like."

Anthony stood and kicked the chair back to its former position. "Just find him. It's about time the Yorkshire highwayman is brought to justice."

When they reached the cove, Parson Hollander was out of the cave and engaged in conversation in French with a group of seven or eight men. Two small boats had been pulled up on a narrow strip of sand that bordered the cliff just above them. The parson waved to them as they climbed down.

"Sarah, Jack...over here!" His voice sounded stronger than it had since his arrest.

Sarah walked toward the men cautiously. If they hadn't wanted to deal with Jack, they would probably be even less inclined to deal with a woman. A woman, a boy and an old man. They didn't make a very impressive trio. He hoped the parson had been right about the men holding some regard for him.

The leader of the group was a surprisingly handsome man of about fifty years with long, iron gray hair. He was dressed in thigh-high boots, a claret velvet coat and a plumed hat, looking more like a courtier than a contrabandist. He removed his hat with a flourish as Sarah approached.

"Mistress Fairfax, may I offer my congratulations," he said in heavily accented English.

She looked at him in surprise as he continued. "My good friend the parson has been telling me about your exploits. I wish I could be there one of these nights to see you riding like a fury over the moors."

Parson Hollander held his hands up apologetically. "Sarah, this is Mÿnheer Van Vleck, the...er...man who is going to help me get out of the country. I had to tell him about you, my dear. They're willing to take me across, but in return they demanded to know the identity of the highwayman."

Van Vleck smiled expansively. "It is just a matter of a little—how do you say—*insurance*," he said. "You can't be too careful these days. The war has made this business too risky for my taste—too many king's men hiding behind every boulder."

Several members of the group scanned the shoreline anxiously. All looked to be much younger than their leader, and none were nearly so well dressed.

"Surely you don't think the parson would betray you to the king's men?" Sarah asked.

"The parson—no. But until yesterday I had not made the acquaintance of your determined young brother here," he said with a nod to Jack. "Nor of you, *mademoiselle*. But I *had* heard of the daring of the masked rider."

"Well, now you have met us all," Sarah said firmly. "You know our secret, and you can trust our word that the king's men will never learn of your activities through us."

The smuggler nodded. "It will be a pleasure doing business with such a beautiful confederate."

Sarah looked around at the band of men who were eyeing her with grinning faces. She had no desire to be a *confederate* of such a group. But this was where her criminal adventures had taken her. She was paying the consequence for the path she had chosen to revenge her father's death. And what was worse, the parson was paying an even higher price. She wanted to finish up her business and get out of here.

"I believe you said fifty guineas. Is it a bargain?" she asked, her voice hard.

Van Vleck set his hat back on his head and looked amused. "A bargain it is, little lady."

"You'll wait here until I bring the money?"

"We'll give you two days."

"What if we need more time?"

He rolled his eyes up the cliff. "You're crawling with king's guards up there. We'll risk it for two days, and then we're gone."

Jack, who had been silent during the entire exchange, pushed in front of Sarah. "You'll have your money in two days."

He took her arm. "Let's get out of here, Sarah. I'll go with you back up the cliff. Will you be all right, Parson?"

Parson Hollander nodded. "I'll be fine. I think I'll just go on back in the cave and rest a spell."

Jack's strong hand supporting her felt good to Sarah. There were advantages, she decided, in having her little brother grow up.

"It's been a pleasure meeting you," Van Vleck called as they made their way over to the rocks. He watched them until they disappeared over the top of the cliff, then turned to his men, the congeniality gone from his tone. "You two," he said, pointing to the men nearest him. "Follow them. Be sure they don't talk to anyone in uniform. If you see anything suspicious, report back here at once."

Anthony worked a piece of dry bread back and forth between his thumb and fingers until it made a powdery trail on the table. He had no appetite whatsoever and had already drunk more ale than he could handle with a clear head. After talking with Oliver and the sheriff, he had ridden hard to get back in time to sup, only to be told by a sympathetic Millie that neither the master nor the mistress would be joining him at the table. Sarah had not been at the table at noon, either. He had not seen her since the strained encounter at the stables this morning.

"May I fill your glass, sir?" Millie had been a hovering presence during the entire meal and gave the impression that she wouldn't mind accompanying him for the rest of the evening.

"No, thank you. Do you know where Mistress Fairfax is?"

Millie's blond curls bobbed as she shook her head. "All I know is that she went out. Walking, I think. Though I can't imagine what she'd be doing out this time of day. It's passing dark."

Anthony wiped the last of the bread crumbs from his fingers. "And you're sure she hasn't come back? How long has she been gone?"

Millie reached across him to collect one of the plates, making sure her soft bosom brushed along his arm. "Mistress Sarah comes and goes as she will, my lord. Nobody keeps much track of her."

Except Jack, she could have added. But everyone in the household had been told by Thomas Fairfax not to mention his young nephew to any of the king's men, including their visitor. Millie did not understand the why of it, but she was fond of her position at Leasworth and didn't want to do anything to endanger it. Although... She made a thorough survey of the elegant gentleman at the table. He certainly was a fine one. Fancy and well muscled at the same time. And clothes grander than any she had ever seen. If she could engage Lord Rutledge's interest to the point that he would take her back to London with him, she could probably find much better employment than any that Yorkshire would have to offer.

"You've hardly eaten, sir," she observed as she removed the rest of the plates.

"I'm sorry, Millie. It's no fault with the food. I'm just not very hungry tonight."

"Perhaps you need another kind of nourishment, sir," Millie suggested.

Anthony looked up at her round face. Her smile was cheery and her body was pleasingly full. Sarah was probably off this very minute with her suitor and perhaps lover, Partridge. It would serve her right if he took advantage of Millie's offer. But he found himself answering, "It appears I've lost my appetite for all kinds of sustenance tonight, Millie."

The girl did not appear in the least disheartened by his refusal. She lifted a heavy platter in each hand and turned to leave, calling back over her shoulder, "I'll be in the scullery a couple more hours if you change your mind, luv."

Anthony couldn't help but smile at her boldness. Was there something in the air of Yorkshire that made the women so audacious? There was definitely nothing diffident about Sarah's nature, either, in spite of her Puritan garments.

She was bold enough, at least, to be keeping two men in harness at the same time. He took a long gulp of ale, then grimaced as it hit his rocky stomach. It wasn't ale he needed at the moment, nor food, nor a kitchen maid. He needed to talk with Sarah and get things straight with her. He didn't know if she'd been deliberately avoiding him all day, but she wouldn't be able to do so indefinitely. As soon as he found her, he wouldn't let her go until she had answered his questions. He would demand to know just exactly what was her relationship with Henry Partridge. And if he didn't like the answer, he was not above using every weapon in his arsenal in order to make her change her mind. The very thought turned his blood to lava.

Sarah was bone weary. All day long her mind had jumped from worry about Jack to confusion about Anthony, interspersed with sudden vivid memories of their lovemaking the previous day. Then to her great relief, Jack had appeared, but he had told her that she herself would have to go meet with the band of smugglers. And that, most probably, she would have to ride again as the masked highwayman in order to get the money they demanded. Which meant that Anthony's continued presence put her in jeopardy. She wished she were a simple village maid like Norah Thatcher. Then she and Anthony could enjoy a long night of lovemaking under the stars without any thought to the consequences. She smiled at her own whimsy. In truth, life wasn't that simple for the village maids, either, she told herself, remembering Merry Thatcher's haggard face.

But at any rate, she wasn't a village maid. She was John Fairfax's daughter and Jack Fairfax's sister, and the world would never be simple for her. She had best keep that in mind and forget about the incredible things she had discovered in Anthony's arms. She would try to stay out of his way and hope he would give up on her and go back to London.

She couldn't wait long to act. When she had brought the parson his food tonight, Jack had been with him and had agreed with her that it wasn't healthy for him to stay much longer in the damp cave. The moon would rise full tomorrow night. With luck, she would find an easy prey along the Old North Road and be done with it.

It was late. She and Jack had stayed talking by the light of the small fire in the cave while Parson Hollander dozed in uneasy sleep alongside them. Her uncle would be asleep by now, and she hoped their guest would have followed suit. She closed the big front door of the manor house behind her. Walking carefully so her riding boots would make no sound on the flagstone floor, she passed the entrance to her uncle's library and headed for the curved stairway at the end of the hall.

She flinched as a strong hand pulled back on her shoulder. "Where've you been?" Anthony asked without preamble.

Sarah turned around slowly. He looked almost as tired as she felt, but his dark, handsome features still made her heart speed up. His hand on her felt as heavy as an anvil, but she stood up straight and said haughtily, "I'd be happy to tell you where I've been as soon as you give me one remotely sensible reason as to why that would be your business."

She was in her blue riding habit again, the same one Anthony had slowly stripped from her silky skin yesterday. And she was angry. Her eyes gave off purple flashes. The speech he had been preparing all evening deserted him utterly.

"Perhaps this will suffice," he murmured, seizing her against him and taking her mouth in a demanding kiss.

Desire blazed through him like wine poured on a fire. He didn't care anymore where she had been, even if she had come directly from the bed of Henry Partridge. He just wanted her. Scooping her up easily in his arms, he climbed the stairs to his bedroom. Tonight would be his—theirs. The morning would be time enough to sort out the rest of it.

Chapter Nine

Sarah blinked sleepily and took a minute to remember that she was in Anthony's bedchamber. The sun was shining brightly through the cracks in the shutters. It had to be well past dawn. She started up in a panic, only to be pushed back down into the feather bed by two strong arms.

"Where do you think you're going?" he asked.

She brushed the hair back from her face. It was in a hopeless tangle. "Let me up. I can't be here, Anthony. Someone will find us...my uncle..." She looked about her helplessly.

He lay beside her and pulled her up against his chest, planting a kiss on her shoulder. "First things first. How are you this morning?"

They were both warm and naked under the coverlet and Sarah took a moment to enjoy the sensation. "I'm very fine this morning, Lord Rutledge," she said with a provocative smile. "And how are you?"

"I'm...hungry."

Sarah pushed against his chest. "You see. It's past time for breaking fast. I've got to get out of here."

Anthony slowly shook his head. "No."

Impatiently she gave him a kiss on the lips. "You said you were hungry."

He nodded, then lifted the covers above them. His potent dark eyes swept the length of their entwined bodies. "I'm hungry for this," he said in a low voice that reverberated in the pit of Sarah's stomach.

A pulse started to beat in her throat. "I can't... Anthony..." she pleaded.

He dropped his hold on the blanket and moved his hand to capture one of her breasts. Molding it with his palm, he bent his head to fasten himself at the peak. "I'm hungry for this," he repeated.

Swift surges of feeling were traveling down her body, but Sarah made one last plea for sanity. "If my uncle should find us..."

Anthony reluctantly loosened his hold on her nipple, giving it a light kiss as he withdrew. "Your uncle and the entire rest of the household think you have gone off on one of those seaside walks you're so dedicated to. And they think I have returned to my bed—indisposed. Which is true, by the way." He kissed her neck and then her soft cheek. "I'm *indisposed* to do anything this morning other than make love to you."

Sarah laughed. When she was by herself, she could think of all kinds of reasons why she should stay several leagues away from the devastating Lord Rutledge.

But here in his arms, everything seemed right. Everything seemed possible.

"I would have thought you'd had your fill of me by now, my lord," she teased.

He was, in fact, pleasantly sated after their night together. The first desperate coupling had been followed by a much more leisurely and exquisite experience, which had sent them both into benevolent slumber. He captured her legs with one of his and let the hardened heat of his body provide her answer. "I'm beginning to think, Sarah, that it's going to take a very long time before I get my fill of you."

"But you're going back to London."

"Perhaps I'll just have to take you with me."

His tone was serious, but the implication of the words was more than Sarah wanted to deal with at the moment. She answered lightly. "My uncle might have something to say about that."

Anthony boosted his body over hers, crushing her breasts against the light hair of his chest. His tone remained serious. "I don't know what will become of us, Sarah. I only know that I can't imagine getting on my horse and riding out of your life."

Sarah's throat closed. How could this have happened to her? She had never paid much attention to the ballads they sang extolling the wonders of true love. It was not something she had ever expected to experience. Certainly not within the space of a few short days and certainly not with a close friend of the man she most hated in the world.

She offered her lips, and he took them gently. His body moved against hers, seducing. He threw off the covers and knelt above her to begin a lingering tour along her breasts and stomach, then lower as she gasped and clenched the bed sheets for support.

When a slow flush suffused her white skin he swiftly entered her, holding himself tense until he felt the tremors inside her that meant he could abandon his control and lose himself in delirium.

Afterward, they lay together, the light sheen of moisture on their bodies cooling rapidly. Anthony reached down for the covers and wrapped them once again in their own little world of warmth. It was something very close to perfection, but they couldn't stay there forever, and both of them knew it.

"You never answered my question last night," Anthony said finally.

"What question?"

"About what you'd been doing out at that hour."

Sarah was silent for a moment. "As I recall, I asked you to give me a reason why I should tell you."

For the life of him, he could not read her. She was as passionate as any woman he had ever known when he made love to her. Yet at times she would become as chilly as a North Sea gale. How Charles would laugh. London's most experienced rake had finally fallen in love, and the object of his affections was as inconstant as a French dance hall girl.

"I would have thought that what we shared last night would be reason enough," he said gravely.

Sarah closed her eyes to shut out his accusing expression. He was right. What they had shared was enough reason for there never to be any more secrets between them. But she had to keep her secrets for just a short while more. Then, she fervently hoped, they could be together with no more evasions, no shadows.

"You have the right to ask me questions, Anthony. But at the moment... Well, for one thing, that hunger you were talking about earlier, I think it's in earnest this time. How about if we see if we can still get some breakfast from the kitchen?"

Anthony felt a constriction in his chest. She still was hiding something, and he suspected that it had to do with Partridge. He had deliberately put the man out of his thoughts last night, but now he realized that he could not continue on with Sarah until the matter was cleared up. If Partridge turned out to be the bandit they sought and Sarah had been somehow involved...

"Sarah, I'm sorry, but I need to have you tell me one thing."

She closed her eyes. She didn't want to lie to him anymore. "All right," she said slowly, turning her head to meet his penetrating gaze. "What do you want to know?"

"Lord Rutledge!" The knocking on the door was discreet but insistent.

"Damnation," Anthony muttered. He slid out of the bed and reached for a night robe. "Get under the covers. I'll get rid of them."

It was Thomas Fairfax, and Anthony felt an unaccustomed wave of embarrassment at the realization that the kindly old man's niece was hidden away in the bed behind him. It occurred to him briefly that in London such a thing wouldn't have given him a second thought. "What is it, Sir Thomas?" he asked.

"Captain Kempthorne is awaiting you downstairs. I wouldn't have awakened you, but he said you were expecting him and that it was urgent he speak with you immediately."

Anthony nodded and thanked his host for the message, then hastily shut the door. He'd forgotten all about Oliver. And about everything else for most of the night. But it was time to get back to reality. He turned to the bed as a red-faced Sarah surfaced cautiously from beneath the feather tick. "I have to go," he said, pulling on his clothes. "But we'll resume this discussion later."

Sarah nodded. The moment of truth had been delayed, at least for a few hours. Perhaps it would give her time to think about just exactly what she could tell Anthony without being entirely false to him. "Yes...later."

He leaned over the bed to plant a firm kiss on her lips, then he was out the door. Sarah sank back into the pillows with a sigh. She wished she could stay there all day until Anthony came back in the evening to make more delirious love to her. But she had to get food down to the cave, and she had to find Jack and make plans. By tonight she would be miles from this bed, and instead of a bold cavalier, her companion would be a blade of the sharpest steel.

Oliver was examining the large oil portraits of previous generations of Fairfaxes that dominated one wall of the great room. He turned as Anthony entered, excitement tingeing his normally passive expression. "My friend the slugabed," he called, walking to meet Anthony in the middle of the room. "I couldn't believe it when they told me you were still sleeping." He asked no questions but gave Anthony an inquisitive look.

"I drank too much ale last night," Anthony replied shortly.

Oliver shook his head. "Try another one. I've seen you drink an entire regiment under the table and be up hawking before dawn."

Anthony walked over to the fireplace and dropped heavily into one of the large leather chairs. "It's none of your business, Oliver. The honor of a lady is involved."

"It usually is with you, Anthony." He sat in the chair across from Anthony's. "It's just that I thought we were supposed to be on a mission here."

"We are. One thing has nothing to do with the other."

Oliver's eyes narrowed. "You said 'lady.' Is it Fairfax's niece?"

Anthony nodded.

"I'm sorry, Anthony, but if she's involved with this Partridge fellow, then one thing definitely does have to do with the other."

Anthony straightened in his chair. "What have you found out?"

"Our informant in Cottleswoode says that someone held a meeting with the smugglers."

"Partridge?"

"Well, someone who fits the description you gave me—tall, blond, good-looking chap. It seems he made arrangements with their leader to take the parson out of England."

"So we've got him."

"We should be able to catch him in the act. The smugglers want fifty guineas for the job, and he told them he'd be back out on the road to get it for them."

"Excellent!"

"Aye." Oliver smiled like a cat at a fishbowl.

"When do you think he will strike?" It felt good to be taking some action. Anthony didn't like the soft spot that had developed in his gut in the past few days. If they could catch Partridge and prove that he was the highwayman, his duties for the king would be finished. Then he could concentrate on what he was going to do about Sarah. It might be rough for her to see her friend arrested, but Anthony retained enough confidence in his abilities to think that he could soon make Sarah forget she had ever even met the man.

"I'd wager it will be soon," Oliver said. "They can't keep the priest hidden away forever. You said you saw

Partridge near here the other day. Maybe there's someone here who could give us word about his movements.''

Anthony thought for a moment. His attempts to discuss Partridge with Sarah had proven spectacularly unsuccessful. But Oliver was right. If Partridge came and went freely at Leasworth, others must know about his activities. The eager-to-please face of Millie popped into his mind. It seemed likely that she would be one to keep her eye on a handsome young visitor. "I have an idea of someone I could ask," he said.

Oliver rubbed his hands together. "Good. In the meantime, we'll start to patrol the Old North Road each night."

"There's a lot of lonely road to cover."

"I know. The surest way would be to find Partridge and follow him. Or at least find out when he is planning to make his move."

"I'll see what I can learn. You keep in touch with the informant in Cottleswoode. The bandit will likely be back in touch with the contrabandists to let them know when to expect the money."

"That's a good point. We'll keep it covered." He stood up to leave. "And now you can continue whatever activity I interrupted with my arrival."

Anthony looked up at his friend. "You don't approve."

Oliver shrugged. "It's none of my affair. But just remember that you saw the girl with the man we are now virtually certain is the highwayman. Getting involved with her doesn't make a lot of sense, if you ask me."

Anthony stood. "That's your problem, Oliver. You don't understand that 'sense' is not a word easily applied to matters of the heart."

Oliver shook his head sadly. "You're wrong, my friend. I know that lesson only too well."

Anthony was sure that Sarah would have long since left his bedchamber, but after his discussion with Oliver he found himself mounting the wide stone steps, hoping to find her there. His bed was empty and tended, the damask drapes tied back into place. The room looked empty without her.

He made his way down to the dining hall, casually looking for her in the rooms he passed, but she was nowhere around. These regular disappearances of hers were annoying. Equally annoying was the knowledge that he had never before felt the need to keep such close account of anyone.

The breakfast platters had all been cleared, but Anthony had a hollow ache in the center of his stomach that had to be filled. He walked through the servants' dining hall and into the pantry. Millie was there, standing on a small step stool putting away dishes.

"Good morrow, sir," she beamed.

She looked less inviting to him than she had before his long night with Sarah, but he remembered that he had considered her a possible source of information.

" 'Tis a good morrow, Millie, m'dear, when I can start it out with your sweet smile."

The dimples deepened in her cheeks and she cocked her head coquettishly. "Why, thank ye, sir. You've a smile yourself that can brighten a maid's morning."

"Do you think I could get a bite of something to eat, though it be well past the hour?"

Millie jumped down from her stool, nodding vigorously. "Of course you may, Lord Rutledge. Anything you wish for."

"A piece of mutton or whatever's easy and at hand. And perhaps you'll sit by me a moment while I eat it." He settled himself against a cupboard.

Millie's blond curls bobbed up and down as she bustled around the pantry readying a plate. "You're feeling better then, sir?" she asked.

"I beg your pardon?"

"Well, yestere'en . . . you said you weren't hungry. And then this morning they said you'd taken to your bed."

"Oh . . . aye, I'm feeling better. 'Twas a temporary indisposition."

Millie's breast pressed into his arm as she handed him a plate heaped with a variety of cold meats and a vegetable pasty. She looked up at him through her long blond lashes. "I'm right pleased that you're feeling better. It's hard to think of a fine gentleman like yourself doing poorly."

Anthony forced himself to return her suggestive smile. "It's hard to stay indisposed when I'm receiving such good care," he said, employing the slick tone he had reserved for the quickest and emptiest of his court conquests.

"I'd be willing to take *very* good care of you, sir. Just say the word."

Millie kept her breasts positioned so close to his plate that he was almost reluctant to reach for a piece of food, hungry as he was. He moved imperceptibly away from her. "I'll remember that, Millie. It's not often I get an offer from such a pretty lady."

Millie blushed. "Sink me, sir. I'm sure a gent like you has lots of prettier girls down in London."

Anthony hastily took a bite of pasty before Millie could crowd in on him again. "A few as pretty, maybe," he said with his mouth full, "but not prettier. The clime here in Yorkshire must promote beauty. Your mistress is another example."

A frown furrowed a little line between Millie's pale eyebrows, and Anthony hastened to add, "She's almost as lovely as yourself."

With the girl's smile restored, he quickly gulped down another few bites of food, then asked casually, "So I suppose that between you and Mistress Fairfax, you have all the swains in the vicinity beating a path to Leasworth."

Millie looked down modestly. "I see my share, sir, I'll have to tell you. But Mistress Sarah, she's not one for the lads."

"No? But she has a regular suitor... Master Partridge. I saw them together the other day."

Millie looked up slyly. "I could tell you a thing or two about Master Partridge. Yes, I surely could."

Anthony kept his expression even. "I'd be interested to hear them."

Millie looked around cautiously. Behind her in the kitchen Bess and the other kitchen servants were preparing candle molds and beginning to boil the fat to fill them. "Perhaps you'd care to meet me in the summerhouse later on," she said softly, slowly licking her full lips as she looked at him.

Anthony felt as if the greasy piece of cold mutton he'd just swallowed had stuck in his throat, but he managed to answer pleasantly, "Fine. At what hour?"

"Sunset. It's the hour for romance, don't you know?" She giggled.

Anthony put his plate down on the counter. "Perhaps I'm not quite as recovered as I thought. I can't eat another bite. But I'll see you later...in the garden at sundown."

"I'll be looking forward to it, sir," Millie said with a little curtsy and another annoying giggle. Then she turned and bounced off into the kitchen.

The fickle weather of the coast had turned again. Sarah shivered and the wind snapped at her cloak as she climbed down to the cave. She tried to hurry, feeling guilty that her morning revels with Anthony had delayed the parson's breakfast. She had lain by herself in Anthony's big bed for several minutes after he had been called away, trying to come to terms with the upheaval of her life that had taken place in the past few short days.

She felt as if she were being twisted around and around like a maypole until she no longer knew in which direction she should be headed. First there was her remorse over the problems she had caused the parson. Then there was this incredible new emotion she was experiencing with Anthony. And complicating it all were her worry over Jack, her guilt about deceiving Anthony, her concern about getting the money to send the parson out of the country...

She had finally forced herself to leave the comfortable bed and get up to face it all. One thing at a time, Bess always said. And the first thing was to get food down to the parson and Jack.

They were waiting for her huddled around the fire. It was a good deal colder than it had been since they had brought the parson down here. If the weather was turning, it was more important than ever that they get the parson out of this place.

"You're late in coming, Sarah," Jack noted. He studied her for a moment. "Did you sleep past the hour?"

It was a measure of how thoroughly Anthony had entered her life that this time Sarah did not even blush under her brother's scrutiny. "No. I just had occupations up at the house."

Jack looked at her speculatively but didn't make any further comment.

"How are you feeling today, Father?" Sarah asked, turning to the parson.

"Better. I'm able to move about again with very little pain."

His actual movements were less promising than his words, Sarah noted as he reached with difficulty to take the food she was offering. "I'm glad to hear it, but I still think it's urgent that we get you out of here as soon as possible."

Jack tore into a slab of bacon with relish. "Will it be tonight?" he asked her.

She shook her head. "Not if this storm kicks up the way it's threatening."

Jack glanced sideways at the parson and spoke in a low voice. "It's got to be soon, Sarah."

"I know. Tomorrow is the full moon. We'll hope this squall will blow on past today and bring in the clear weather by tomorrow night."

Jack nodded. "Do you think you could work on that, Parson, with your special contacts?" His eyes went up toward the ceiling.

Parson Hollander smiled gently. "Let me talk with the contrabandists again. I'll try to persuade them to take me without payment."

Sarah reached out to pat his hand. "You just worry about getting better, Father. And say us a little prayer for a clear night. Leave the rest up to me and Jack."

She turned to leave and Jack walked with her to the cave entrance. "Tomorrow it is, then?" he asked.

"Tomorrow it is," she answered grimly.

* * *

Sarah was as anxious as Jack to get the parson out of the country, but she felt as if the gathering clouds had given her a reprieve for a day. By the time she got back to the big house, it was midday, but the sky had turned almost as dark as night. There would be no venturing out for the next several hours, which meant she would just have to stay at home and entertain their guest, a prospect she found arousing in a fashion she was still beginning to learn.

She made it back to the house just as the storm hit with great icy sheets of water blowing in from the sea.

Her uncle met her coming out of his library. "Ah, there you are, Sarah. We've been worried about you, or I should say, our visitor was worried. He's been prowling the house like a caged animal looking for you."

He crossed the hall to help her off with her wet cloak. "I felt the need for a walk this morning," Sarah said.

The tale sounded weak to her own ears, but her uncle did not seem to think anything amiss and continued briskly, "I told Lord Rutledge that you've been running up and down those cliffs like a mountain goat since you were a child. You and Jack, but of course I didn't mention Jack. Though, my dear, I think it's about time we set Lord Rutledge straight on that score. Surely you no longer think he could be of any danger to your brother?"

Sarah pulled her chamois gloves from her frigid fingers and let her uncle take them along with her cloak. She had been thinking along the same lines as her uncle this morning, but she wasn't sure exactly how to broach the subject to Anthony. She didn't want him to get the idea that she told lies at every turn, especially since she had several matters that she was still forced to conceal from him.

"I'll tell him about Jack soon, Uncle. But I'd rather do it myself, if you don't mind."

"I don't mind at all. It's just that I feel bad deceiving the man like that. He seems a decent chap. And I think he has his eye on you, Sarah, which could prove to be a very favorable match. Yes, indeed."

Sarah had been furious with herself for letting the exact same thought enter her head, so she spoke more sharply than she intended. "Don't be silly, Uncle. What a preposterous idea. Lord Rutledge is merely being courteous during his stay here. Soon he'll be heading back to London and forget all about us poor country folk."

"I don't know..." Her uncle shook his head. "His concern this morning was a sight more than courtesy."

"He's not even of our kind, Uncle Thomas. He's not a Puritan."

"Well now." Thomas scratched his gray goatee reflectively. "I never thought I'd say it, but somehow those kinds of distinctions just don't seem to make the difference they once did in this country. It's one thing we have to thank the king for—the new tolerance. He just may be right that a person's religion is not the factor that determines his character."

Sarah was dumbfounded. After all the fighting and sacrifice of the Fairfax family for the Puritan cause... "But, Uncle," she began.

"No, you listen to what I'm saying, Sarah. That man is taken with you, and if you feel the same way, I don't see any reason why it couldn't work out. First, though, I think you'd do well to clear up this matter and tell Lord Rutledge the truth."

"Tell me the truth about what?" A voice came from the stairway, startling them both.

Thomas looked at his niece, whose eyes pleaded with him to let her handle the situation. "Er...about my niece here," he said in a loud voice, "and her confounded habit of venturing out in the most inclement weather. She's near frozen to death and wet in the bargain."

Sarah gave him a look of thanks. "I'm just an outdoors person," she said quietly.

Anthony finished descending the stairs and crossed the hall to take one of Sarah's hands and bring it to his mouth. "You do splendidly indoors, as well, if I recall," he murmured so that her uncle could not hear.

Sarah pulled her hand away, but the chiding look she intended to give him somehow turned itself into a smile. Anthony straightened, his eyes twinkling. "Your uncle's right. Your hand is like ice. We must get you some warm ale."

"You'll have to excuse me," Thomas said. "I've accounts to do with my overseer and have asked to have our meal sent into us." He looked from Anthony to

Sarah, smiling contentedly. "I trust you two young people can find some pleasant occupation for a rainy afternoon?"

Anthony and Sarah shared a smile. "We'll be fine, Uncle," Sarah said.

"And you get yourself something warm to stave off the sickness," he admonished.

"Yes, Uncle."

"I'll be sure she gets taken care of, Sir Thomas," Anthony said, keeping his face straight.

Thomas Fairfax gave a satisfied nod and turned to walk back to his library.

They had hidden themselves away in the solar, barricading the door against any unwanted intrusions by the servants. Anthony had prepared a tray with enough food for the entire house staff, and they'd managed to consume a goodly portion of it. Now they lay in a pleasant state of satiation on a heap of pillows in front of the fireplace. Outside the storm threatened to rattle the sturdy brick house off its very foundation, but they were cozily ensconced underneath a quilt Sarah had brought from her bedchamber.

Neither one had brought up their unfinished conversation from this morning. They had talked instead about London, the revival of the theaters, philosophy, religion, farming, which oddly enough seemed to be a favorite topic for Anthony.

"So they've actually written *books* about planting things?" Sarah asked in amazement.

"Volumes," Anthony answered with enthusiasm. "I've never had the chance to try the theories out myself, of course, but I'd like to give it a try someday."

"It's hard to imagine you settling down as a gentleman farmer," Sarah teased, rubbing her finger along the rough cleft of his chin.

Anthony grabbed the finger and bit it gently. "Why not?" he asked lightly, then became more serious as he added, "Perhaps it's exactly because I've been such a wanderer for much of my life that a place of my own seems so appealing."

"The king has rewarded most of his closest supporters with lands. Why hasn't he done so for you?"

"Oh, the king has been most generous with me. I've a bigger fortune than my father ever had before the war. So I suppose one of these days I shall purchase a place for myself."

"You'll want to be near London, I suppose?" Sarah probed.

"I don't know." He looked down at her and snuggled her more closely in his arms. "I haven't thought about it that much yet. No doubt I'll have to go to war first."

"To war!" Sarah struggled in vain to sit up, but Anthony tucked her back down on his shoulder.

"To fight the Dutch. The conflict is heating up again."

Sarah frowned. "You men and your wars. Will you never be done with them?"

Moonrise

Anthony turned to press his body over hers. "Well, I don't have to go fight it this afternoon, dearling."

Sarah shifted her legs to let them fit more closely with his. "I'm glad to hear that," she murmured.

"Will your uncle come looking for you if we stay in here too long?"

She shook her head. "He loses himself in his books for days. Now, if someone sent word down to the kitchens to Bess, she'd be up here in a minute, meat cleaver in hand."

"Meat cleaver?" Anthony asked, pulling up from her to look down at the more sensitive parts of his anatomy.

Sarah gave a firm nod.

His eyes went back up the length of her body to stop on her slightly swollen lips. "It's worth the risk," he said with a sigh, and bent to kiss her.

Chapter Ten

When Anthony awoke, the storm was still lashing against the glass windows of the solar. It appeared that night had fallen, though the sky had been so dark all day it was hard to tell the hour. Certainly it was past sundown, and he had missed his rendezvous with Millie. He hoped the provocative little maid would have known enough not to venture out in the garden in such weather. He didn't want her angry with him. Though he was not planning to take advantage of her offer of her charming body, he did want to find out the details she could provide about Henry Partridge. Briefly he considered getting up to go look for her, but as Sarah moved against him sleepily, he changed his mind. Millie and her information could wait until tomorrow.

Oliver pushed his trencher away with a sigh of contentment. The villagers may not have proven very co-operative in catching the highwayman, but he couldn't complain about the hospitality. For the past two nights he'd been staying at the home of Mayor Spragg.

Though a bachelor, the mayor had an excellent cook, who had just provided Oliver with a breakfast the likes of which he hadn't seen even at court.

It was a good start for the day. Perhaps an omen. It couldn't be too much longer before they learned something more about the bandit. His men had talked to nearly every family in the shire.

There was a weak tapping on the doorframe and Oliver turned around to see Mayor Spragg, bobbing his head nervously.

"Come on in, man. It's *your* house," Oliver bellowed. The timid little man annoyed him.

"It's...uh... Are you finished with your breakfast, Captain?"

"Aye. What's the problem?"

"No problem. A couple of your men are here and want to see you."

"Bring them in," he yelled.

The mayor backed out of the room, bumping against the doorframe as he went. Oliver shook his head. In a moment three of his men entered. They were from the group he had sent to keep watch around Leasworth.

"Has something happened?" he asked, getting to his feet at once.

One of the guards gave a salute. "We've taken two more smugglers, sir. Practically in the garden of the Fairfax manor, they were."

"What were they doing there?"

The man shrugged. "I don't know. Just watching, it seemed."

"Have they said anything?" Oliver felt a surge of excitement. He had known it was going to be a good day.

All three guards shook their heads. "We...uh...tried to persuade them, but so far they won't say a word."

Oliver frowned and reached across the table for his hat. "Perhaps I'll be able to change their minds," he said grimly.

It was midmorning before Anthony could find the kitchen maid. She was scrubbing a fearful pile of pots in the scullery and looking none too pleased about the task. He moved up behind her and put his arm around her waist.

She gave a little jump. "I didn't see ye coming, sir."

"You're hard at work."

"A frump's work," she said with a sour expression.

"Not when you're doing it, Millie," Anthony said lightly, trying to restore her cooperative mood of the previous day. "I'm sorry about the storm. We missed our appointment."

Millie shrugged. "It was probably a bad idea—a gent like you with a girl like me."

Anthony shifted uncomfortably. He didn't want to mislead the girl, but he did need to know what information she might have. "Well now, I wouldn't say that, Millie."

She turned around and looked up at him. "You mean you really *are* sorry we didn't meet yesterday?"

"Of course." Anthony felt as if his smile was plastered on his face.

Millie gave a little giggle and rubbed her backside up against him. "Better late than never, I always say."

"We'll work something out," he said hastily. "But in the meantime, remember you were going to give me some information about that Master Partridge?"

"Millie!" The booming voice could belong to no other than the formidable Bess whom Sarah had described so vividly. A short, plump woman appeared in the doorway and Anthony caught himself glancing at her hands in search of a meat cleaver.

Millie stepped adroitly out of the circle of Anthony's arm and turned with a little curtsy. "I was just finishing the washing up, mum," she said demurely.

"I could see just exactly what you were doing, missy, and I think you'd better hie yourself back into the kitchen."

Millie turned around so that Bess couldn't see her face and gave Anthony a wink, then she scooted around the stocky cook and left the room.

"Don't hold it against the girl," Anthony said, irritated at yet another delay.

"It's not the girl I'm likely to hold it against," Bess said with a huff. "Millie can be shameless at times, but I've never known her to do anything without encouragement. She doesn't have to. The offers are plenty as it is."

Anthony was not used to accounting for his actions to a household servant, but something in the way Bess stood watching him with her big bosom heaving with indignation made him feel as though he had just been caught stealing tarts from the cooling shelf.

"No matter what it may have looked like, ma'am, I'm not interested in your maid," he said soberly.

Bess took a step toward him. "No?" she said, stabbing him with her intelligent brown eyes. "Then see that you keep your hands off her."

Jack had insisted on walking back with Sarah to the house. "No one will see me," he'd assured her. "I'll be careful."

She hadn't minded the company. She was in a wonderful mood, in spite of the task that awaited her that evening. She and Jack both avoided that particular subject as they made their way up the cliff.

"Remember the time you and the carpenter's son were pretending to be smugglers?" she asked him fondly.

"And made a boat out of his father's wood scraps that took us about two yards offshore before it crashed to pieces on the rocks? Aye, I remember," Jack said ruefully.

"That's when I knew that you weren't cut out for a seagoing career," Sarah said with a laugh.

Jack didn't reply. The truth was he had been thinking more and more in recent days about exactly that— a seagoing career where a lad without a fortune and with a disgraced name could earn a place for himself in the world. But he hadn't as yet shared his plans with

Sarah. He knew she would be opposed to any course that would take him so far away from her mothering.

"You look tired, Sarah. Are you feeling all right?"

She nodded happily. "I'm feeling...*wonderful*, Jack."

He looked over at her, surprised by the vehemence of her answer. "It's the king's surveyor, isn't it?"

She nodded and gave a little sigh. "I know you think me foolish to get involved with someone who's so different from us, but—"

Jack held up a hand to interrupt her. "Sarah, I am only myself now learning that in matters of the heart, we don't have much say in our direction."

Sarah reached out to squeeze her brother's hand. "Thank you for understanding."

Jack returned the squeeze. "We've always understood each other, big sister. Nothing's ever going to change that."

They were nearing the hawthorne hedges that marked the boundaries of the Leasworth gardens. "You should go back, Jack," Sarah said. "I don't want anyone to see you."

"I just want to sneak around back and say hello to Bess. Then I'll be on my way. Don't worry. I know how to stay out of sight."

They walked quietly around the outside edge of the bushes, Sarah peering anxiously through every opening to be sure no one was out in the garden. As they reached the back side of the property, she grabbed

Jack's sleeve. "There's someone there," she whispered. "In the summerhouse."

They stopped and Jack craned his neck to see over her head and get a look at who it was. Though the day was clear after yesterday's storm, it was still cold enough to see their breath, which made it seem a bit too cold to be entertaining in the summerhouse. "Who is it?" he asked.

Sarah had turned white and was clutching at the neck of her cloak.

"Sarah?" Jack asked in alarm. "What is it?"

She nodded her head toward the summerhouse, where it was now clear that two figures were entwined in what looked like a very intimate situation. "It's Anthony," she said, her voice barely audible. "He's with the kitchen maid."

Anthony made an effort to smile engagingly at Millie as she preened in front of him. "Do you like my new dress, Lord Rutledge?" she was saying. "Mr. Spragg brought it all the way from York."

"The mayor?"

Millie giggled. "He's been sweet on me for nigh on two years now, but he's too old and rat-faced for my taste." She sidled up to Anthony. "I like a well-made gentleman like yourself. I'd wager you could get much grander clothes than this in London."

"London's a fine place for fashion these days," Anthony agreed impatiently. "Now, Millie m'dear. You were going to tell me some things about Henry Partridge. Remember?''

Millie batted her long blond lashes and looked coyly up into his face. ''And what would you do for a poor country girl who gave you valuable information that she's not supposed to tell?''

''Who said that you were not supposed to tell?''

She gave another of her annoying giggles. ''You have to answer my question first.'' She draped her arms around Anthony's neck, then went up on tiptoe to kiss his cheek, saying in his ear, ''Are you going to be nice to me, Lord Rutledge, if I'm nice to you?''

She smelled of onions and unwashed linens, in spite of her new dress. Anthony found himself wanting to pull her arms from around him and escape back to the house. The hoyden probably didn't know anything about Henry Partridge anyway.

He reached for her hands. ''Millie, I'm afraid—'' he began, then stopped as they both heard the sound of a horse galloping right across the Leasworth garden toward them. Anthony looked out through the wooden slats of the summerhouse. ''It's Captain Kempthorne,'' he said, for once relieved to be interrupted by his friend.

He slid Millie's arms from around his neck and descended the two wooden stairs that ran all around the structure. ''Kempthorne!'' he called. ''Over here.''

Oliver brought his horse right up to where Anthony was standing and dismounted practically before the animal had stopped. ''They told me you were out here.''

He glanced over at Millie and turned back to Anthony with one eyebrow raised. "I need to talk with you."

Anthony took Millie's hand to help her down the steps. "Our...er...meeting will have to wait until later, I'm afraid, Millie."

Millie's lips pursed into a pout of disappointment. "I don't mind if the other gentleman stays," she said with a hopeful tone.

Oliver gave Anthony a look of disbelief.

"Be a good girl, Millie, and go on back to the house." He gave her a gentle push on the bottom. "I'll see you later tonight."

Millie looked up at him with a bold smile. "I'll be looking forward to it, sir," she said, and scampered off to the house.

"I can't keep track," Oliver said dryly. "Wasn't it the Fairfax girl who had you in a lather the last time I saw you?"

"She still does," Anthony said grimly. "This was purely work."

"Oh, pardon me for not being able to tell the difference."

"The girl was babbling on about knowing secrets about Partridge and I had to see if she was telling the truth."

"Did you find out anything?"

"No. As usual, you came just at the wrong moment."

"Well, it may not matter anymore."

"Why not?" Anthony could tell that Oliver, behind his typically impassive expression, was excited.

"We caught two smugglers last night, practically right here under your nose."

"Here?"

Oliver nodded. "We're having...uh...trouble making them talk, but the point is that they're here. It must be to pick up the parson."

"And if they have come for the parson, the highwayman has to somehow get them the payment for his passage," Anthony finished.

They both smiled. "I reckon it will be tonight," Oliver said.

"Are you ready for him?"

"Aye. I've brought some more men down from Hull. We'll have the Old North Road so lined with guards a field mouse would have trouble getting across it."

"You want me there?"

"If you want to be in on it when we bag the fox."

"Aye," said Anthony grimly, picturing again Sarah in Henry Partridge's arms. "I want to be in on it."

For more years than anyone could remember, the Old North Road had sliced across the lonely Yorkshire moors, a vital artery of communication from the bustling factories of the south to the more tranquil farming territories of the north. Merchants seeking trade, clerics carrying their messages of salvation, politicians making a rare tour of their home boroughs—on any given day the traffic along the highway was as varied as any London street. But it was the fancy carriages of the newly restored aristocracy that had drawn the masked highwayman. Polished black equipages with the family coat of arms on the side or great lumbering coaches complete with uniformed grooms. Sarah had been meticulous about robbing only those she knew could afford the losses, the nobles who were sharing in the profligate luxury of Charles II's glittering court.

There had been times when she had returned empty-handed rather than stop a cart of some poor tradesman's worsteds on its way to York. But it appeared that tonight she was in luck. From her vantage point on Topper's Bluff she could see a smart two-horse carriage making its way slowly along the deserted road. A lone driver was the only escort. Yesterday's storm had blown away, leaving in its wake a crystal-clear, mild night, with a brilliant moon that had just made its appearance on the far horizon.

Sarah turned to Jack with a bleak smile, the first she'd had since seeing Anthony with Millie this afternoon. "Parson Hollander's prayers have been answered one final time, little brother. The weather's perfect, and this pigeon is ripe for the plucking."

Jack looked around him nervously. He had an uneasy feeling about this final job and was wishing fervently that he had forced Sarah to stay behind. She'd been moody and quiet since the scene at the summerhouse, and he didn't know what to say to comfort her. They had certainly both heard the tales of the shameless behavior favored at court these days. They had just never thought it would affect them all the way up in Yorkshire. He made one last effort to dissuade her.

"Let *me* go, Sarah. It's my last chance, you know, to get some of the excitement for myself."

Sarah gave her brother a knowing look. "You're still my subordinate, Jack Fairfax, and you'll not stop taking orders just because the campaign is about to end."

Jack could see the beginnings of the familiar gleam in her eyes that said she was ready for the chase. It had always amazed him that his Puritan sister, who to all the world presented the picture of charity and humility, could suddenly turn into a high-stakes gambler thriving on danger.

She was dressed all in dark gray—boots, hose and shirt—and her light hair was hidden beneath a wide-brimmed gray felt hat. A kerchief covered the whiteness of her slender neck and another was tied lightly around her chin, ready to be pulled into place to hide her face up to her steady gray eyes.

"I'm not feeling good about this one, Sarah," Jack persisted. "Let's go in together."

Sarah reached to soothe Brigand as he pranced nervously, eager to be let loose. "I've kept you out of this up to now, Jack. It doesn't make sense to turn you into a criminal on our last run."

Jack threw up his hands in exasperation. He hadn't won an argument with his sister since he was a baby. There was no reason why tonight should be any different. "I could just go on down with you. You wouldn't be able to stop me," he said.

Now her expression became grim. "Brigand and I work best alone, Jack. If you interfere, you could put us all in danger."

The brother and sister glared at each other for a moment. "Promise me you'll not try it," Sarah demanded.

"Oh, all right. But tell me what I can do to help you."

"You can keep watch at the other side of the bluff to be sure no one else is coming while I relieve these good people of their unnecessary trinkets."

He reached out to put a hand on Sarah's arm. "You're the only sister I've got, you know," he said, his voice thick. "I'll thank you to take care of yourself."

"Don't worry, Jack. In another hour we'll be on our way back to our beds."

"Now there's a pleasant thought. I told Norah to wait up for me," he teased. He waited for the expected admonishment, but Sarah merely reddened and looked away from him.

He wondered what his sister would say if she knew of the conversation he had had with Norah earlier that day. He hadn't really asked Norah to wait up for him tonight, but he had asked for a different kind of commitment—to wait for him while he went off to battle. While talking all those long hours with the parson in the cave, he had made the definite decision to join the navy. He'd depended on Sarah for too long now, and it was time he did something to fend for himself. Norah had made no promises. She had looked at him with those big, sad eyes of hers and told him that he would forget about her the minute he stepped foot on a ship. But he didn't think so. Those long autumn nights in the meadow would not easily fade from his memory.

"Jack, are you listening to me?" Sarah's tone revealed something of her agitation.

"Yes. I'll head down the other side of the bluff and block the road. I'll pretend to be injured or something if anyone comes along."

"Don't take any risks. Just delay them and make a lot of noise to warn me."

"I'll be fine. You're the one who needs to be careful."

Their horses danced together and they embraced without words. Then Sarah wheeled Brigand around and headed down the steep side of the cliff toward the road.

She hadn't wanted to admit to Jack that she was uneasy about this final job, too. She was sure it was just superstition, knowing that it was her last time. Still, a little chill of warning went down her back as she headed toward the road. The world that had looked so promising to her as she lay with Anthony this morning had turned dark. It was beginning to look as if she had been seduced and taken for a fool by a true expert. She was honest enough to admit that she had participated fully in the experience, had enjoyed it, too. But she had also invested far too much of her soul. She wondered if Anthony would regale the court with tales of his Yorkshire conquests when he returned to London.

At least it looked as if tonight would be an easy hit. In the bright moonlight she could see that there was only one passenger, an elderly gentleman who lolled against the side of the carriage, apparently asleep. She couldn't ask for better circumstances.

Her usual pattern was to study her quarry thoroughly, then wait for the moon to disappear beneath some clouds to give herself a little extra advantage. Tonight she didn't feel the need for the extra precaution. The target was too easy, and besides, even if the victims got a better than usual description of the masked bandit, it would no longer matter. After tonight, the Yorkshire highwayman would never be seen again. Positioning herself behind a copse of trees conveniently located just at a bend in the road, she waited.

She hardly had to tell Brigand when the right moment came. He charged out onto the road like one of hell's furies, causing the two carriage horses to rear up in terror. The driver had all he could do to handle them, giving Sarah plenty of time to move up close and position herself next to him, her saber ready in her left hand, and in her right, a flintlock pistol that was trained on his chest. "Stand and deliver!" she rumbled, the voice coming from low in her chest.

The driver put the reins of the still-prancing horses in his left hand and raised his right toward the sky. "Don't shoot," he pleaded in a quavery voice.

Sarah felt a wave of elation. The driver sounded as old as his passenger. There would be no foolish heroics from this mark. She was practically assured of an easy victory.

A gentleman with a huge white wig poked his round face out the side of the carriage. "What's going on?" He sounded sleepy and irritated.

Keeping one eye on the driver, Sarah moved Brigand a couple of paces backward. "Your money and your jewels," she barked.

"Good gracious me," the man babbled. "Don't shoot, knave. I'm just a poor country gentleman."

The man's wig alone was worth fifty guineas, and Sarah noted the shiny new spring carriage, the latest in traveling comfort. He might be a country gentleman, but he was not poor. "Hand out what you have," she said with a flourish of her saber, "or I'll skewer you for my breakfast."

The head disappeared inside and in a moment a hand came out with a leather pouch. "Throw it on the ground," she ordered. It hit the dirt with a soft thud. "And the pin in your cravat."

The jewel fell next to the bag of money, glinting in the moonlight. Sarah gave a satisfied nod and turned to the driver. "Now drive as if the devil himself were holding on to your tail," she told him. "And perhaps you and your master will live to see another day."

The driver didn't wait to ponder the matter. He lashed the horses with the reins and urged them on with a harsh sound in the back of his throat.

Sarah was left in a cloud of dust, but she hardly noticed. A great feeling of peace had come over her. The job was done. The career of the masked rider was over. Brigand stood stock-still as she jumped to the ground to retrieve the evening's spoils. The purse clinked and felt heavy. She did not even bother to look inside. It didn't matter anymore. The stickpin itself would be enough to get Parson Hollander out of the country. Tucking the items inside her shirt, she pulled herself up on Brigand's back.

She had heard nothing from the south. Jack must not have encountered any other late travelers. What luck. Everything had gone perfectly tonight.

Anthony and Oliver looked at each other in disbelief. "This *is* Henry Partridge, isn't it?" Oliver asked. He pointed to the horse and rider his men had surrounded farther down the road and brought up the cliff to them. The captive's hands were bound behind his back and his lip was bloody.

Anthony nodded. There was no mistaking the lad's blond hair and chiseled features.

"Then who's that?" Oliver pointed over the bluff to the dark figure whom they had just watched rob the coach of Phineas Willoughby, sixth Earl of Dandridge.

"Partridge's accomplice, I guess," Anthony answered. "It doesn't matter. We've got them both now."

"Or we will have shortly." Oliver turned to his men. "You three guard the prisoner. The rest of you men split in two. Half will come with me over the cliff to head him off if he starts to run. The others will go with Lord Rutledge straight down after him."

Oliver flashed Anthony a smile. This was sport such as they had not had in a long time. "Do the plans meet with your approval, my lord?" he asked.

Anthony did not share his friend's zest for the hunt, but he nodded his consent.

Oliver stretched up in his stirrups, eager to be off. "All right, men, let's go get him."

Sarah held Brigand steady while she peered down the road after the departing coach. They hadn't appeared to be the type who would cause problems, but she preferred to be sure they were headed away from her before she turned her back. When she could no longer see even dust rising at the end of the long, straight stretch of road, she signaled to Brigand to turn and head south. She would meet up with Jack, and then they would ride swiftly back to Leasworth.

Now that the danger was past, the exhilaration of success turned once more into melancholy. What was waiting for her back at Leasworth? Anthony didn't know she had seen him. Would he try to resume his affair with her as if nothing had happened? Or had he now moved on to the riper charms of Millie? Brigand began to dance skittishly beneath her, and Sarah forced her thoughts back to the present situation. Riders were behind her on the road, a lot of them, coming hard. Angry with herself for having lost her concentration, she turned Brigand off the highway and headed toward the bluffs. Her heart beat out of rhythm, but she did not panic. She had never yet seen the horse that could out-run Brigand.

She let the stallion stretch out into a gallop, reck-lessly ignoring the uneven terrain and hillocks in their path. Brigand knew this countryside. She'd let him pick the course. Turning her head she could see the pursu-ers—at least ten of them. They left the road at the same point she did, but Brigand's headlong pace was pulling her ahead of them.

She put her hands alongside her horse's neck and bent low, giving him free rein. They had to be Kemp-thorne's men. They'd probably been patrolling the highway each night. Why hadn't she thought of that possibility? It was too late now, but, thanks to Brig-and, she shouldn't have any trouble getting away. She just hoped that they hadn't encountered Jack.

She reached the edge of a series of bluffs. Sarah straightened and pulled on Brigand's reins to urge him to take the southern route around them. The horse turned to the left, then took a great jump as a fallen log suddenly appeared in the path. To Sarah's horror, she could feel one of his hind legs catch when they cleared the obstacle. He stumbled, and Sarah's stomach took a sickening drop. Three, four more paces and it was ob-vious that something was terribly wrong. Brigand slowed in confusion, then stumbled again, listing to the right.

Behind her the sound of the riders' hooves had be-come thunderous. Sarah looked about her with alarm. Brigand was hurt, and she could not keep trying to make him run. She pulled back on the reins and almost in the same instant jumped to the ground. A limestone crag just above her head showed eerily white in the moonlight. Her limbs were shaky, but she ran straight for the cliff, determined to climb to safety. She clawed at the rocks, her riding boots slipping over the smooth stone. A small bush growing at a right angle out from the cliff made a perfect safety rope. She clutched it and pulled herself upward. The pressure in her ears merged with the noise from behind her. She took a gasping breath that was cut in half when two strong hands grabbed her shoulders and hauled her backward.

She fell hard, the jolt knocking her teeth together. Pain shot along her backbone. Suddenly someone was straddling her and a gloved hand pressed down hard on her throat, cutting off her air.

"Don't move!" her captor said.

And as in some kind of terrible nightmare, Sarah recognized the deep voice of Lord Anthony Rutledge.

Chapter Eleven

Anthony felt as if he'd been kicked in the stomach. Her hat had fallen off, releasing the wave of soft hair he had that very morning felt across his chest. The silk mask had slipped down far enough to show the pert nose and high cheeks he had covered with his kisses.

He couldn't move, and Sarah seemed frozen to the ground beneath him. In a daze, he heard someone say, "It's a woman."

"Anthony, are you all right?" Oliver ignored Sarah on the ground and turned to give his friend a concerned look.

"It's Sarah," Anthony said in a choked voice.

"I know. She rode like the devil. How was anyone to know it was a woman?"

Anthony looked down at her. Her gray eyes beseeched him. "You mean it was her all along?" he asked Oliver. "*She's* the highwayman?"

"It looks like she and Partridge were partners. There were two highwaymen, it appears. Or I should say one highwayman and one highwaywoman."

Anthony shook his head, dazed. "Where's Partridge?"

"They're bringing him."

He stepped back from Sarah, who was slowly sitting up. He felt a humming behind his ears as a tremendous anger started to build. She'd completely taken him for a fool. She and her blond lover. After he'd protected her from Oliver's questions, she'd made sweet love to him. This morning she had lain in his bed and murmured words of passion, all the while knowing that she would be riding the road tonight to commit a crime against the king's justice. Her words came back to him. "*I'm* the only one who rides Brigand." What a bloody fool he'd been.

Oliver jerked her to her feet, his huge hands biting into her upper arms. She tried to pull away. Anthony watched his big friend holding Sarah's slender body as if it were a chicken leg. She grimaced with pain, and Anthony was furious with himself for caring.

"I'm the bandit you're seeking," she said, sounding out of breath. "Master Partridge had nothing to do with any of the crimes."

Still lying, the deceitful bitch. His stomach turned. He thought he'd finally found a woman who was different, but he should have known better. His mother had taught him early on that there was nothing more cold and calculating than the heart of a woman. He should have followed Oliver's example and remembered the lesson.

There was movement among the men as the three guards arrived with the other prisoner. The most burly of them dismounted, then reached up and dragged Jack off his horse, throwing him facedown on the ground. He shoved him toward Sarah with his boot. "Get on over there," he growled. When the fallen man didn't move, the guard gave him a vicious kick in the side.

Sarah cried out. Tearing herself out of Oliver's grasp, she ran to kneel beside Jack and pulled him into her arms. His face was bloodied and his eyes half-shut. "My poor darling, what have they done to you?" she cried.

The words dropped on Anthony's hardening heart like lead weights. He wanted to get up on his horse and ride off to lick his wounds like a battle-scarred dog. But he had responsibilities to fulfill. "There will be no mistreating of the prisoners," he said gruffly.

The man who had kicked Jack looked for confirmation to Oliver, who shrugged and nodded. "Lord Rutledge is in charge of this investigation. You'll take your orders from him," he said.

Sarah looked up at Oliver in disbelief, then over to Anthony, who was staring down at her with eyes full of disgust. "*You* are in charge?" she asked.

Anthony walked over to stand directly above her. His words were as cold as frozen steel. "King Charles asked me to personally take charge of catching Yorkshire's infamous highwayman. It seems I've caught him two, instead. He'll be pleased."

"No." Sarah couldn't believe her ears. It wasn't possible that Anthony had been hunting her. Not this man who had wooed her so gently and introduced her to the delights of love. Not this tender lover to whom this very morning she had been about to pledge her heart.

"It's all right, Sarah." The words were slurred as Jack reached up a hand to give her a comforting pat.

Sarah rocked him in her arms as tears of betrayal and despair stung her eyes. There was no hope left for her, but she couldn't let them take Jack. "I'm the person you want." She addressed the words to Oliver. She couldn't bear to look at Anthony. "I'm the masked highwayman. This boy has had nothing to do with it."

Oliver's stern expression did not waver. "It appeared to us that he was posted as a lookout for you tonight. I guess it'll be for a judge to decide." He looked to Anthony for orders but, after seeing his friend's stricken face, gave the commands himself. "We'll separate the prisoners," he said. "You men start out tonight to London with Partridge. The rest of you will ride with me tomorrow to escort the girl."

"I tell you, he's done nothing," Sarah screamed, clutching Jack as two men roughly pulled him away from her.

"Let me go with them, Sarah," Jack said, still sounding groggy. "Uncle Thomas will get us help. Just take care of yourself."

"He's hurt," she said angrily to one of the men who were trying to pull Jack to his feet. "He should be seen by a doctor."

Anthony's face was implacable as he watched her plead for her lover. The guard hesitated and looked up for confirmation first to Oliver, then Anthony. Oliver waited for Anthony's response. "Go ahead," he said. "Take him."

Sarah slumped back to the ground. The two guards half dragged Jack over to his horse and started to assist him up into the saddle. A third man pulled Sarah to her feet, wrenching her arm and making her cry out. Jack was halfway on his horse, but he turned at the sound of her cry and sprang at the two men on the ground. "Don't hurt her!" he yelled, lashing out with his boots. It was a useless gesture. He was a powerful man, but his hands were tied behind him and he was no match for the six guards who engulfed him within seconds. He took a knee in his midsection and several blows to the head before finally crumpling to the ground.

Sarah put a hand to her mouth in horror and tears filled her eyes. "Please don't hurt him," she sobbed.

Anthony snapped an order. "Tie him on his horse and get him out of here."

He took a quick glance at Sarah. Moonlight glinted off the tears that were streaming down her cheeks. He turned away.

The guards boosted Jack back up on his horse. He slumped over the saddle but turned his head toward Sarah.

"Don't make trouble, Sarah," he said, words slurred. "I'm all right."

She turned to Anthony with a final entreaty. "Please, Anthony, don't let them take him. He's not in any shape to ride."

Anthony merely nodded to the guards, who put Jack's horse between them and started off. Sarah watched them go with deadened eyes. Then from behind she heard a familiar whinny. She turned to see Brigand coming painfully toward her, his right hindquarter dragging ominously. She scrambled up and threw her arms around his neck, her wet cheeks drying against his bristly warm hair.

From a distance, she heard Oliver speak. "The horse's leg is broken." She closed her eyes and tightened her hold.

"Aye. Lend me your pistol," Anthony agreed in a low voice.

Sarah looked up in horror as Oliver pulled her, more gently this time, away from the horse. Anthony was checking the load on the flintlock. "You can't kill him," she said. The words were barely audible.

Too dazed to struggle, she let Oliver lead her a few paces away. Then he turned her face into his big shoulder so that she was not able to see. There was another long whinny, followed by the deafening sound of a shot. Sarah collapsed against the captain amid an explosion of pain. It was as if the shot had gone directly into her heart.

Anthony waited in the sheriff's roomy parlor. He had sent word to Leasworth. He didn't look forward to his meeting with Thomas Fairfax, since he was virtually certain the old general knew nothing of his niece's perfidy. The whole situation would have to be handled with great diplomacy so as not to alienate an important Puritan ally to the king.

He rubbed his burning eyes. He and Oliver had not slept last night after arriving back in Wiggleston. Sarah had been taken to the sheriff's house under guard. He wondered if she'd been able to sleep. She hadn't said one word after he'd shot Brigand. Anthony had avoided looking at her, letting Oliver ride at her side.

Henry Partridge was already on his way to London. Today they would have to sort out just exactly who his family was and see if he had any moneyed support behind him. If he didn't, he probably would be a candidate for the gibbet at Newgate Prison, which was fine with Anthony, particularly in his current mood.

As for Sarah, it was hard to tell how it would all play out. The king might want to go easy on her in gratitude for her uncle's help at the time of the Restoration. Or he might decide she should meet the same fate as her father. Anthony told himself he didn't care. He only hoped Charles would never discover to what extent she had played Anthony for a fool.

The door opened and Oliver came in looking weary. "When do we leave?" he asked.

Anthony pushed himself back in his chair. "I've a favor to ask."

Oliver rolled his eyes. "I suspected you might."

"Will you take charge of her?"

Oliver's expression became sympathetic. "She got you bad, didn't she?"

Anthony didn't answer.

"Of course, my friend," Oliver continued after a moment. "I'll take her. But aren't you going back to London?"

"Not directly. I'll send the king a written report. I'm not in the mood for the court just now."

"What are you going to do?"

Anthony shrugged. "I'll probably head to France for a few weeks." His voice had a raw edge. "Who knows, I might go visit my devoted mother and thank her for the lessons she taught me."

"Travel will do you good." Oliver nodded his approval. "You *will* recover, you know. All those ballads about dying of a broken heart are just folderol. Eventually the wounds heal. I'm a living example."

"What about healing a *poisoned* heart?" Anthony asked with a bitter smile.

"It takes a bit longer, but it, too, mends," Oliver said grimly.

Anthony sighed. "Are they bringing her here?"

"Aye. You said her uncle would want to see her. Are you going to be all right? Do you want to leave now?"

"No. I can stand to see her treacherous face one more time. As long as I know it will be the last."

There was a knock on the door followed by the entry of two guards holding Sarah between them. She was still dressed in the male clothes from the night before. They were smudged with dirt, as was her face.

"Why didn't you let her clean herself up?" Anthony asked with disgust.

One of the guards shuffled his feet and answered, "Captain Kempthorne said we wasn't to let her leave the room, sir."

There was a commotion outside the room and Thomas Fairfax came up the wooden steps to the door. "What's the meaning of all this?" he asked.

Anthony's aching head began to throb. "General Fairfax, I'm sorry to have to inform you that your niece has been arrested for highway robbery."

Fairfax looked at Sarah in astonishment as Anthony continued. "It appears that she and Henry Partridge have been conspiring to rob innocent people of their valuables along the Old North Road."

Thomas Fairfax's face was ashen. "Henry Partridge?" he asked in confusion.

"Aye, your niece's... suitor."

Fairfax shook his head in bewilderment and turned to Sarah. "What's going on, Sarah dear?"

Sarah's eyes misted when she looked at her uncle, but became hard again when she looked back at Anthony. "Go ahead and tell them about Henry Partridge, Uncle. There's no point in trying to keep it secret any longer."

Thomas addressed Anthony. "Henry Partridge was just a name my niece foolishly invented. The man you must be talking about is Jack Fairfax, Sarah's brother."

"Her brother?" Oliver and Anthony asked at once.

Anthony's eyes went to Sarah. "Your brother?" he asked softly.

"Yes," she said, her gray eyes filled with loathing. "The boy your men beat bloody last night and dragged off to prison is my brother."

Chapter Twelve

Whitehall Palace,
June 1666

"So, my friend, you've finally decided to face me again after your Yorkshire debacle." The unmistakable, drawling voice belonged to King Charles and Anthony turned around to greet him with a smile. The king had entered without fanfare as a crowd waited in the great banquet hall. Anthony dropped to one knee.

"Oh, posh," Charles said in response to the gesture. "Come embrace me, Rutledge." He held his arms out wide and Anthony stood and let himself be pulled into them.

"I've missed you, sire."

"Then why did you stay away these many months?" the king asked peevishly. "I'd banish you again for your indifference, except that I haven't had a decent game of chess since you left."

Anthony knew that Charles valued him as much more than a chess partner, but it was not in the king's nature to say so directly. He looked around at the throng of elegant people who made up Charles's sumptuous court. Courtiers and retainers preened and showed off the latest fashion while pages and chamberlains and cupbearers scurried around with their myriad duties. Across the banqueting table the obsequious master of harriers engaged in deep conversation with the pretentious Viscount Gilby, and over in a discreet corner of the room, Sir Jeremy Elliot was hovering over the nearly exposed bosom of the Earl of Strickland's new young wife.

On the ceiling above them were the Peter Paul Rubens panels honoring the rather uneventful life of Charles's grandfather, James. The voluptuous figures and vibrant colors dominated the decor of the room.

Suddenly Anthony felt very distant from it all, though he didn't know if the feeling was due to his long absence or to everything he had experienced since the last time he had been at court.

"If you'll recall, sire, it was you who sent word to Paris that I was to remain there with the mission negotiating terms for French assistance against the Dutch."

"Ah, yes. That boring little war. It's become quite tedious, Anthony."

"We weren't able to make much progress, I'm afraid," Anthony said.

"There, you see! Depriving me of my finest chess opponent, and to what avail? I'm half inclined to call the whole thing off."

Charles's ever present retinue of ministers and secretaries and hangers-on gave a collective gasp.

"Could you do that, your majesty?" Anthony asked with amusement.

"I don't see why not. I'm the king, aren't I?" He looked for confirmation to the group of avid listeners, some of whom nodded.

Anthony had planned to wait until a more private moment, but he decided to seize the opportunity. "It would certainly make you a more *popular* king with the people."

"Eh?" Charles had spied the Lady Castlemaine, his beautiful and treacherously clever mistress, holding her own court at the far end of the hall. "Ah... you were saying, Anthony?"

"Only that the Dutch wars have been a dreadful burden on the common folk, sire, and it would be a great relief if the war taxes could be lifted."

Charles shifted his attention back to Anthony. "Have you become a politician during your absence, my friend?"

Anthony shook his head. "No, but my visit to Yorkshire turned me into a bit more of a humanitarian, I believe."

Charles gave a delighted hoot of laughter. "Yes, tell me about Yorkshire, Anthony. Tell me how the notorious highwayman, whom it took a whole troop of my dragoons to capture, turned out to be a woman. And how an entire village was able to keep the identity of the bandit and her accomplice secret from two of my most skilled officers.''

Hiding his irritation, Anthony met the king's mockery with an assured smile. Self-confidence was the only manner to assume when dealing with Charles. The days of exile were long past, and court life had become a constant pursuit of comforts and pleasures, but the king was still possessed of a sharp mind, and he did not suffer fools lightly.

''I confirmed Thomas Fairfax's loyalty,'' Anthony said calmly. ''And I caught your moonlight bandit. I believe those were the tasks you had assigned me.''

Charles smiled as he looked into Anthony's younger version of his own intense brown eyes. There was more to this story, and Anthony most clearly did not want to tell it. Which meant that it would prove very interesting, indeed. He looked down the hall to where the Castlemaine was charming her usual retinue of the most attractive men at court.

''We must talk more after dinner, my friend,'' he said. ''For now, the Lady Barbara is awaiting me.''

These days when he slept, Jack no longer dreamt of Bess's chestnut-stuffed capons and apple tarts. He didn't even dream about Norah's plump breasts and rounded belly. He dreamt instead that he was in the middle of the stream that ran through his uncle's property. It was a sweltering summer day, and he had come tired and sweaty from the fields. Now he was in the middle of the stream, plunging again and again into the cool depths of the water. His body tingled, and he felt clean and invigorated.

Then he would awaken to his stifling cell, the sixth he had occupied since his arrest many weeks ago. Or months. He had lost track of the time. He would give anything just to be clean once again, to rid himself of these vermin-infested clothes and scrub his skin until it returned to a normal color. He spent a good deal of his time thinking about clean water. It was, after all, a better subject for his thoughts than most others he could choose—home, Norah, the future, real shoes. His own had been stripped from him his first week at Newgate, before they had moved him into the Tower.

The hardest topic for his thoughts was Sarah. In all this time, no one had been able to tell him what they had done to her. Sometimes he would picture that big soldier's hands on her, and the rage would become almost unbearable. He would beat his fists against the rough stone walls in sheer frustration over his helplessness. He didn't care what they did to him. Perhaps Sarah's fears had been right and he had been doomed to this fate since the death of his father. But he wished with all his heart that there was something he could do to save her. His merry, kind, beautiful, spirited sister, who had fallen in love with the wrong man and had ridden once too often into danger.

A faint, flickering light appeared through the barred window of the cell. Someone was coming, carrying a torch to see his way through the gloom. Jack got to his feet. His legs were wobbly. For the first few weeks he had tried to move around his cell, flexing his stiffening muscles, but of late he had found little incentive to stir himself.

"Jack Fairfax?" a disembodied voice asked.

"Yes, in here." The sound felt strange in his throat.

With a creak of iron the cell door opened. "You're to come with us."

There were only two guards. A couple of months ago, Jack might have considered trying to overpower them, but in his current condition, he had no choice but to follow meekly along. He supposed this was the end. He had had no trial, seen no lawyer, heard not a word of his sister or his uncle. But this was King Charles's justice, the same that had taken his father's life. He didn't expect more.

"Where are you taking me?" he managed to croak.

The guards didn't answer. They led him through the claustrophobic halls of the prison down two flights to the ground and the outside. He took a deep breath. The fresh air smelled as sweet as a lilac bush in May. He stopped to fill his lungs to the maximum. But the guards were impatient and hurried him along with ungentle tugs on his arms.

He thought they would be heading out of the prison grounds toward Tower Hill. But instead they led him to one of the more comfortable buildings off the Tower courtyard. It was here that the highest-class prisoners of the king were kept, where the notorious Anne Boleyn had spent her last days.

"Where are we going?" he asked again, his voice finally sounding more normal.

One of the guards gave a grunt of irritation, but answered, "They said you was to be able to see yer sister."

Elation and a kind of deadly fear sluiced through his body at the same time. Sarah was alive, and healthy enough if they were allowing him to see her. But the very fact that they *were* allowing him to see her very probably meant that this was, indeed, the end. It was strange. In these past long days in his cell, he had thought he would welcome the moment. Anything to end the interminable bleakness of his current existence. But now that the event was at hand, he found it agonizing to think of. He felt the sunlight on his face and the life coming back into his limbs.

They reached the door of the neatly constructed building with its heavy Tudor beams and wattle roof. The guards pushed Jack ahead of them. Her cell was on the second floor. A warder came to open the door. He saw with relief that the cell was much more comfortable than the ones he had been subjected to over the past months. It was more like a small bedroom, complete with cot and even a table. But the air was oppressive and the thick bare walls and barred window left no doubt as to the purpose of the chamber.

At first he didn't see his sister, but gradually his eyes grew accustomed to the dim light, and he saw that she was curled up at one end of the cot, looking almost like a pile of rags.

"Sarah!" he cried, and ran across to take her in his arms.

She reacted slowly to his presence, reaching a hand out to touch his face as if he were a ghost. "Jack?" she asked in a quavery voice.

"Yes, it's Jack. Sarah, are you all right? Have they harmed you?" Through the filthy dress she wore, he could feel the bones of her back and shoulders. Her face, too, was much thinner and drawn, making her eyes look huge.

"It's really you?"

"Yes, my dearest sister."

"How did you get here?"

Jack nodded at the guards who stood just inside the door. "They said I could visit you."

She touched his shoulders, his arms, his chest. "I don't understand. Are you free?"

Jack shook his head. "No. I was brought here under guard."

Sarah couldn't believe what she was seeing. It was as if her vivid dreams of the past several weeks had suddenly materialized. This was Jack, sitting with her, holding her. And he was all right. He was safe. The bruises he had received when they were captured had disappeared from his face, though she noticed a new scar at the corner of his lip. "You're healthy? You've been treated well?" She wanted to know everything that had happened to him in these past months all at once.

"I'm healthy. As to the treatment, let's just say I've enjoyed better hospitality in my life." He looked at her with something like his old grin.

Sarah felt a swell of happiness. Whatever they had done to him, they hadn't managed to beat the good humor out of him. "Why did they give you permission to visit me?"

Jack looked away uneasily. He wouldn't tell her his suspicions as to the reason for the boon. "I don't know. They won't tell me anything. Perhaps they're moving me to another cell or another prison."

Sarah's hands stopped in midair. She looked at his averted eyes with mounting horror. "But you don't think so," she said.

Jack pulled her against his chest. "I just don't know, Sarah. The important thing is that I'm able to see that you're all right."

Sarah drew away from him. "You think they're going to kill you," she stated in a hard voice.

Jack could not mask the truth in his eyes. "It's in God's hands now, Sarah," he said gently.

Tears filled her eyes, but her voice was strong with loathing. "It's not God's hand that commands your fate, Jack, it's the king's. And his henchmen. Treacherous, deceitful men like Lord Anthony Rutledge."

Jack's eyes grew sympathetic. "Have you heard anything from him?"

"Of course not," she said bitterly. "Nor do I expect to this side of hell."

Jack gave a sigh. "The man was only doing his assigned duty."

Sarah looked at her brother in astonishment. "And I suppose it was his *assigned duty* to seduce me into his bed?"

"No. It was wrong for him to accept the hospitality of our home under false pretenses, and it was wicked of him to lure you to his bed with false words. If I ever get out of here, I will be duty-bound to demand satisfaction."

The idea of Jack, even grown as he was, proving a match for Anthony's experience and skill struck Sarah as absurd. "You will do no such thing," she said. "If we get out of here, I want you to take me far away—far enough away so that there would be no chance of ever setting eyes on Lord Rutledge for the rest of our lives."

"Perhaps to the New World," Jack suggested, a far-off look in his eyes.

"We could go to the Plymouth colony," Sarah added, a flush of excitement showing on her pale cheeks. Many of the Puritan leaders who had been friends of their father had taken their religious beliefs and started a new life in the land they were now calling Massachusetts.

"Perhaps Uncle Thomas would go with us, and together we could establish our own plantation."

"There are several families in Wiggleston who would go."

"I could take Norah," Jack said softly.

It was a nice fantasy, and for a moment the brother and sister held each other and envisioned a far-off time when they would be reunited in a better place. But a gruff call from one of the guards brought them crashing back to reality.

"Fairfax! It's time to go."

Sarah grabbed at Jack. "They can't take you yet," she said, her words tumbling out in a panic. She looked pleadingly over at the guard. "Please, just a few more minutes..."

Jack felt a tremendous calm settle in his middle. The waiting was over. He didn't want to leave Sarah, but it was as he had said before, he would have to entrust her to God's hands. Gently he pried her fingers from his arms. "It's going to be all right, Sarah. Whatever happens, I want you to know that. If this is the end for me, then I will be going to a better place to watch over you and await you with our father and mother at my side."

Sarah began to sob and her head fell heavily against his chest. "Don't leave me, Jack," she pleaded.

"No one can part us. You and I are sister and brother for all eternity."

He stood, his eyes dry. The peace that had flooded through him seemed to radiate out into the room. Sarah crumpled onto the bed. He lifted her chin and looked into her eyes. "I'll always be by your side, Sarah. I promise."

"I love you, Jack," she whispered.

He gently stroked her hair, then he was gone, leaving Sarah soaking the rough covering of the cot with her tears.

Anthony had thought coming back to Leasworth would be painful, but for the first few days he had been so busy, and in such uncharacteristically constructive activity after the idleness of court, that he had little time to feel sorry for himself.

Today he had a shadow. A noisy one.

"How did you learn that, my lord?" the boy asked for at least the tenth time in the past hour. It was little Benjamin White, who had appointed himself as Anthony's official entourage during his visit to Wiggleston.

Anthony answered patiently, "Remember I told you that over in France near a city called Paris they're starting to study these things—how to plant a crop so it will grow better, how to alternate things so you can make the season last longer?"

Benjamin's rapt face bobbed up and down. "And you lived over there, right, sir?"

"Aye." There was no point in telling the boy that his interest in the science of agriculture had started years ago as an antidote to the useless existence of his mother and her like. After spending time surrounded by the frivolous minds and deceitful natures of his mother's friends, it had been a relief to arrive at the academy and listen for a spell to people who were trying to make a difference in the world, not with ships and guns, but with knowledge.

When he had left Yorkshire last winter, he had been drawn back to the academy. He couldn't explain why. He was not a farmer—he didn't even have any land of his own. It had had something to do with his travels around Leasworth with Sarah . . . and the faces of those children. Wars and taxes would come and go, but the secret to increasing prosperity in this part of the country lay in the land.

Of course, most of the people around Wiggleston were suspicious of him, and loath to take his suggestions. But here and there he had made a little progress, and a few converts to the new ideas. Such as Benjamin here. Benjamin would be a modern farmer, no question about it.

"So, how is it to have your father at home again?" he asked the boy.

Benjamin beamed under the brown thatch of hair. "My ma is home again, too. She's quit her job over at the Wyeths'."

"Shouldn't you be at home helping out?"

"My da' says if I be helping ye, I can stay as long as I likes. He says he owes you a debt."

"You tell your da' that he doesn't owe me anything."

"He says you talked to an *admiral* to help him get out of the navy."

"Your father never should have been sent to the navy in the first place, Benjamin. There are plenty of men who want to go off to sea without taking away ones who need to stay behind to take care of their families."

"Well, anyways, I'm to stay and help you as long as you need me."

Anthony hid a smile. "You've been a great help, Benjamin. But I don't think I need you more today. I'm heading back to Leasworth."

"Will you be out tomorrow?"

Anthony hesitated. Would it do any good? Sometimes it seemed that all his efforts in Wiggleston were sheer folly. Once he left, the people would go back to the ways they always knew. Why did he care, anyway? Perhaps he should just give up and go on back to court, where he would at least make the king happy playing chess with him and joining him in his new passion for horse racing.

"I don't know yet, Benjamin. I've already talked to most of the folks in the area. I'm not sure there's much more I can do."

"You're not leaving?" The boy's clear blue eyes grew sad.

"I'll have to be leaving one of these days, Benjamin. But I won't go without saying goodbye. Now you get along home to your family."

Benjamin planted his bare feet firmly in the dust of the road and stretched his hand out to Anthony. "You're the most—" he screwed up his face as he searched for the right word "—*important* man I've ever met."

With a solemn face, Anthony shook the little hand, then watched as the boy turned and scampered away down the road.

Important. That was exactly how he had felt over these past few weeks helping to remedy the problems of one little town. First with the king's taxes and then with his agricultural improvements. Not all, but some of the farmers around Wiggleston had agreed to try the new system of rotating crops rather than leaving fallow fields to replenish the soil. And he had told them about planting fodder crops and letting the sheep graze them, filling the earth with natural fertilizers.

These people were not stupid. He had learned a new respect for them and their knowledge of the land. And he had discovered that he liked working side by side with them. He understood now even more fully how Sarah must have felt, providing what she could to the villagers, even if it meant going against the law and putting herself in danger.

He suspected that after this court life would be anti-climactic and boring. When he had returned from Paris, the court had seemed all too trivial. And the ladies . . . But of course, that was another matter. He had not been able to find a lady to interest him in all these many long months. Which did not surprise him. None of them had cat's eyes and a temperament to match.

He reached the turn into Leasworth and spurred his horse ahead when he saw Arthur leading Oliver's horse into the stable. "The visitors have arrived?" he called.

Arthur dashed over with a big grin. "Yes, sir. It's a happy day for Sir Thomas, I reckon."

Anthony dismounted and threw his reins to the beaming boy, then walked swiftly up to the house. They were waiting for him in the great room—Thomas, Oliver... and Jack, standing by the mantelpiece looking thin and white, but otherwise healthy.

As he entered, Jack said in a surprised voice, "Rutledge!" Then he looked to his uncle for an explanation.

"Anthony is staying here, Jack."

Jack's chin dropped in disbelief. "This is some sort of cruel joke! You mean to tell me that you are playing host to the man who's responsible for Sarah being locked away in a filthy cell all these months?"

Thomas got up from his chair and walked over to his nephew. "He's also the man who has just had you released, my boy."

Jack looked from Anthony to Oliver, who nodded his confirmation. "It was Anthony who arranged to have you sent into the navy instead of being tried and possibly hung for robbery."

Jack looked as if he'd swallowed something disagreeable. "I don't understand..."

"It wasn't really that difficult," Anthony interrupted. "According to your sister, you never were really involved in the robberies. It was just a matter of talking to a few of the right people."

Jack had not entirely recovered after the months in prison, and his knees suddenly felt weak. He walked over to sit down in a nearby chair. "Could I talk to Lord Rutledge in private?" he asked Oliver.

Oliver looked over at Anthony, who nodded. "Leave us," he said.

Oliver got up to leave the room, followed by Thomas, and the big double doors closed behind them.

Anthony walked over and took a seat opposite Jack. Jack rubbed his knees for a moment, then looked across at Anthony and without wasting words asked, "What about my sister?"

Anthony was somewhat taken aback. There were certain aspects of how he had handled his relationship with Sarah of which he was not proud, having had many months to analyze them. If he had been her brother, he would have had the same insulted, angry look in his eyes that Jack had this minute.

"Your sister committed robberies on the king's highway. There's nothing I can do for her other than fulfill the promise that I already made to your uncle."

"Which is...?"

"That I will petition the king that she not be put to death for her crimes."

Jack was silent for a moment, then said bluntly, "She was in love with you."

The words hit Anthony like a punch in the jaw. "I don't think so," he said stiffly.

"She went to your bed. Do you think Sarah is a woman who would do that unless she were in love?"

Anthony was feeling increasingly uncomfortable. The months in prison had aged Jack, and he no longer looked like a boy. He was Sarah's brother, and had a perfect right to be calling Anthony to account for his actions. Still, they were talking about a person who had committed a capital crime. "She lied to me," Anthony said, trying not to sound defensive. "All the while she was in my bed, as you put it, she was lying."

Jack shook his head. "Not about that, no." He stood up and went to stand by the fireplace, leaning on the mantel for support. "Sarah lied to protect me, that's true. She did so many times over these past few years. But you can't judge her unless you know what it's like to live as we did for so many years with the nightmares of seeing our father killed—not knowing if we would be next."

"The king would never have killed children."

"We had no way of knowing that. Sarah has spent the better part of her life trying to protect me and make things better for those around her."

Anthony had told himself much the same thing many times since he had last seen her, her hands bound, riding double on Oliver's horse on her way to London. But it didn't change the fact that she had deceived him, played him falsely.

"Your sister has many admirable qualities, but she is also a liar and a thief, and now she's facing the consequences."

There was no hint of softening in Anthony's expression. "Put me back in prison and let her go," Jack pleaded.

Anthony threw up his hands in exasperation. "It's not up to me to let her go. *I'm* not the one keeping her there. She's broken the law, the *king's* law. I was able to get them to send you off to the navy instead of prison because of your age and because it was evident that you were only an accomplice."

Jack was silent for a long moment. "She thinks I've been executed," he said, his voice tightening as he remembered that last painful scene in his sister's cell.

"What!"

"The guards took me to see her, and we both thought I was on my way to Tower Hill."

"Good God, she must be in agony." In spite of himself, Anthony felt her pain. Jack was more important to Sarah than her own life.

"Can you at least get word to her that I am free?"

Anthony nodded. He had vowed that once he left Yorkshire this time he would forget all about the bloody Fairfax family, but this much at least he could do. "I'll see that she's told."

Jack walked back over to his chair and sat down heavily. He studied the man across from him. He had spent the last several months in prison hating Anthony Rutledge, almost as much as his sister professed to the last time he saw her. The man had come into their home under false pretenses, deceived his uncle and seduced his sister. He had planned to call him out if he ever saw him again. But his anger was strangely dissipating. There was a look in Anthony's eyes when he talked of Sarah. And when he had exclaimed over her suffering at thinking that her brother was about to die, Jack had seen pain in Anthony's eyes, too.

It was possible that Sarah had been wrong about Lord Rutledge. Possible that he hadn't seduced her for his own base purposes, but had instead developed real feelings for her, as strong as the ones she had developed for him.

Obviously, Uncle Thomas must not think of the baron as treacherous or he would not have him staying here at his home. Of course, Uncle Thomas didn't know that Anthony had made love to Sarah, a fact of which Jack intended to keep him in ignorance. The older generation never really understood about these things.

"Will you go see her yourself?" Jack asked cautiously.

"No, but I'll send word. I promise."

"You intend never to see her again—to let her rot away in prison . . . for years, perhaps?"

Anthony's hands gripped the armrests of his chair. "It's not my affair."

"She's been in there for months now and hasn't even had a trial."

"Aye. It's an unusual case. I think the prosecutors don't quite know what to do with her. I've told your uncle that he should appeal to the proper authorities to get things moving more quickly."

Jack watched Anthony's hands open and close on the carved lion heads at each end of the chair arm. The baron was decidedly not indifferent to Sarah's fate, and Jack felt a surge of hope. "My uncle knows few people in London anymore. It would take someone of your stature to make a difference."

"These things have to be worked through the assizes. They take time."

"She's not well."

Anthony's head came up sharply.

"What do you mean?"

Jack's eyes looked steadily at Anthony. "When I saw her she was so thin that at first I thought I was looking at nothing more than a pile of rags on the bed."

"Was she ill?"

"I don't know. I only know that she's wasting away, and if she's left there many more months there may be nothing left of her to save."

Anthony looked over at the fire crackling in the giant hearth. For a while he stared at the dancing flames. Finally he turned back to Jack and said, "I'll talk to the king and see if I can get them to act on her case."

"You won't go to her yourself?" Jack asked again.

"She wouldn't want to see me, Fairfax." Anthony's expression was bitter.

Jack gave a half smile. "You may be right about that. Sarah has very definite opinions about things, and she doesn't easily change her mind. But if she knew what you have done for me, I think she would talk with you."

Anthony gave a final pummel to the wooden lions, then pushed himself up. "It would be to no purpose, believe me. But as I say, I will try to get her case reviewed."

Jack was still not satisfied, but the interview was clearly over. He stood also, and after a moment offered Anthony his hand. "Thank you," he said simply.

Anthony took the gesture for the peace offering it was intended to be and gripped Jack's hand warmly. "You are satisfied to be entering the navy?" he asked him.

Jack's smile grew broader. "It's the exact course I had intended for myself for some time. I just could never get up the nerve to broach the subject to Sarah."

Anthony's answering smile was sad. "Your sister took good care of you."

"Yes, she did. She was mother, father and sister all together. She's an extraordinary person."

Anthony made no reply. He finished the handshake, then clapped Jack on the shoulder. "I've arranged for you to have a month here before you're to report."

"Thank you, sir. Perhaps we can continue this discussion at a later time."

"I'm afraid I've said all I care to on the subject, and I'll be heading back to London shortly."

"But, surely—"

Anthony held up his hand. "I understand there's a young lady—a Miss Thatcher—who's looking forward to welcoming you home. I believe she's waiting down by the kitchens."

Jack felt an instant glow. He wanted to make a further attempt to persuade Rutledge to get involved with freeing Sarah, but perhaps he had gotten far enough for their first meeting. And Norah was waiting.

Chapter Thirteen

"It's damned *tiresome* of you, Anthony. You finally fall in love with a woman, and then it turns out she's a felon—currently in residence in one of my prisons."

Anthony had waited until Charles had beaten him in their first game of chess and was in a good mood before bringing up the subject. "She hasn't been convicted yet."

"Are you saying she's innocent?"

"Not exactly, but—"

"Oddsfish, Anthony. I have an entire court full of *uncomplicated* ladies. Why couldn't you have chosen one of them? Listen, my friend..." Charles made an expansive gesture with his arms. "I'll give you your pick, whichever one you like. Except Lady Throckton," he added as an afterthought. "I think I rather fancy her for myself."

Anthony smiled. "You're very generous, your majesty. But I'm not pleading Mistress Fairfax's case for my own purposes. I don't intend that I shall ever see her again."

Charles gave his friend a shrewd look. "You badgered me for days until I lowered the taxes in her uncle's shire. You spent weeks in various legal manipulations to free her brother. You deliberately let me beat you in chess so that I will look favorably on her case. And you say you don't intend to see her again?"

Anthony didn't bother to deny the accusations. "No, I don't."

Charles stretched and reached up both hands to scratch underneath his huge wig. "You, my friend, are either trying to cozen me, or you are a bigger fool than I have ever taken you for."

"I'm not trying to deceive you, sire. As to the fool—that may well be so."

"Damn these hairpieces. This one itches abominably. Where's my chamberlain?"

"You sent him to bed over an hour past, sire."

"Ah, so I did." He got up from his chair and went over to a huge chest inlaid with mother of pearl. "Help me off with this blasted thing, Anthony."

Anthony went to stand beside him and lift off the heavy periwig of curly dark ringlets. The king himself opened one of the cupboards and took out a satin nightcap from the drawer to cover his nearly bald head. "There, that's better. Now what were we talking about?" Charles looked at Anthony with an infuriatingly blank expression.

"Mistress Fairfax."

"Ah, yes. Well, you'll have to marry the girl, that's all there is to it."

Anthony took a step backward. "I beg your pardon?"

"You want her out of prison, as I understand it."

"Well, yes, but—"

"Then marry her. It's about time we got you settled down, Anthony. Once she's the Lady Rutledge, we'll arrange for a pardon of some sort." Charles gave a regal wave of his hand. "My ministers will figure out the details."

"But, your majesty..."

Charles walked back over to the chess table and sat down. "Come on and sit down, Rutledge. I'm going to beat you legitimately this time."

"Your majesty, I don't think you understand—"

"Hurry up, man. If you've a marriage to plan I'll be out a chess partner again for a spell, so let's get to it."

Anthony walked slowly back to the chess table, his mind awhirl. He almost didn't hear the king's next pronouncement.

"It's a tidy estate and I was going to give it to Norfolk, but he hasn't been very nice to me of late. And since you seem so taken with Yorkshire. Yes, it would be the perfect wedding present. I'll have my ministers draw up the papers in the morning. Are you listening to me, Anthony?"

Anthony sat down hard. "An estate, sire?" he repeated in a daze.

"Of course. I'd always meant to find one for you, but the matter kept slipping my mind."

"I have to think about this, sire," Anthony said slowly.

Charles leaned across the chessboard. "Nothing to think about, man. You'll enjoy marriage, Anthony. It's not as bad as they paint...a bit restraining at times, but if one can overlook the conventions..."

On any other occasion, Anthony would have greeted the king's pithy description of the state of matrimony with the derision it deserved. Though the king was unfailingly kind to his hapless, unattractive Portuguese queen on the rare occasions that she made an appearance, there was no pretense of a relationship between them. Charles was more than satisfied with his bevy of mistresses.

The king finished moving the chess pieces back into place as Anthony looked on in stunned silence.

"I believe the opening gambit is yours," Charles said smoothly.

Oliver found Anthony still at a table in the great banquet hall, a full two hours after the other diners had departed. Two kitchen terriers lay at his feet, no doubt hoping the lone diner might still have some scraps to share. His only companion was a nearly empty pitcher of ale.

"What in the name of Saint Stephen are you doing in here all by yourself, Rutledge?" Oliver pulled out a chair directly across from Anthony and turned it around to sit on it backward. "What's wrong with you?" he asked, eyeing his friend with a frown. Then he held up his hand. "No, wait... don't tell me. I know the signs. It's got to be a woman. And since you've been celibate as a monk since Yorkshire, I would say it has to be the beautiful Mistress Fairfax."

Anthony looked up with bloodshot eyes. "Mind your own business, Kempthorne."

He reached for his goblet, but before he could lift it from the table, Oliver shot out his huge hand and stopped him. "You've had enough, my friend."

Anthony gave a lopsided grin. "I can still *think*, can't I?"

"Not cogently, to all appearances."

Oliver held firm to the goblet, so Anthony let it go and instead grabbed the pewter pitcher. "I'm in the mood to get roaring drunk, Oliver. You can join me or you can go away." Ale dribbled down each side of his mouth as he tilted the pitcher and drank.

"Why don't you put that stuff away and just admit that you're in love with the chit?"

Anthony closed his eyes and swayed in his chair. "No such thing as love..." he said, his words slurred.

Oliver stood up. "If that's the case, you won't be interested in my news."

"Newsh..." Anthony repeated drunkenly.

"I came to tell you that the prosecutors have started proceedings on Mistress Fairfax's case."

Anthony sat up straight and blinked his eyes.

Oliver leaned one hand on the table and bent close to his friend. "They're asking for a sentence of death."

When Anthony had fought his first battle with then Prince Charles against the Republicans at Worcester, he had been a raw youth of sixteen. His stomach had formed itself into a mass of knots that it took a full day of battle to dissolve. But he couldn't remember his insides feeling any more agitated than they did now as he walked behind the prison warder on his way to Sarah's cell.

It had taken Oliver most of yesterday to bring him back to sobriety. They had gone together to the prosecutor's office to inquire into Sarah's case, which was as Oliver had reported. The evidence was firm, and the Crown intended to demand the full measure of punishment.

Anthony thought about going back to Charles, but visions of the king's mocking dark eyes changed his mind. The king had made his offer. Now it was up to Anthony to accept or reject it.

With the alcohol at last out of his system and his headache beginning to abate, Anthony realized that there really was nothing to decide. The instant Oliver had said the words "sentence of death" he had known that he simply could not bear to think about living in a world without Sarah.

The king had been right. Oliver had been right. He was in love with her, pure and simple. He wanted her in his life, in his bed, in his heart. For now and always.

He knew that she wouldn't welcome his proposal. She had had months for her sense of betrayal to fester. He had made love to her under false pretenses. He had arrested her and her brother. He had shot her beloved horse, though that had been due to no fault of his own. He had not contacted her in prison all these many weeks, had offered no help, no comfort.

She had no way of knowing how hard he had worked to better conditions in Wiggleston. She didn't know that he himself had gone to bring Parson Hollander out of the cave when his location had been revealed by the smugglers. That he was responsible for clearing the parson of all wrongdoing and returning him to his parish. She didn't even know that Jack was alive and free. He would have to tell her about all these things, but first he would have to make her listen to him.

The harsh scrape of the cell door against the stone floor jarred his edgy nerves. A solitary beam of light illuminated the dim room, and Sarah stood in the middle of it. She looked more like a ghost of the lady he had loved those many months ago than a flesh-and-blood woman. But her eyes were not those of a ghost. They stared at him first with shock, then swiftly changed to a glare of unrelenting hatred.

"You!" she gasped, bracing herself against a table behind her.

"Surprised to see me, my love?" He was at a loss as to how to approach her. A wall of animosity surrounded her, thicker and more palpable than the clammy stone walls of the cell.

"Not surprised," she said. "Disappointed. I had hoped by now you had been blown to bits by a Dutch frigate."

Anthony gave a reluctant smile. She had lost none of her spirit, in spite of the fact that she looked, as Jack had said, overly thin and unwell. "I've managed to stay out of that particular war so far. You see, I have some unfinished business yet in the world of the living."

That stubborn chin of hers went up a notch. "Not with me, you don't. Our business was finished long ago."

"Perhaps not." His blood warmed as he looked at her. Even in dirty clothes and with the pallor of prison on her skin, she looked dignified, her classic beauty unmarred. He started toward her.

"Leave me be, Anthony."

She held up a slender hand as if to ward him off, but he knew now, finally, that no matter what it took, he would make her his again. "Now there's a problem, my sweet. It appears that I can't let you be." He was an arm's length from her, and there was thunder in his chest. "Were old Mephistopheles himself chasing me away, I'd not be able to let you be," he said, pulling her into his embrace.

She did not resist. Sweetly, her mouth opened to his, soothing his heart like rainfall on a dusty garden. He deepened the kiss, drawing her warmth inside himself. Her body melded to the contours of his own. Even through the curtain of desire that fogged his mind, it registered with him how fragile she felt through the heavy wool dress. A wave of guilt swept through him. Why had it taken him so many months to come to his senses about her? How could he have left her here at the mercy of the filthy vermin who were guarding her cell? If they had hurt her...

He brought his head up sharply at the sound of a tin cup scraping across the bars of the door.

"Glad to see ye enjoying yerself, yer lordship. But ye'd best finish it off right quick. I can only let ye have a few more minutes."

Anthony wanted to knock the warder's black teeth through the back of his throat, but he maintained an outward calm. Keeping Sarah out of view, he walked to the door and spoke in a low, deadly voice. "My good man, if I see you looking into this room again before I summon you, I will cut out your eyeballs and roll them in my next game of bowls. Do you understand?"

Anthony watched as sweat began to roll down the warder's face. The thought of his squinty eyes on Sarah day and night made him want to be sick. He turned back to Sarah. "Have they...bothered you, Sarah? Hurt you?"

She looked about to answer, but then, to his horror, her knees buckled and she started to sag. He was at her side in an instant, lifting her in his arms. "Sarah!" he cried. "What is it? Are you sick?"

With reluctance he placed her on the room's filthy cot. He wished he could take her from here this minute, but first he had to get her to listen to his proposal. Her response to his kiss had been encouraging, but now she was looking up at him with the same hostile expression as before. "What are you doing here, Anthony?" she asked.

He had to break through to her somehow. Stroking her hair back from her forehead, he said gently, "I've come to take you out of here."

Her laugh was sardonic. "In case you've forgotten, *Lord* Rutledge, your king has other ideas for me. If the royal prosecutors have their way, I'm to have my head smitten from my body."

It was unthinkable. His eyes went to her slender neck, and he tried to imagine it poised on the axman's block. It gave him another wave of nausea. "That's not going to happen, Sarah. You're leaving here with me... today."

"Oh, certainly. I just walk on out past the guards? A condemned prisoner?"

Anthony took a deep breath. The moment was here, and he had no idea how she would react. "Not as a condemned prisoner. As my wife."

Her face went ghost white. "Your wife!"

He reached for her hand, but she snatched it away. He should have led up to it more slowly. "I knew you might be opposed to the idea, but it's the only way, Sarah. Marry me, and you can leave here today, a free woman."

She backed against the wall, her gray eyes lethal. "I'd sooner rot a thousand years in hell."

Anthony didn't know if he wanted to shake her or make love to her. Or both. He had known that it wouldn't be easy to convince her to marry him. Now he understood that it would be nearly impossible. Furthermore, the prosecutors were busy at work on her case. He didn't have time for a slow courtship that would bring her around to favoring the idea. Besides, he had resolved that she wouldn't spend another night in this place. He would just have to take matters into his own hands.

He held up his hands, palms toward her. "Just think about it, Sarah," he said with a calm he was far from feeling. "The important thing is for you to get out of here before they can present evidence on your case in the courts."

"I asked you to leave me alone, Anthony." With surprising strength she pushed him out of the way and got up off the bed to walk to the door. "Warder!" she called. There was no response from the dim hall.

Anthony stood behind her and put his hands on her shoulders. "Sarah..." he began.

She turned to face him, backing away from his touch. "After your threats, he probably won't come back until you call, so if you would be so kind." She made a gesture toward the barred window.

With a sigh of exasperation Anthony leaned toward the window and called loudly for the guards. Still there was no answer. He stepped closer and grasped the bars, and to his surprise, the door started to swing open. "They've left it unlocked!" he said with astonishment.

Sarah eyed him suspiciously. "What trick is this, Anthony? I'm not leaving this cell."

Anthony frowned. " 'Tis no trick of mine. Maybe it was just an oversight by the guards. I'll go see what's going on."

"Good riddance, my lord," Sarah said, marching across the room to sink down heavily on the bed.

Anthony paused for a moment. "I'll be back, Sarah. Think about what I said."

He pulled open the heavy door and left. At some point during the course of his interview the knots in his stomach had dissolved and an exhilaration had taken their place. He had seen her again, and kissed her. And though she had obviously suffered from her confinement, she had not lost one whit of her spirit.

He would have her out of this place, with or without her consent. The Tower must have a vicar or a curate of some sort who could perform the ceremony. He would wed her bound and gagged if need be.

The two guards who had led him here were nowhere in sight, nor was the warder who had spied on them earlier. He made his way along the nearly black hall toward the pitch torch at the top of the stairs. He could hear movement from inside some of the cells, but there was not a single guard. Puzzled, he ran down the stairs to the ground floor. No one appeared to challenge his movements.

Out on Tower Green he looked about him, trying to decide which would be the likely building to house the office of the Keeper of the Tower. He had met the man at court and felt he could count on his help.

The Old White Tower was directly in front of him. He turned in a circle, trying to get his bearings in the labyrinth of buildings that made up the Tower complex. The air was heavy and today seemed overly filled with grime, even for London. And it was strangely quiet. Even the birds were quiet. Or rather, he realized as he looked around the yard, there weren't any birds. Neither was there a guard at the front gate. What in hell was going on?

He turned toward the south. What he had noted as an unusually heavy haze this morning had turned to an ominous black. And instead of hovering over the overly crowded streets of the old City, it was billowing out to engulf the entire east side of London. He stood watching the sky for several minutes as the significance of what he was seeing slowly dawned on him. London was on fire.

Sarah had put on a brave front, but now that Anthony was no longer present, she rocked back and forth on the bed, the tears streaming down her face. Her hands and arms were shaking as if she had a bad case of the ague. After Jack, she had thought she could bear anything. She had known that she would not so much as flinch as they marched her up on the scaffold. None of that mattered anymore. But she hadn't reckoned with seeing Anthony again. His arms had felt the same around her. His features were more striking than ever. It almost took more strength than she could muster to convince her mind and her senses that inside that attractive facade beat a false heart. He had lied to her and had pretended to be falling in love with her while all the while he was spying on her family and plying his same seductive talents on her maid. His efforts had resulted in the death of the only person she truly loved in this world. She would *never* accept his offer of marriage.

After a few minutes, she began to calm down. The tears stopped. The shaking became less noticeable. She took some deep breaths, trying to compose herself. She wanted to be strong in case Anthony carried out his threat of coming back for her. She glanced over at the door. No guard had come to lock it. In fact, it was still a couple of inches ajar. How very odd.

She swung her feet to the floor and stood, walking unsteadily across the room. Peering through the bars, she saw no sign of anyone. Slowly she turned around. The room itself looked peculiar. The late-afternoon light had a different quality to it, darker, grimier than usual. The window was too narrow for her to see down to the ground, but the slit of sky that showed through was a strange yellow gray color.

Finally, she heard sounds down the long dark hall. They would be coming to lock her in again, no doubt, having discovered their mistake. She sat down on the cot to wait. But instead of the repulsive face of the guard, it was Anthony who appeared when the big door scraped open. His expression was stern and determined.

"Don't argue with me, Sarah. Something's happening—something big. There are no guards left anywhere, and it looks as if half the city has turned into an inferno."

"What are you talking about?"

"London's burning. You can see it from below on the green. We've got to get out of here."

"Are you saying that the fire could reach the Tower?"

"I don't know. All I know is that it's an opportunity meant for the taking. We're leaving—now."

Sarah hesitated. She wished she had a clearer head. She wished the air were not so heavy.

Anthony grabbed her arm. "You can come along with me nicely, or I can carry you. It's up to you."

Sarah took a quick glance around the tiny cell that had been the total extent of her world for so long. "I'll come," she said.

The previous spring the king had written a formal warning to the Lord Mayor and aldermen of the dangers inherent in the current practice of piling one rickety wooden house on top of another in the narrow streets of the city. Fires were a constant fact of life. A neglected iron cooking tray or a careless soap boiler could spell disaster within a matter of minutes in the crowded neighborhoods of Cheapside or Cripplesgate. So plumes of dark smoke amid the ever-present haze over the city were not that unusual. But as Anthony led Sarah out of the building where she had been housed for so many months, it was obvious to them both that this fire was beyond anything London had ever seen.

"We'll head down to the river," Anthony said. His voice was calm, but urgency showed in the way he pulled her along with him with little regard for the fact that her legs were not accustomed to the activity.

He steered them toward the ancient Traitor's Gate which had only recently been reopened to bring in building materials for the Tower renovations.

"What do you think has happened?" Sarah asked, struggling to keep up with his pace.

"I don't know. I saw a few fires on my way here, but nothing out of the ordinary. Now it looks like all hell has broken loose."

They reached the stone gate near the water entrance. It was wide open with not a yeoman guard in sight.

"Come on!" Anthony shouted. He had hoped to take her to Kensington, where he had arranged rooms at a comfortable inn. He had pictured her there, imagined the two of them sharing one of the inn's huge feather beds in a wonderful honeymoon reconciliation. It was still his intention, but first he had two hurdles to conquer. He had to cross half of London through a veritable holocaust. Then he had to convince Sarah to forgive him and agree to become his wife. At the moment, he didn't know which obstacle loomed more intimidating.

They made their way down to the edge of the river, which was crowded with boats of every kind. It seemed as though the people of London were leaving *en masse*. Anthony shouted to several vessels that passed by, but no one paid him the least attention.

He stopped a prosperous-looking gentleman who was making his way down the bank carrying a heavy satchel in each hand. Anthony grabbed his arm. "Your pardon, sir. Can you tell me what the conditions are to the north?"

The man shook his head. "It's bad, unimaginable. I've come from St. Bride's parish and it's virtually destroyed."

"Where's it coming from?" Anthony said, raising his voice to be heard over the increasing cries of the panicked citizenry.

"It started up in Pudding Lane in the heart of the city, but by now it's blazing every which way."

"Is there passage through to the east?"

The man set his load on the ground and rubbed his hands together. "I don't know, sir, what with the lady and all." He nodded his head toward Sarah. "I'd try the river, I think."

The man picked up his satchels, impatient to be on his way. "It's the river for me," he said, "even if I have to swim all the way to the Channel."

Anthony looked around them. It seemed that there were a hundred people clamoring to get on every small boat that went by. The gentleman was right. If the river was their choice, they would have to swim.

"We'll try it by land," he shouted to Sarah. She looked too exhausted to give an opinion. He hoped she would be able to keep walking, because they wouldn't get far if he had to carry her.

They reached Moorfields with a human river of refugees—coal men, milkmaids, tinkers, drapers, fishmongers, old and young alike—all fleeing with what they could carry in their two hands. The ground was littered with discarded goods that people had tried to carry away and had abandoned. Smoke stung their nostrils as ashes and bits of scorched paper and cloth floated down around them. The eerie quiet of the deserted Tower had been replaced by the roar of flames, the splintering of buildings and the fearful cries of the victims.

In the background they could see the smoking ruins of the great cathedral of St. Paul's. The heat had been so intense that the lead roof of the huge church had melted down around its walls.

Anthony stopped as Sarah faltered. Even under the layer of soot that covered her from head to toe, she looked deathly pale. "I don't think I can go on," she said, coughing.

He looked around them. The conflagration was raging outward in every direction. No course looked promising, especially with Sarah in her weakened condition. "We'll have to give the river a try," he yelled. "Can you make it back there?"

She nodded, but clung heavily to his arm as he turned south again to the Thames. It appeared that several thousand others had reached the same conclusion, because this time when they reached the water, it was utterly full from bank to bank with anything that could float. Pleasure craft, fishing boats and ferries competed with upside-down sedan chairs and vegetable crates carrying throngs of panicked citizens away from the heart of the blaze.

Anthony's spirits sank. Perhaps he never would have the chance to plead his case with Sarah. She looked as if she were at the very end of her strength. Lifting her in his arms, he jostled his way through the group of people crowding precariously on a shaky wooden dock. "Please," he begged. "I have a sick woman here. Please let us through."

Even in the midst of panic, there was a modicum of chivalry left. From down below he heard a gruff voice calling, "Over here, sir. I can take you and yer lady."

At the edge of the wharf was a small boat half-filled with vegetables. Four people huddled at one end, including the man who had called to him. Without a moment's hesitation, Anthony secured Sarah in his arms and leapt into a pile of cabbages. "I'm much obliged to you," he gasped. "I'll make it worth your while."

"You just see to your wife, sir," the vegetable seller said kindly. "She's looking right poorly."

"Aye. Thank you, I will." He sank back into the cabbages with Sarah cradled in his arms as the man pushed away from the bank and started slowly out into the stream of traffic, away from the Tower, away from the inferno that was the city. It had proven to be a bit more complicated than he had thought, but the first step in his plan was accomplished. Sarah was free. Now came the more difficult task. He would start by telling her about her brother.

"Sarah," he said softly. "I've some news for you that will make you feel a sight better."

She lay inert in his arms, and he shifted to see her face. Her head lolled to one side and her eyelids rolled back. Sarah had fainted.

Chapter Fourteen

Sarah awoke groggily, but she knew instantly that she was not in her cell. Instead of a hard straw mattress, she was resting on a satin-covered feather bed, and it couldn't have felt any better if she had been in heaven floating on a cloud. Perhaps she was, she thought for the briefest of moments. But instead of sky over her head there were heavy oak beams and plaster. Instead of the heavenly songs of the angels, she could hear the crackle of a hearth and a faint clatter of pans from a kitchen somewhere below. She turned her head. This definitely was not heaven, for dozing in a chair by her side was Anthony Rutledge.

He sensed that she was awake, and sat up straight, blinking his eyes a couple of times. "How are you feeling?" he asked softly.

"Where am I?"

"An inn in Kensington. We had quite a trip here, but I'm afraid you missed out on most of it."

"The fire . . ."

"Aye." Anthony's voice was grim. "The fire's still raging to the east. They say the king himself has gone out to fight it with his brother James." It was hard for Anthony to imagine the elegant Charles battling the heat and ashes and chaos. Perhaps his friend had retained more of the spirit from his days of exile than Anthony had given him credit for.

But Sarah was not interested in hearing about the king. "All those poor people…losing their homes, their belongings…"

"Many have lost their lives," Anthony added soberly. "It will take a long time to recover what London has lost these past three days."

Sarah struggled to sit up. "Three days!"

"You've been asleep since yesterday, dearling. The fire started on Sunday, they say, but began to blaze in earnest on Monday, the day I went to get you at the Tower. Today is Tuesday."

Sarah shook her head as if to clean out the soot inside. Someone had already cleaned it off her body. She was washed and wearing a soft cotton dress that she had never seen before. It fit her perfectly and was cut in a plain style such as she might choose herself. Picking the easiest of the dozens of questions that were crowding her mind, she asked, "Where did these clothes come from?"

"The innkeeper's wife was kind enough to purchase them for me."

"You mean … since we arrived here?"

Anthony looked at her steadily. "No, yesterday morning. I had already surmised that you would not want to be wearing your prison clothes on your honeymoon."

Now Sarah did pull herself up to a sitting position. The events of the previous day were coming back to her, and she was regaining some of her spirit, if not her strength. "You had my answer on that subject back at the prison, Anthony. It hasn't changed."

Anthony's expression did not waver. "Before we discuss it any more, Sarah, I have a surprise for you. Are you feeling up to it?"

"What are you talking about?" Her voice was cold.

Anthony stood. "I'll be back in a moment."

Sarah closed her eyes and sank down again into the blissful softness. She wished she felt stronger, but whatever strength she had would have to do. She needed to get out of here. She was free now, and with the confusion in the town, it would undoubtedly be days or weeks before anyone even knew she was gone. Somehow she had to make her way back to Yorkshire. From there she knew she could count on Uncle Thomas to help her get out of the country, perhaps using the same route they had planned for Parson Hollander. Her throat closed as she thought of the kindly old parson, but she swallowed down the tears. She couldn't afford to think of the parson...or Jack. She had to gather her wits about her and take action.

Her muscles cramping, she rolled over and got off the bed. She had to make her body work—Anthony could return any time. She was about halfway to the door when it opened. Her shoulders sagged. She would have to wait for another chance to escape.

"Sarah!"

The voice was not Anthony's. In fact, it was a voice she had thought never to hear again in this world. Her head snapped up. Jack was there, his broad shoulders filling a substantial part of the doorframe. His hair was longer, and he had on strange clothes that made him look more like a cavalier than the Puritan boy she knew. But it was Jack, alive and well and grinning at her.

She took a couple of faltering steps and then was snatched up in his arms and swung around in a circle. "Jack, it's really you!" she cried, tears bursting forth.

A dry voice from the door said, "Have a care, Jack. She's not as hearty as you are accustomed."

The brother and sister turned their heads toward Anthony, and Jack immediately released Sarah from his embrace and took a step back. "I'm sorry, Sarah. I didn't hurt you, did I?"

Sarah flung her arms back around him. "Oh, Jack, you ninny! How do you think you could hurt me? Let me feel that it is really you—in the flesh."

He hugged her to him, more gently this time. " 'Tis I—in the flesh. Not quite as much flesh as before I enjoyed the king's hospitality those many months, but little by little it's coming back. Lord Rutledge has fed me well.''

Sarah looked from Jack to Anthony, her jaw dropping. "What is going on here?" she asked, giving up her hold on Jack and backing away from both men. She felt the bed behind her and leaned against it for support. She could hardly fathom what was happening.

"I was never set for execution, Sarah. On the day they let me visit you in prison, it turned out that they were releasing me into the custody of Lord Rutledge to be enrolled in the royal navy."

"The navy!"

Jack gave another of his irrepressible grins. "It's a sight better than the gibbet, don't you think?"

Sarah felt a churning inside her stomach. "You arranged this?" she asked Anthony.

Anthony kept his voice light. The emotion between the brother and sister already filled the room, and Sarah looked as if she were about to faint again. "I'm told the navy is the perfect place for promising young lads who want to get out from under the thumbs of their overbearing older sisters."

Jack laughed and went to Sarah's side. "Come sit up here on the bed, older sister, before you collapse, and I'll tell you all about it."

He boosted himself on the high bed and lifted her up next to him. Sarah listened in wonder as Jack recounted the story of his release from prison and return to Leasworth. When he reached the part about his commission in the navy, his voice rose with excitement. She realized that Anthony's joking words had more than a ring of truth. Jack *was* looking forward to joining the navy, even though it meant leaving her so soon after they had been reunited.

She leaned against his shoulder. It was broad and hard with muscle, a man's shoulder. And Jack must begin to live a man's life. But any sadness she may have felt was far overshadowed by the miracle of his being alive. Which was actually no miracle at all, but rather the work of Anthony Rutledge.

"I'm happy for you, Jack. Though it's hard to lose you again now that I've just gotten you back."

"I'll be back in your hair on leave before you know it. We'll be stationed in Hull, just a stone's throw from the estate that Anthony..." Jack stopped and looked up at the man he sincerely expected to become his brother-in-law. "Perhaps I should give you two some time alone," he concluded.

Sarah grabbed his arm. "Don't go. I want to hear about Leasworth and Wiggleston. How are the people doing without the...you know, extra help? And Parson Hollander? I've had nightmares about him dying all alone in that dreadful cave."

Jack gently removed her hand from his arm and stood. "We'll have time to talk about everything. For now, I'll just tell you that by intervention of the king's good friend Lord Anthony Rutledge, the Wiggleston taxes have reverted to prewar rates. And Parson Hollander is once again happily organizing people's lives from his old parish. The charges against him have been dropped."

"Also thanks to Lord Rutledge?" she asked her brother, almost not wanting to hear the answer.

Jack nodded. "Also thanks to Lord Rutledge. Now, I think the two of you should talk."

Sarah felt a churning inside her stomach. "We've nothing to talk about." The words were intractable, but her tone was not as certain as it had been a few minutes ago.

Jack put his hand on his sister's cheek. "For once, big sister, just try to listen to what he has to say." He bent to kiss her and spoke softly for her ears alone. "And for once, Sarah, you might try listening to your heart, as well."

Then he was gone, and Sarah sat staring after him. Anthony had resumed his seat in the chair he had been occupying when she awoke. He folded his arms and waited for her to speak.

"You've been busy," she said haughtily, scooting back to get a firmer seat on the bed.

Anthony nodded, but still didn't speak.

"I suppose I should offer you my thanks," she said after a moment.

"Gratitude is not what I want from you, Sarah."

Her head went up. "What, then?"

"I told you . . . at the Tower."

"That ridiculous proposal? Well, I'm free now. It won't be necessary for you to make the sacrifice."

"You're still a fugitive from justice."

"Then I'll leave the country."

Anthony gave a snort of exasperation. "What a stubborn wench you are, Sarah Fairfax. Tell me now, just how do you propose to leave the country?"

"The same way Parson Hollander would have left."

"So... you would involve the parson and Jack and your uncle and start the whole thing all over again? I can't keep rescuing you from the king's gaolers forever, you know."

Sarah glared at him. "You lied to me."

Anthony barked a laugh. "Would you like to draw up an accounting of just exactly who lied to whom... and how often?"

A flush crept up over the prison pallor of her face. "They were different kinds of lies."

Anthony felt his ire building. He stood and began to pace the room. "Is that so? Please enlighten me, Mistress Fairfax, as to the *differences* between lies. I've had little experience with such distinctions."

Sarah looked down at her hands. It was true. She *had* lied to Anthony. But at the time she had told herself that her falsehoods were justified, whereas his had been perfidious. Now she was not as sure. Her mind was a muddle. "You lied in order to get me into your bed," she said finally, coming to the core of the hurt that had been with her all these months in prison.

Anthony stopped pacing and faced her with an out-raged expression, his hands on his hips. "Of all the ad-dlepated ideas..."

"You can't deny it. You were trying to spy on us!"

Anthony drew in a deep breath. "Sarah, what hap-pened between us had nothing to do with my duties in Yorkshire. From the minute I set eyes on you, I wanted you. As I got to know your loyalty, your indepen-dence, your sense of caring, I wanted you even more."

"You wanted information about my family, about the highwayman."

"Aye, but not from you." He started toward her, his eyes riveting. "From you I wanted a little piece of that vibrant spirit that showed through everything you did, every word you spoke. I wanted to share feelings and sensations that I'd felt with no other woman."

He stopped less than an arm's length away. His mus-cled chest rose and fell as if he had just run the length of the city. His knuckles were white where his hands had formed themselves into fists.

"No other woman but the kitchen maid, you mean."

Anthony relaxed his hands. Now he was back on safe ground, since he had done nothing of reproach with the silly maid, Millie. In fact, his case was suddenly look-ing more positive. If his judgment was correct, the glint of fire in Sarah's gray eyes was due to pure and simple jealousy.

"The kitchen maid?" he asked innocently.

"You know very well whom I mean...Millie, the scullery maid." She turned her eyes away from his. "The pretty one."

He began walking slowly toward her. "I did not see another pretty face my entire stay in Yorkshire. I was too busy looking at yours."

Sarah glared at him. "But not too busy for a tryst in the summerhouse."

Anthony paused. He had almost forgotten that particular incident. At the time he would have been distressed to learn that Sarah had witnessed it. But it was turning out to be a fortunate circumstance. He advanced more confidently.

"I met Millie at the summerhouse because she had promised me information about the mysterious Master Partridge. There was nothing between us, nor would there ever have been."

"Why should I believe you?" she asked softly.

He took the final step to her side and drew her up until her face was just inches from his. "You don't have to believe me, Sarah. But believe your own heart."

He took her hand and pressed it between her breasts. Together they felt the vibrations from deep inside her. "Believe this," Anthony murmured as he bent her back into the feather bed and claimed her mouth.

Sarah closed her eyes. His lips were the most life-giving sensation she had felt in all her weeks in prison. They sent waves of warmth radiating throughout her. She could feel the rough masculinity of his unshaven cheek against hers, the whiskers of his chin chafing her sensitive lower lip. He moved against her, his hands caressing her through the thin cotton of her dress. Other than petticoats, she was wearing no undergarments. If Anthony had washed and dressed her, he had already seen her naked.

"Sarah," he asked hoarsely. "I'm not hurting you?" He pulled his head back to look down at her with belated concern. "I shouldn't be doing this...you're not well."

The hard lower portion of his body pressed against her softness. After months by herself, with no touching, no contact with those she loved, her senses were heightened. Just the small amount of stimulation had already started a flush of heat up the sides of her body. Inside her an ache began to build, urgent and demanding.

"I'm well enough, Anthony," she said simply.

He waited for no further invitation. The fire had kindled too quickly. They were suddenly too close, too aroused for preliminaries. Within moments he had rid himself of his clothes and, lifting her skirt and petticoats above her waist, joined their bodies together. She made a sound of yearning inside her throat, then pulled his head back to her mouth. His lips mashed against hers, then his tongue picked up the increasingly frantic rhythm of their mating. In only a few moments she began to shake, the tremors starting deep inside her and radiating outward to the tips of her limbs. Anthony stiffened and tightened his hold on her as they reached a peak and held it for endless seconds out of time.

Then it was over. They lay sated, exhausted. Anthony spoke first, tiredly. "We belong together, Sarah. Can't you see it? Don't you *feel* it?" He rolled to one side and smoothed down her dress, but made no move to hide his own nakedness. Her eyes were closed, and she lay still and quiet for so long that he became alarmed. "Sarah," he asked, cupping her chin in his hand, "are you all right? I've not hurt you?"

Her eyes opened, luminous with a sheen of moisture. Slowly she shook her head. "You've not hurt me, unless it's possible to die of a burst heart, for I believe mine did so a few minutes back."

Relieved, he kissed her mouth. "As did mine, little one." He kissed her again, and again. He felt like a thirsty man whose thirst remained unquenched no matter how often he drank. "Now what are we going to do with these two burst hearts of ours?"

Sarah did not respond to his smile. "I would give mine away," she said gravely.

"Would you now?" His smile became utterly tender.

"Except that the one I would give it to doesn't want it."

Anthony started up in surprise. "Now why do you say that?"

"Because he is a man who believes in having many ladies, not one. He espouses the virtues of infatuation, rather than love."

Anthony settled back down, resting his head against her chest. "He sounds like a rogue."

"A knave," she agreed.

"A veritable scoundrel. I shall run him through when I catch up with him."

He had busied himself undoing the tiny buttons down the front of her dress. "I wouldn't ask you to be quite so drastic," she said, sounding a bit breathless.

"To what fate would you have me condemn the rascal?" he asked, his lips following the path of white skin his fingers were unveiling.

"Perhaps we could put off deciding that until a more opportune moment," she said, now decidedly breathless.

He had bared her breasts and was paying them the attention their previous urgency had prevented. "I can't imagine a moment more opportune than this," he said happily.

The dreams had come again. Her father awaiting the executioner's ax. But this time the flimsy wooden scaffold was on fire. Flames leapt up around the platform and Sarah could hear the screams of the onlookers as the entire structure collapsed in a shower of sparks. She wanted to scream herself, but she was in a river, and no one could hear her over the lapping of the waves. Suddenly strong arms plucked her from the water and held her above it so she wouldn't drown. And they enfolded her in a hazy blanket of warmth and rocked her gently, then more insistently....

"Sarah, wake up!"

Sarah opened her eyes and looked up into Anthony's face bent over her with concern.

"You were dreaming, dearling," he said tenderly.

It was night, and she and Anthony were in a warm cocoon formed by the feather bed and a thick quilt that had appeared from somewhere. Looking around the room she saw that the fire had been built up, and a tray of food and ale had been placed on a nearby table.

"Are you all right now?" Anthony asked.

She nodded. "I have dreams sometimes...about my father. At the end."

Anthony tightened his arms around her. "It's understandable. That was a horrible thing for you and your brother to go through."

Sarah shuddered. "Sometimes when I wake up, I feel so lost...so alone."

"I don't want you to ever have to face those dreams alone again," he said, wiping tendrils of damp hair back from her forehead.

Sarah didn't respond, but snuggled deeper in his arms. "How long have I been sleeping?" she asked after a moment.

"Three or four hours, at least."

"You wore me out," she teased.

He looked concerned. "You've a right to be worn-out. I should never have made love to you in your current condition. I ought to be run through, after all."

"Ah, yes." Sarah pushed herself up so that their heads were level. "The last bit of conversation I remember, we were discussing a proper fate for a fellow who prefers infatuations to love."

"A scoundrel."

"Indeed."

"Personally," Anthony said carefully, "I think he should be condemned to a life sentence."

Sarah was not sure if she liked the prison analogy so soon after her own internment, but she believed she liked the import behind the words. "A life sentence at hard labor?"

Anthony leaned over and kissed her neck. "Not *that* hard."

She gave him an exasperated little push. "You are an infuriating man, Lord Rutledge. I've a mind to go ask my brother to take me out of here."

"Your brother, Mistress Fairfax, is already on his way back to Leasworth."

"What!" Sarah sat up. "He left without saying goodbye?" She jumped out of bed, ignoring her nakedness, and ran to throw open the shutters of the window. "He's gone...you're certain?" she asked, looking down at the street as if she would will him back to the inn.

Anthony dragged the quilt off the bed and went to stand behind her, wrapping it around them both. "My darling Sarah, what would your fellow Puritans say to see you hanging out the window of an inn without a stitch of clothing."

"They'd say I'd been corrupted by an agent of the devil."

"I've been promoted, it seems," Anthony teased.

Sarah gave a sigh. "I don't know if I will ever get completely used to your irreverence, Anthony. But enough of your teasing. Tell me about Jack."

"Well, someone had to go on ahead to Leasworth to make the preparations."

"Preparations for what?" Sarah couldn't believe that after all the months of separation and the anxiety over his fate, Jack would leave her so soon.

"Why, for the wedding."

"For the wedd—"

Anthony turned her around to face him. "For the last time, Sarah Fairfax. Will you marry me?"

Sarah looked out the window. To the east the night sky was still illuminated with the flames of the burning city. She spoke slowly. "Our Puritan preachers will be saying that this is the wrath of God—His vengeance for the licentious ways you cavaliers have brought to London."

Anthony felt his heart freeze. "And you, Sarah?" he asked tensely. "Is that what you believe?"

She looked up into his face with an expression full of love. "My father never believed in a vengeful God. Nor do I."

Anthony waited.

"I believe in a God of love, one who for mysterious reasons we'll never fully understand has brought us together. Two people from two different lives, but sharing one love."

"Now there's a theology I won't debate," Anthony said with a smile.

She put her arms around him and leaned her head against his shoulder. "Though it does seem wicked to be so happy when so many people are suffering."

Anthony kissed the top of her head. "Let's look at it this way. There has been more suffering caused in this country over these past few years by differences among people than by any number of fires. So our *alliance* is one step closer to bringing harmony back to England."

Sarah smiled. "So it's an alliance you want now, is it?"

"Aye. A union of a Roundhead and a Cavalier."

"A Parliamentarian and a Royalist," she corrected gently.

"How about—" he bent to nibble the edge of her ear "—a man and a woman?"

She nodded, then blushed.

"So are you finally ready to give me an answer to my question, you stubborn, infuriating, beautiful, incomparable woman?"

Her gray eyes looked into his. "The answer is yes," she said.

Anthony gave a whoop and lifted her up in his arms, letting the quilt fall to the ground. He nudged the shutters closed with his shoulder, then started toward the bed.

"This is one civil war treaty," he said, "that is going to be properly celebrated."

Epilogue

Wiggleston,
October 1666

"Till death do you part." Parson Hollander finished the last words of the simple Puritan service and smiled benevolently at the handsome couple standing before him. "You may kiss the bride, your lordship," he added gently.

Anthony felt an unaccustomed wave of emotion wash over him. Until recently he had never expected to be reciting the vows he had just taken with Sarah. In fact, he had scoffed at the whole idea of sanctifying a union by standing up in a church and making promises. But suddenly he felt as if his whole life had been leading up to this very moment. His heart had been waiting these thirty long years to find the one true match that would carry him unto death and beyond.

He turned and looked into Sarah's shining, clear eyes. If he had not known before what it was to love, he did in that moment.

"Kiss me, my husband," she said. And he did, thoroughly, in front of her uncle, Jack, the parson and even Bess, whom he could see watching them with the sharp look of a mother fox guarding her den.

Then there was chaos as Jack came to claim a kiss from his sister and the rest of the congregation crowded forward to offer their own good wishes.

It was several minutes before he could get her back in his arms, but finally he managed to pull her off to the side of the church and share another, only slightly more private, embrace.

"Are you happy, my love?" he asked softly.

"Aye, my bold cavalier, I'm happy. Though I almost feel as if I don't deserve all of this. It's so much..."

Anthony kissed her nose. "A little bit of that Puritan guilt working its way to the surface?" he teased.

Sarah shook her head. "*I'm* the one who committed the crimes, and Jack is the one who has to go off to sea."

"Jack *wants* to go to sea, dearling. He's grown up, remember?"

They looked across the room at Jack and Thomas Fairfax talking with some of the other wedding guests. Sarah glanced to the back of the room, where Norah Thatcher was holding on to the arm of Mayor Spragg.

"I can't believe that Norah threw him over, just when he's about to leave," she said.

"Norah's a practical lass. With Millie gone from Wiggleston for good, she had an opportunity to grab the best catch in town."

"You can't mean to say that Mayor Spragg is a better catch than Jack!"

"Jack and Norah could never have been together that way, Sarah. You know that. She'll have a chance at a good life with Spragg."

Sarah hugged Anthony to her more closely. "I just hope that someday Jack finds the happiness we have found in each other."

"You've no regrets at marrying a king's man?"

Sarah flushed. "It was gracious of the king to send me such a wedding gift."

"The stallion is superb," he agreed. "A mount worthy of its mistress. What are you going to call it?"

Sarah looked up at him sideways, a sly twinkle in her eye. "There will never be another Brigand, but I had thought, perhaps . . . Bandit."

Anthony winced, then pulled her against him to speak low in her ear. "I know that I'll have no luck at taming the mistress," he said ruefully. "I won't even try. But as to the horse, how about if we name him Buttercup?"

Sarah smiled and turned her face for his kiss.

* * * * *

Claire Delacroix's UNICORN TRILOGY

The series that began with

UNICORN BRIDE

"...a fascinating blend of fantasy and romance."
—*Romantic Times*

and

PEARL BEYOND PRICE

"...another dazzling Delacroix delicacy." —*Affaire de Coeur*

now continues with the November 1995 release of

UNICORN VENGEANCE

"An irresistible romance..." —*The Medieval Chronicle*

If you would like to order your copy of *Unicorn Bride* (HS #223) or *Pearl Beyond Price* (HS #264), please send your name, address, zip or postal code along with a check or money order (please do not send cash) for $4.50 for each book ordered ($4.99 in Canada), plus 75¢ postage and handling ($1.00 in Canada) payable to Harlequin Books, to:

In the U.S.	In Canada
3010 Walden Avenue	P.O. Box 609
P. O. Box 1369	Fort Erie, Ontario
Buffalo, NY 14269-1369	L2A 5X3

Please specify book title(s) with your order.
Canadian residents add applicable federal and provincial taxes.

HUT-3

Harlequin Romance ®

AVAILABLE IN OCTOBER—A BRAND-NEW COVER DESIGN FOR HARLEQUIN ROMANCE

Harlequin Romance has a fresh new eye-catching cover.

We're bringing you an exciting new cover design, but Harlequin Romance is still committed to bringing you warm and contemporary love stories that are sure to touch your heart!

See how we've changed and look for these fabulous stories with a brand-new look:

#3379 Brides for Brothers
by Debbie Macomber
#3380 The Best Man
by Shannon Waverly
#3381 Once Burned
by Margaret Way
#3382 Legally Binding
by Jessica Hart

Available in October,
wherever Harlequin books are sold.

Harlequin Romance ®—
Dare To Dream

HRNEW

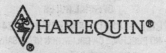

OFFICIAL RULES
PRIZE SURPRISE SWEEPSTAKES 3448
NO PURCHASE OR OBLIGATION NECESSARY

Three Harlequin Reader Service 1995 shipments will contain respectively, coupons for entry into three different prize drawings, one for a Panasonic 31" wide-screen TV, another for a 5-piece Wedgwood china service for eight and the third for a Sharp ViewCam camcorder. To enter any drawing using an Entry Coupon, simply complete and mail according to directions.

There is no obligation to continue using the Reader Service to enter and be eligible for any prize drawing. You may also enter any drawing by hand printing the words "Prize Surprise," your name and address on a 3"x5" card and the name of the prize you wish that entry to be considered for (i.e., Panasonic wide-screen TV, Wedgwood china or Sharp ViewCam). Send your 3"x5" entries via first-class mail (limit: one per envelope) to: Prize Surprise Sweepstakes 3448, c/o the prize you wish that entry to be considered for, P.O. Box 1315, Buffalo, NY 14269-1315, USA or P.O. Box 610, Fort Erie, Ontario L2A 5X3, Canada.

To be eligible for the Panasonic wide-screen TV, entries must be received by 6/30/95; for the Wedgwood china, 8/30/95; and for the Sharp ViewCam, 10/30/95.

Winners will be determined in random drawings conducted under the supervision of D.L. Blair, Inc., an independent judging organization whose decisions are final, from among all eligible entries received for that drawing. Approximate prize values are as follows: Panasonic wide-screen TV ($1,800); Wedgwood china ($840) and Sharp ViewCam ($2,000). Sweepstakes open to residents of the U.S. (except Puerto Rico) and Canada, 18 years of age or older. Employees and immediate family members of Harlequin Enterprises, Ltd., D.L. Blair, Inc., their affiliates, subsidiaries and all other agencies, entities and persons connected with the use, marketing or conduct of this sweepstakes are not eligible. Odds of winning a prize are dependent upon the number of eligible entries received for that drawing. Prize drawing and winner notification for each drawing will occur no later than 15 days after deadline for entry eligibility for that drawing. Limit: one prize to an individual, family or organization. All applicable laws and regulations apply. Sweepstakes offer void wherever prohibited by law. Any litigation within the province of Quebec respecting the conduct and awarding of the prizes in this sweepstakes must be submitted to the Regies des loteries et Courses du Quebec. In order to win a prize, residents of Canada will be required to correctly answer a time-limited arithmetical skill-testing question. Value of prizes are in U.S. currency.

Winners will be obligated to sign and return an Affidavit of Eligibility within 30 days of notification. In the event of noncompliance within this time period, prize may not be awarded. If any prize or prize notification is returned as undeliverable, that prize will not be awarded. By acceptance of a prize, winner consents to use of his/her name, photograph or other likeness for purposes of advertising, trade and promotion on behalf of Harlequin Enterprises, Ltd., without further compensation, unless prohibited by law.

For the names of prizewinners (available after 12/31/95), send a self-addressed, stamped envelope to: Prize Surprise Sweepstakes 3448 Winners, P.O. Box 4200, Blair, NE 68009.

RPZ KAL